D0897937

What I Know

Also by Andrew Cowan

Pig
Common Ground
Crustaceans

Andrew Cowan

What I Know

SCEPTRE

First published in Great Britain in 2005 by Hodder and Stoughton
A division of Hodder Headline

The right of Andrew Cowan to be identified as the Author
of the Work has been asserted by him in accordance with the
Copyright, Designs and Patents Act 1988

A Sceptre Book

1 3 5 7 9 10 8 6 4 2

A CIP catalogue record for this title is available from the British Library

ISBN 0 340 71306 2

Typeset in Sabon by Hewer Text Ltd, Edinburgh
Printed and bound by Clays Ltd, St Ives plc

Hodder Headline's policy is to use papers that are natural, renewable
and recyclable products and made from wood grown in sustainable
forests. The logging and manufacturing processes are expected to
conform to the environmental regulations of the country of origin.

Hodder and Stoughton Ltd
A division of Hodder Headline
338 Euston Road
London NW1 3BH

for my mum and dad

I

My name is Mike Hannah and I am forty years old. I am forty today, which isn't an age to which I've ever attached any kind of significance. I don't suppose my life is about to begin here, it will simply continue. My best years are no more behind me than they ever were.

I am forty years old and lying near-naked on the wood laminate floor of our dining room, gazing up to the bedroom of a girl who has just washed her hair. Her house, which she rents, backs on to ours and until today, until I felled the trees that enclosed our garden, I would not have been able to see her, not from here, though her window has always been visible from our youngest son's bedroom and the room in our attic. She is a student and shares with two others, a boy and a girl. There are many student houses in our area. Many family homes, too.

My own family is me, my wife Jan – which is short for Janette – and our two sons: Jack, who is ten, and Ben, nearly six. They are good boys, without secrets, and the youngest was born here. Jan was pregnant when we moved in and it was her pregnancy, I'm sure, that hurried us into buying before we were certain. Our impressions on first viewing were of tightness and gloom, and even at that time the trees – which are conifers – were too dense and too tall. They displaced the air, or seemed to. Going into the garden didn't quite feel like going outdoors; you wouldn't breathe any easier.

It is mid-evening now, mid-May, and this day began for me early – soon after five – when I woke from a dream about Sarah, who's a girl I once knew in a house I once shared, when I too was a student. In the lives of most men, I imagine, there is somewhere a Sarah, and perhaps you dream of one also. I don't dream of mine often – not as much as I used to – but always something stays with me, a kind of disturbance, a day-long mood I can't shift. Usually the details are quick to dissolve, but this time I remember a squash court, everything white, and the fact that I was losing. I don't remember my partner. Sarah tapped my arm and asked if I was receiving her phonecalls. *I've placed a tap on your phone, yes*, I replied. She was conversational. I shouldered my racquet and answered her questions. I dealt with her coldly, but then she laughed and I smiled. I looked into her eyes. And that was all – it wasn't lurid or sexual – but when I woke I reached for Jan's hand and I squeezed it. She rolled away from me, still sleeping, and quietly I crept downstairs in my T-shirt and shorts. I was afraid I might disturb Ben, who had gone to bed with my presents, all set to surprise me.

My birthday of course wasn't meant to be different, in any way 'special', though for the sake of the boys there would be breakfast in bed, with my presents and cards, and they could pamper me all evening – fetch my notional slippers and pipe – if that's what they wanted. But otherwise there'd be no celebrations, no party or friends. I would go to work as I normally did, if I had work to go to.

I am a private investigator, and business of late has been slack. My wife is a teacher of maths.

'What's there to celebrate?' I asked her.

'You?' she suggested.

'Not much then,' I laughed, and she stared at me. She was disappointed, possibly angry. It wasn't only myself I was refusing to celebrate, but my life, and that also meant Jan. It has been eighteen years for us now; sixteen since we married.

The morning was still, hushed and unflustered, and I sat for a while on the bench in our garden. Sunlight caught the tops of the trees and the chimneys beyond them. Nothing moved, a few birds were singing. It should have been peaceful. And yet I felt pressured, uneasy, as if I had things to attend to. Which is a feeling I don't often get until evening, when Jan goes out to her yoga, or to the theatre, or else retires – usually early – to write in her diary. I mean those evenings when I have no excuse but to be home. It is then I start drinking, though not excessively so, just sufficient to take the edge from the restlessness that builds once the boys are in bed, the vague sense of alarm. I drink, and I read, and I wander the house, my circuit of windows. Sometimes I list all the things I ought to get done soon.

And this morning, feeling a chill on my legs despite the blue sky, hemmed in by the trees and thinking of Sarah, I found myself listing again, and settled at last on something for Jan, something 'auspicious'. I tipped away my coffee and went back to bed, impatient now for the boys to come through. There's a tool-hire place just over the river, and as I lay watching the ceiling, my wife softly breathing beside me, I decided I would need a bowsaw, a three-foot axe and a chainsaw. I would need to reschedule the rest of my day.

The trees were planted by the Sommers, who lived here before us; I suppose I should mention them.

They were closed-in, unwelcoming people who valued their privacy and showed little interest in anyone else's. Their trees were tall for a reason, and when Jan hopefully asked, as she often did on our viewings, 'So what are the neighbours like?' Mrs Sommer flatly replied, 'We never see them,' and pressed on with her tour. She asked nothing about us. Her husband didn't stir from his armchair. There was a fire blazing beside him, a floral display in the dining room, coffee percolating in the kitchen. Their children – a girl aged twelve and a boy of fourteen – were concealed in their bedrooms, studying. It was an estate agent's idea of good presentation, the illustration of a homelife that might one day be ours, and of course it was stifling. We wanted to damp down the fire, open the windows, send the kids out with their friends. We wanted Mrs Sommer to smile.

But she was watchful, defensive, and had a habit, I noticed, of touching or moving whatever we happened to glance at – her ornaments, a book, even the kettle – as though to reassure it: *don't worry, you won't be staying here.* And in fact most of the correspondence between us – our solicitor and theirs –

concerned the ownership of fittings and fixtures: door handles, shelf brackets, window locks. When eventually they moved it was to a larger house just three streets away – in Benedict Avenue, where some friends of ours live – and they took almost everything with them. What they did leave behind was a lot of bad feeling. That and a small bunch of daffodils – displayed in a plastic cola bottle, the top end scissored off – which Jan immediately dumped in the garden.

By then our dislike of the Sommers had deepened to loathing; we found them exhausting. I remember the issue of who should pay to have the loft timbers treated. They were infested with woodworm, or had been. It was a petty dispute, finally too petty for the solicitors to deal with, and involved Jan in several sour phonecalls that left her red-faced and shaking – and feeling, she said, as if she too was infested, riddled with the Sommers' mean-spiritedness. In the end we gave in, or made a principled decision – as Jan saw it – not to sink to their level, and spent the following six years – as I see it – attempting to hide or remove every trace of their time here.

And it has all been cleared now – their Artex and carpets and fire surrounds; their bath suite and kitchen; their colours and woodworm. We had the attic converted into my office. The conifers were the last thing on our list. And really we ought to be celebrating: we have worked hard to get to this point, to establish this house as our own.

The student has just switched on her desklamp, though the sun is still bright in the garden, filling the space where the trees were, slanting low through this window. She is dressed in a white towel, folded and tucked just over one breast, just under one arm. Her shoulders are sheeny with wet and her hair is bunched up in a smaller towel, a loose heavy turban. She is pacing to and fro, talking into a mobile, and as I follow her movements I can hear Jan's voice on the landing, tired and impatient – eight o'clock ratty – chivvying Ben towards bed, arguing with Jack. He is taking his bath, while I am laid out on this floor, wearing only my pants, a bag of frozen peas underneath me. They are numbing the small of my back, though the pain is beginning to seep now to my legs. Something went wrong as I undressed from my day in the garden, as I bent to tug off a sock. Jan had insisted I shed my soiled clothes before climbing the stairs; I wasn't to trail my dirt on the carpet. But then a muscle exploded; that's what it felt like. I yelled and lay down, and I haven't moved since.

It was Jack who saw to my socks, solemnly peeled them away. Jan went for the peas and parcelled them up in my teeshirt. She eased them beneath me and said not a word, as if finally a point had been proven. The tools, the ladder, the electrical cable: all of these had concerned her, though of course she couldn't have predicted the sock, this kind of calamity. My back was never a problem before.

'Sad dad,' said our youngest, experimentally stroking my forehead, and I smiled at that, or tried to, then noticed his brother, half hiding behind him. His face was cautious, alert, absorbing this new information about me, and he was ready, it seemed, to bolt at any moment. 'Would you fetch me some aspirins?' I asked him, and that he did gladly. The medicine cabinet, he knows, is out of bounds, but I had given permission; I was still his father. He returned with the pills, some water, an air of self-importance. 'Good lad,' I told him. In the garden too he had made himself useful.

Straight home from school, both my boys had come out to watch me, up there on my ladder in my hard-hat and goggles, my gauntlets and ear-muffs. The trees by then were three-quarters felled. On either side of the lawn, stumps and roots were all that remained. The branches and trunks were stacked high on the grass, enough debris already to fill up two skips – which is a job I had down for next weekend, and which will now have to wait, if Jan will bear with me.

The mound of branches was springy. Ben clambered half-way and sat flexing against them. Jack kept a sensible distance. And when I noticed them watching I'll admit I was glad of the audience, and suddenly proud of the wreckage I'd caused. It's a truth I believe about being a father that it's mostly performance. Perhaps it's different for you. Maybe it's different with girls. But once the love is acknowledged – and I try not to shy from it – I can't think what else is required but acting the part, giving the boys something more to believe in than wizards and ghosts, wrestlers and Santa. All of which have their place, I wouldn't deny them. And though I'm not a natural disciplinarian, playing Dad is a role I do feel at home in. It makes me feel more solid than I actually am, when what I actually am – who knows? – is a boy just like them, as full of fears and strange notions, though without their illusions, and with no one of my own to look up to.

When the next branch fell I called Jack forwards to clear it, and soon Ben was also involved, pretending to help him, making a nuisance. But Jack was eager, he didn't complain, and though the branches were whippy – awkward to carry and layer – he stacked them up neatly. He began a new pile. I stripped that tree to its trunk and came down from the ladder. I told the boys to stand back and get set to shout 'timber!' But the chainsaw was slackening and wouldn't slice cleanly; it ripped and gnawed, repeatedly jammed. It was slow, sweaty work and of course it grew boring. Ben stood dreamily for a while just watching, then wandered off with his thoughts. Jack stuck it out an hour or so longer – another two trees – looking increasingly miserable and hot, until at last Jan emerged from the house with some water. She gave him the glass and stroked his bare arm. 'You're getting a rash,' she said. 'I think you'd better come in now.' And after a moment's hesitation, that's what he did; he stepped out of a role he'd grown tired of and went abruptly indoors.

Jan gazed around at the garden, surveyed the neighbouring windows. 'I suppose you know what you're doing,' she said.

'Making you happy?' I replied, and she pressed her mouth to a smile, then started to laugh. She shielded her eyes.

'Did I need making happy?'

'You never liked these trees.'

'No,' she conceded, and picked up a stray branch. She tossed it onto the pile. 'But I wasn't unhappy, Mike,' she said, and walked slowly back to the house.

Up in her bedroom the student has now loosened her hair, dabbed the wet from her shoulders and neck, and is considering herself in a mirror I cannot quite see. Snug in her towel, she is stooping a little, probing round her eyes with her fingertips. In one hand she is holding a hairdryer.

This is where she sits when she's studying, framed by the window, the upper casement hinged open. She smokes Marlboros and works on a laptop. She types quickly, using all of her fingers. I have noticed these things, peering down from my attic, or closing Ben's curtains at bedtime. And on several other occasions I have seen her wrapped in the towel, wafting with the dryer as slowly she strokes the damp from her hair. I have seen this, and yet I have not, until this evening, been reminded so sharply of Sarah, who often came to my room in the house we once shared, still wet from her bath and dressed, I remember, in a leopard-print gown.

Mine, she said, was the only room in the house where the light and mirror and the wall socket came together just so. It was ideal for drying her hair. And in this, as in other things, we were conspiratorial. Each time she appeared I would swivel from my chair, leave my typewriter, and stretch out on my bed – my mattress on the floor – to watch her. Sometimes we talked. Often we didn't, and Sarah accepted my watching as I accepted these interruptions, her presence in my room. It was intimate, cosy, and though her gown was loose and sometimes revealing, what I enjoyed as much as those glimpses, I think, was sharing her privacy, quietly spectating, as I enjoy even now watching my wife dress to go out, smoothing the seat of her trousers, fussing with hemlines, adjusting her straps. That is, I enjoy watching Jan when she is most absorbed in herself, least conscious of me, when she is most like a stranger.

Every marriage is a mystery. I wouldn't be the first to think that, nor to suppose that most are stalked by regret, the melancholy thought of what they are not. Perhaps Jan also wakes and feels sorry; perhaps she dreams of some other. It wouldn't surprise me. I'm not sure it would bother me. She is talking now on the phone in the kitchen, her voice a low murmur, the door shut between us, and as I lie here – made drowsy by my day in the garden and the ache in my back – I feel no curiosity about this. Instead I let my eyes rest on the student and wonder how it might be if the voice I can hear was not Jan's but Sarah's. I picture Sarah ending the call, opening a bottle of wine, coming into this room. Her face is much as it was; I cannot conceive of her older. She places a glass at my side and steps across me and closes the curtains. Her movements are sleek and the word I think of is 'feline'. She turns and smiles and flips the hair from her eyes. She asks if I would like my dinner re-heated.

I do realise these are not adventurous imaginings. But what comes over me then is something like vertigo, a dizzying tilt in my mind, because of course none of this could occur. If Sarah not Jan was my wife then I would not be the same person, or in the same place. Every point in my life would have been different. I would not have acquired the same habits, grievances, faultlines, and probably I would not be in the same job. I might not be a father, and certainly there would be no Jack or Ben.

What exactly there would be I cannot imagine. All I know is what I have, and what I have is surely enough, as much as I might ever have wished for. I am comfortable. My life, as I say, is not about to end or begin here. It may not even have come to its mid-point: married men, as we know, live longer lives than the single. I used to be encouraged by this, but now I'm less certain. Contrary to what you might think, I do love my wife, and she, I'm sure, loves me, but I cannot pretend to find our life interesting. It has ceased to be a story to me, if it ever was. There's little sense of a plot being revealed, no hint of surprises in store, and often it seems the only kind of 'what next' we might reasonably expect is the worst kind of catastrophe. Which is a thought that keeps me awake at nights, fearful and sometimes, I'll admit, hopeful.

The last of the sun is glinting over the rooftops; in a moment or two it will dip completely from view. I'm not sure of the time: the old clock on the shelf needs rewinding. My feet are in shadow. My bag of peas has defrosted and the shirt wrapped around them is damp. I would like to soak in the bath now, perhaps stretch out on our bed with a beer, a bottle or two for my birthday. And I am hungry. But the slightest movement towards lifting myself is too painful. Ben, I can hear, is listening to his story tape, the same cassette he plays every night. Jack is busy at his computer. I take a long breath and try calling to Jan, but even the effort of that is too much; my voice trails away and she does not respond. I don't know where she is in the house. It seems I must lie here and wait.

The student has switched off her desklamp. A milky veil of sky is reflected in her window and she is standing, I realise, directly behind it. Her forehead is almost touching the glass. She is looking down at our garden. Perhaps she has only just noticed that something is missing. For almost two years she'll have risen each day to a view of our trees, and closed her curtains on them each evening, and what she'll be contemplating now is wreckage and emptiness. Those are the exact two words in my head and they don't seem, as maybe they ought, unduly melodramatic. Our garden is six feet wider all round, unenclosed and unprotected, and I am now as conspicuous to her as she is to me, but also, I suspect, more exposed to myself, more plainly on view, than is probably good for me.

And perhaps, after all, my age today is a factor, leaving me open to thoughts such as these, because suddenly it seems I have created far too much space, more than enough to get lost in, and when I try calling again to my wife the oddest, least welcome thing happens. I find I am weeping, overcome by a grief I don't recognise, which seems misdirected, nothing I ever asked for or wanted. The student needs only to glance up to see me. My wife and children just need to come through this door.

2

The blue plastic clock on the chiropractor's wall ticks loudly. It is ten minutes past nine. Stella in her white tunic and white pumps sits up on the edge of the bench and suggests I might like to undress. She watches me closely, once or twice nods. 'Uh huh,' she murmurs, 'okay.' I avoid meeting her gaze. There's a wall-sized mirror beside me, a door wedged open behind her. I concentrate on my buttons, my belt-buckle and zip, the least painful way out of each garment. In the adjoining room a male voice is asking the questions I have just answered for Stella. 'And your health generally?' he concludes. 'Any problems?'

'I'm on anti-depressants,' a woman replies.

'But physically?' he says.

The woman doesn't answer him. I glance across to the door and find her reflection in the sheen of a wallchart. She hasn't yet removed any clothes.

'You can keep your socks on,' Stella tells me.

'Right,' I say, and drape my trousers over a chair. It was Jan who dressed me this morning, pulled on my socks, tied the knots in my laces. 'And my pants?' I ask quietly. 'Shall I keep them on too?'

Stella nods, unsmiling. She shuffles back on her buttocks and spreads her legs slightly. She pats the bench in between them. 'Then if you'd just like to stand here for me please. Facing that way.' She indicates a wall lined with pictures of sports stars, framed certificates of competence, laminated diagrams of the ankle and knee joints, the pelvic girdle and spine. On her desk is a tub of coconut oil and I look over at that – at her finger-smears in the cream – as she briskly explores the small of my back, prodding and probing until I give out a gasp. 'Just here?' she says, and I wince.

'Yes.'

She is satisfied, cheerful, and shifts her weight forward again. I glimpse a bare knee to each side of me. She is close enough now to slip her arms under mine; she could rest her head on my shoulder, whisper into my ear. 'Okay then,' she says crisply, 'when did you last take a good look at yourself?'

'Sorry?'

'Walk across to the mirror,' she says, and I take half a step away from her, gingerly bring my left leg alongside, another half-step, my left leg again. 'That's good,' she says, and slips down from the bench. 'Keep it going.' Her reflection appears just behind me; our eyes briefly meet in the glass. 'Can you see the tilt in your posture?' she asks, and at first I suspect there must be a kink in her mirror, a fault-line somewhere near to my midriff. My lower body seems magnified, my chest and shoulders pinched thin, hardly wider than the breadth of my hips. But this of course is how I am built; the picture's a true one.

I have the calves and thighs of a rugby player, the upper half of a boy.

With an upturned palm Stella swiftly indicates the coordinates of my hips, shoulders and sternum, as if my body were also a diagram, the illustration of a typical sub-category of male physical decline. 'You see how everything slopes?' she says, and clearing my throat I say that I do. But it isn't only the definite lean of my trunk to the right. My skin is post-mortally white, and there is grey in my stubble, dark rheumy pouches under my eyes. I am hairier than I once was, and puffier. My knees, I notice, are dimpled, and there's a roll of soft flesh round my middle. Once, lying in the bath some time in my mid-twenties, I found I could 'pinch an inch' and embarked on a short-lived programme of sit-ups and swimming. There have been many such programmes since, and many more resolutions to watch what I eat, but even so, I've grown heavier, and before me now is a paunch. I could comfortably hold two fistfuls of flab. I am looking at the body of a middle-aged man.

Dressed or undressed, mine isn't a body you'd notice. On the beach or in the street, I wouldn't stand out from the crowd, and I'm sure if we were to meet you'd be hard-pressed later to put together an identikit of my face. Professionally speaking, I have the ideal appearance, I think – unobtrusive, anonymous. I'm neither too tall nor too short. I'm not handsome, but couldn't claim either to be 'interestingly ugly', which is a phrase Jan sometimes uses, though not, I'm afraid, about me. She claims to like ugly. I also lack whatever it is – the energy, self-confidence, conceit – to compensate with 'character' or 'charisma' for my ordinariness. I don't turn heads, and never have done. I am in fact what some of the women in our circle now claim is their fate: invisible. It's what I am used to. Nothing has been lost, and so I really needn't grieve for my youth, as they do. I have no cause for regret or self-pity, whatever the chiropractor's mirror might show me.

Jan however is beautiful, though she would deny this. She is someone who has always turned heads, firstly on account of her hair, which is red and unmissable, thick and long and naturally curled. It has never been styled or cut short, and gives, she feels now, too youthful an impression. From behind she might still be twenty, and what, she asks, must people think when they catch sight of her face? That she is beautiful, I say; a good-looking woman nearing forty with spectacular hair. Mutton dressed as lamb, she says; an old hag in a wig.

She is predictably prone to insecurities about wrinkles, the pouching of her jawline, the crepeyness at her neck. But her neck is still long, her features are strong, and the wrinkles, I say, add character. Which she scoffs at. 'Willowy' is a word that might once have described her. When we met she was pale and slim, graceful, and she remains pale, long-limbed and smooth in her movements, though her arms have begun to thicken and she is broader now in the hips than she once was, which is something I like, as a general rule. But for all that she is beautiful – in my opinion beautiful – I do not often desire her, that spark is not there, and sex between us is infrequent, which Jan does not seem to mind. I wonder in fact if she might be relieved, for sex was rarely something she would initiate, and in eighteen years she has never once had an orgasm, at least not in my presence.

I do not desire my wife, who is beautiful, but find I am attracted this morning to Stella, who is not, though she is certainly youthful, and healthy – and, I'll admit, buxom – which these days would seem to suffice; my gaze is that restless, that indiscriminate. *Sad Dad* said my youngest, and in the week since my birthday this has become the family's nickname for me. I would not disagree, but wouldn't wish them to realise just how 'sad' I am either. Nor would I wish Stella to know.

Looking to our reflection, she places one hand on my right shoulder, the other on my left hip, and gently attempts to make me stand upright. 'You're very twisted around,' she says, and I nod, though momentarily I'm distracted by my underpants, which were fresh from the packet this morning and are already damp-stained – or seem so – where lately I've begun to leak after using the toilet. 'Did you have a bad fall when you were younger?' Stella asks me.

'I don't think so.'

'You're sure?'

'Nothing I can remember.'

She addresses the mirror and demonstrates by touching, her

hands cool and dry, pressing lightly, and in her voice is something like boredom, the half-heartedness of having said these words routinely, to too many others just like me. 'I think it's likely you had a fall playing football, or jumping from a wall – something of that sort? Quite a heavy impact that would've bumped your pelvis out of alignment, possibly without you being aware of it? And probably you've been leaning to the right ever since, to compensate for this twist in your posture, *here*. Which will have affected the way you move, and the way you sit, and put quite a strain on these muscles just here. Especially this one, which has basically had enough and gone *snap*, like you say.'

She clicks her fingers, and again I nod, though I'm fairly certain I said no such thing. My muscle did not *snap*, not audibly. Besides which, it strikes me that what Stella has identified is not a lifelong habit of bad posture but the natural consequence of my straining a muscle a few days ago. My back – like the rest of me – was simply out of condition, unused to such work. There was definitely no fall in my childhood; I was never that boisterous. I haven't always 'tilted'. The only reason I cannot stand upright today is because, for the moment, it hurts me to do so.

These thoughts I keep to myself however. There is no point in objecting, though not for the first time I suspect I am in the wrong place. Stella's practice is one of several in a converted Methodist chapel re-named 'The Holistic Clinic'. The brass plates by the door advertise shiatsu, reflexology, hypnotherapy, homeopathy, acupuncture. There's a herbalist's pharmacy too. And until the clinic was recommended by someone I know, for whom backache is an occupational hazard – he is a writer – I had often wondered what kind of a person would come here.

'If you could just pop across to the bench now,' says Stella, though of course I'm no more capable of 'popping' than cartwheeling. I goggle my eyes at her, puff out my cheeks, and she gives a perfunctory smile then stands to one side and quietly adds, 'In your own time.' Self-conscious, I shuffle into position and painstakingly manoeuvre myself onto my back on the bench, and when at last I am comfortable Stella stands close behind me and takes hold of my head. Her fingers shape to the nape of my neck, the underside of my jaw. She tugs gently, rhythmically, coaxing my neck muscles to lengthen, and the effect is calming, relaxing. My breathing slows, I think I may drowse, and then sharply she twists my head to the right. There's a click. She makes a noise of satisfaction, and cranks to the left. Another click. 'So it was Will Brown who suggested you come to us?' she says.

'Mm.'

'We haven't seen him in a long while.'

'No?'

'I keep meaning to read one of his books.'

'Me too,' I say, attempting a smile, and Stella begins to smile too, then covers her mouth, gives out a long yawn. She comes round to the side of the bench. Her eyes are sleepy, heavy-lidded and wide, and there's a feline curl to the corners that reminds me, I realise, of Sarah. And perhaps after all it is this that attracts me to Stella, her resemblance to somebody else, someone who is lately much on my mind.

Though there is also her tunic. Close-fitting and short, it tucks where she tucks, pulls taut at the buttons. She perches beside me, her leg nudging mine, and I glance down at her thigh, the plump swell beneath the white fabric, and notice also her midriff, her softness. I shift my gaze to the ceiling. She places one hand on my right knee, the other under my calf, and lifts up my leg. She rotates it from the hip, and I close my eyes, clench my hands at my chest. I dig my nails into my palms and begin to count backwards. I feel a chill on my forehead.

The truth is, in eighteen years, only my wife has touched me this freely and I am suddenly fearful I might get an erection. I am not a 'tactile' person, and generally shrink from others who are. I would not stroke someone's arm to console them, for instance, or throw an arm around a friend's shoulder. I don't greet our female friends with a kiss, or ruffle their children's hair. Jan is comfortable with all of these things, but I am not. And people realise, I think: they generally allow me my distance.

Which isn't to say my life is wholly lacking in physical warmth. I do cuddle my boys even now, and my wife and I do often hug – the kind of prolonged, swaying embrace that becomes as hard to leave as a warm bath in winter and which, for us, usually develops into dancing, tickling, horsing around.

This mostly occurs in the kitchen. But I do not 'play away'. In all these years there have been no girlfriends, no 'dalliances' of any description, though there have been 'situations' – mostly in the line of my work – which many other men might have exploited. I have never been that kind of man however, and don't personally know anyone who is. Adultery, I've always thought, is beyond any of us, myself or my friends. We're not risk-takers, and I've heard no rumours of affairs, much as I'd like to. Neither have there been any divorces, not in my immediate circle, though I am aware of at least two mothers in the school playground – well-dressed, professional, harassed – who have in the past year become single parents, assuming sole custody. Interestingly, or worryingly, they're a few years older than I am, and so perhaps that's all still to come; it's the next stage, after the interior redesigns are completed, the back-of-house extensions, and the third, possibly accidental child has been added to the muddle of making a life. It's what comes after we turn forty.

Stella lowers my right leg, rubs her hands briskly together. Humming to herself, she comes round to my left side and lifts up my left leg. She sits on the edge of the bench and distractedly asks me, 'And are you also a writer, Mike? Is that what you do?'

'No, no.'

She gazes down at my fists, clenched on my chest, and turns my leg slowly, a wider circle than before. She is frowning. She readjusts her position. 'What is it you do then, Mike? Did you say?'

'I work in insurance,' I tell her, which in fact is where I began, not long after I took up with Jan. 'I'm a claims investigator.'

'Oh right,' Stella nods, 'I see,' and then she asks nothing more of me. She glances across to the clock. 'Soon be done now,' she says.

3

'So,' Jan says, 'are you up to it?'

She looks in from the hallway and it's plain from her tone that she expects me to say that I'm not. If I was coming I would by now have got up from this mat and probably called for some help with my shoes. The boys are waiting behind her, dressed in their replica shirts and new trainers, their arms and necks greased with sunblock. Jan's dark glasses are perched on top of her head, her red hair spilling out to each side. Her dress is pale blue. The freckles are beginning to show on her shoulders.

'No, I'm coming,' I say, and make a first move towards rising. 'But you go on, I'll catch you, sorry, I was dreaming.'

She leaves without another word; perhaps she doesn't believe me. I hear the careful click of the door, her determination not to be angry, then the boys' piping voices as they head off down the street. They're excited, and I relax, lie back for a while as I was.

It is Sunday, twelve-thirty, and the sun is bright on the houses behind us. Nothing is moving. Nothing, I suspect, will disturb this stillness all day. The light will sharpen and fade, slowly the shadows of the chimneys will lengthen and turn, clouds will form and drift on.

The student hasn't yet opened her curtains. She may not surface till mid-afternoon, and when she does, she'll be dressed, already showered. Her hair will be brushed and tied up. She has, I'm sure, noticed me, the hours I've spent lately on my back on this floor. She hasn't appeared in her towel since the day I took down the trees, and she's begun to draw her curtains early, before it gets dark. She whips them across. I don't mind. I do the exercises set for me by Stella, my few leg bends and stretches, nothing too strenuous. I let myself doze, and I read. Often I gaze out at the rooftops, at the pigeons perched on the aerials, the reflections of sky in the windows.

I could remain here all day, drowsing, but this afternoon is the school's annual 'fun run', in aid of some charity, I can't remember which, and I have promised to be there. I have sponsored my boys fifty pence a lap each, and they will want me to watch them. All the other dads will be going. As will the mums of course, in their sandals and short summer frocks, their bare legs and arms.

Laboriously I turn onto my side and begin to lever myself to my knees. My walking stick is beside me; my sunhat is hanging from a hook in the hall. I have a method for lacing my shoes now, slow but effective. I just need to look for my keys, some cash.

Ours is a high social-capital community, which is a phrase I once came across in a newspaper and then used in a report for a client, a solicitor representing a husband and wife living at that time in London. They couldn't commit to buying a house in our area – in Woodcock Lane, a cul-de-sac, 'unadopted', expensive – until they'd first received a dossier on the neighbours, the crime rate, 'the retail and recreational amenities', the local school's Ofsted performance. Which wasn't such an unusual commission – five per cent of my income now comes in this way, though it's rare that I work quite so close to my own home. Certainly the couple in question wouldn't have known that their investigator was himself a prospective near-neighbour, and they have – I hope – no idea now, though the wife regularly stands near me in the school playground, her youngest strapped into a three-wheeled 'sports' buggy, her eldest a girl in Ben's class. She wears a green felt hat, pink lipstick. I believe she is some kind of artist. We haven't yet spoken and perhaps never will but she seems well-connected, always with someone to talk to, and I trust she understands now what I meant by the phrase. She didn't back then and I remember I had to explain it in a supplementary note.

We are good citizens here. Our streets are tree-lined, and our local park is not often vandalised. The proportion of parents with a university degree is unusually high, and our children attend a school that is 'exemplary', a state-sector 'beacon' for others. We aren't litter-bugs, and we conscientiously recycle our newspapers and bottles and cans. We donate our unwanted clothes, books and bric-a-brac to charity. Sometimes we leave items of unwanted furniture overnight on the pavement with a note for whoever might want them: *PLEASE TAKE!!* We are courteous drivers, and many of us cycle to work, go shopping by bus, take the train when we can. Elections to the school board of governors are genuine contests, and I know of at least three city councillors amongst the other parents in the school playground. The turnout for any election is high in our ward, and whatever the national telethon event you can be sure of several innovative and 'amusing' fundraising efforts round here, often involving the parents of Ben or Jack's classmates, people I might nod to or smile at, but don't in fact know.

And the truth is, for all the many things that do go on, I'm not personally acquainted with anyone who is actively involved, and wouldn't particularly want to be. My own few friends aren't like that, though twenty years ago most of them would have belonged to some campaign or other, some tendency or grouping or humanitarian good cause. There weren't many who didn't. Now I'm distantly friendly with just one card-carrying politico, and even there, carrying the card is just about the limit of his participation, his attachment more nostalgic than heartfelt. We've all of us lapsed into scepticism, indifference, ambivalence, though we're happy enough to co-exist with the enthusiasts and activists, even the churchgoers.

Regarding churches, there are any number around here – a fact noted in my report – and the largest of those is St Luke's, a short walk from the end of our street and built, I would guess, to resemble the nondescript houses nearby. It has the same suburban red brick and pantile, the same unassuming pitch to the roof. It isn't a building you'd notice, despite its great size, and I've never once been inside, though I understand it is well-attended. Sunday turnouts are high, and as I shuffle slowly that way today I keep my eyes lowered. The congregation is milling about on the pavement, savouring the sunshine, buoyed perhaps by the sermon, and my stick, I fear, is bound to draw some charitable interest, some friendly remark.

The kerbside is parked up with their cars, washed and waxed, a few windows just open. The interiors give off a smell of warm vinyl. There are cushions on back seats, ornaments on dash-boards, many other homely touches, and I pretend to take an interest in these as I pass. But there is no avoiding it. I hear my name being spoken, and look round to find the determinedly smiling faces of two people I'm sure I don't know.

I nod and say nothing.

They are standing a little way off, the woman somewhat larger than her husband, a few inches taller, and plumper. She is lurking behind him, the sun glinting from the yellowish tint of her spectacles, her lipsticked smile beginning to falter, and it comes to me then that these are the Sommers. The spectacles, like the smile and the lipstick, are new to her, and on any other day of the week, in any other location, she would not be so friendly, as I suspect she must be aware. Mrs Sommer is someone who will pass me by in the street without so much as a murmur – she did the same to my wife just a few days ago – and when I attempt to meet her gaze now she stares full ahead, as if transfixed by something behind me.

Her husband however takes a relaxed few paces forward and holds out his hand. 'I thought that was you,' he says. His grip is firm, his eyes darting to my stick as we shake. 'I said to Susan, that looks like our friend Mr Hannah.'

He regards me with a keenness that is puzzling, and makes me uneasy, and for a moment I wonder if I ought to be congratulating him, if that is what he expects. It is after all six years since we last spoke, and without the proximity of 'Susan' I am certain I would not have recognised him. On both our visits to their home he remained in his armchair, said next to nothing, and was wearing, I think I remember, a cable-knit cardigan that suggested a far bulkier man than is actually the case. Mr Sommer, I now see, has the leanness of a runner, all sinew and bone, and is much shorter than I would have imagined.

'So how are things?' he asks, grinning expectantly, and I notice – I cannot avoid – the green stains on his teeth, which seem fused by bad hygiene, no gaps in between them. I look away to the church porch, where the minister is talking to a young woman whose back is towards me. Her buttocks are broad, her hair very long.

'Fine,' I say abstractedly, 'things are fine,' and would leave it at that if I could. The only 'things' Mr Sommer will be interested in are his former home and my current lameness, neither of which are his business.

'Go-ood,' he says, rocking back on his heels, pleasantly nodding. 'That's good.'

He is waiting. I bounce the rubber tip of my stick against the pavement. The young woman shifts her weight to one foot, her left hip pressing outwards. 'And yourselves?' I ask him.

'Oh us? We're well. Comfortable, you know.'

I nod, and watch as the girl slips off a shoe. Her tights are cream-coloured. She scratches a toe against her calf.

'Actually,' he says then, clicking his fingers as if just this instant remembering, 'now I think of it, we were in your vicinity only recently – a week or so ago – last Thursday? Friday? We were passing along that way – we don't often need to – and I said to Susan, "Shall we take a look? See if the old place is still standing."'

'And?'

Mr Sommer cocks his head at me.

'Was it?' I ask.

'Oh yes,' he confirms, touching my arm. 'Still standing!' His laugh is sudden and loud and an elderly couple glance over as they walk to their car. They smile indulgently. Perhaps in this company Mr Sommer's laugh is well-known and considered a tonic. The minister too is beaming in our direction; the young woman is peering over her shoulder. 'We were curious though,' he continues. 'We thought we heard some work going on – around the back?'

There's a beep, a flash of sidelights, door locks snapping open, and I watch as the elderly man helps manoeuvre his wife into her seat. 'Probably one of the neighbours,' I say vaguely, and Mr Sommer narrows an eye. He scrutinises me closely. The sun is blazing above us; the light is giddying. I hear the fun run tannoy in the distance and finally I'm too irritated to persist with this. 'Look, I'd better be going,' I say.

'Oh,' says Mr Sommer. 'Oh yes, of course.'

He appears disappointed, but steps adroitly aside, as though to avoid a collision, and reflexively I look across to the porch. But the young woman is no longer there. She is standing next to Mrs Sommer and their arms are linked, their hands clasped together. Pale-faced and watchful, this must be the daughter, just twelve years old when I last saw her, and regarding me now with the faintest of smiles. She is pretty, and though I am not a person who often blushes, I do feel – despite myself, and despite my lack of any religious conviction – quite transparent here, outside their church, my ill-feeling towards the Sommers plainly on view, my interest in the daughter obvious to all.

'Take care,' says Mrs Sommer, whether sarcastically or not I don't know, and as I make to move away her husband touches my elbow.

'God bless,' he says privately, and for the briefest of moments I think I might strike him, but then tighten my grip on my stick, and nod and walk on.

I have never myself attended a church. Other than assemblies in school, I've never once sung a hymn, bowed my head and prayed, listened to a sermon, chorused *amen*. Most of the weddings I've been to, including my own, took place in the registry, and what I recall of those two that occurred in a church is my boredom, and the confusion over when to sit, stand and kneel. I have been to five or six funerals, all of them cremations, none of them especially memorable, even those of my parents. Occasionally on holiday Jan will insist on entering some church or cathedral and gazing around, and we'll be calmed by the quiet, the dimness, the cool stone and high ceilings. The appeal of these places can't be denied, but the appeal is in the acoustics, the lighting and architecture. It's all about the atmospherics.

Professionally I am required to swear countless affidavits in God's name, but privately 'He' does not exist for me, and never has done. My parents weren't believers, and neither would they have called themselves agnostics or atheists. They were indifferent. Religion wasn't something they bothered with. Yet still, they observed the Sabbath. On a Sunday they did nothing; inactivity began and ended their day.

And Sunday morning, with its promise of nothing in store, no demands or commitments, is a peaceful time for Jan and me also, though looming always is the rest of the day when increasingly I will find I don't quite know what to do with myself, what I am for, what is my purpose. I mean other than to be a good father and husband. Sunday for Jan is our family day and she expects me to be there, in spirit and person; she expects me to participate, though of course it doesn't always work out. Lately our excursions have become fractious, unhappy affairs – the kids sulking, their parents bickering – and I have wanted only to be at home, on my own. Except that on my own I am lost, especially on a Sunday. Sadness pulls like gravity. I cannot move.

What might lie behind such inertia I wouldn't like to look into, but the remedy I'm sure is to work. And on Sundays there are opportunities that might not arise on any other day of the week, mostly in the area of personal and industrial injury claims, when my 'targets' – the claimants – are inclined to be less cautious, more complacent or stupid, believing themselves free to behave as they please, unobserved on their 'day off'.

I am thinking in particular of a warehouseman called Thrale, whom I followed one morning in February to a recreation ground in a neighbouring town and videotaped playing Sunday League football, my camera concealed in a sports bag slung from one shoulder, secured under one arm. He played badly, but lasted all game, and captured also on film is a moment at half-time when he hitched up one leg of his shorts, tugged out his penis and casually relieved himself in the misty late-winter air while drinking from a carton of fruit juice. His steaming urine melted a patch of frost in the hard frozen ground. Which was, in its own way, incriminating. No one claiming to have broken two toes as a consequence of being issued with the wrong footwear at work – as he was – could have run more than a couple of strides on such ground. Not that he ran particularly well. He wasn't an athlete.

Coincidentally, Thrale was employed – though no longer – at the same 'home improvements centre' in which I last found a use for my camera, four or five Sundays ago. My quarry on that occasion was a man called Minto, who was suing a local authority – not our own – for their culpability in causing him 'severe and disabling pains in the back, shoulders and neck' as a result of one of their Parks and Gardens lorries reversing into his car.

Filling my basket with items I supposed I would eventually need, I followed Minto and his wife to the Building Materials pallets, where she stood counting – her pen poised over a spiral-bound notebook – as he swiftly loaded a dozen 'major bags' of sharp sand onto their trolley. I guessed – from my own home-improving – what the sand would be used for, and with my hands in my pockets, my feet slightly splayed, posture open, crotch unprotected – all signalling my trustworthiness, I hoped – I was able to ask their advice on laying block paving, and had Minto demonstrate for me and my hidden camera, and so the insurers, his own technique.

Not everyone is quite so trusting, or dim-witted, as Minto and Thrale. But these are just two of several instances of assignments successfully concluded on a Sunday, all of them insurance-related. What I couldn't describe however are the 'matrimonial' cases I've brought to a close then, because for some years there have been none. Sunday is a day when most errant husbands and wives will have far fewer excuses to be absent from home, and I will have less opportunity to gather evidence of their infidelities, or indeed of their innocence. Instead I will schedule my surveillance for later in the week, and trust that they will dedicate themselves for this one day at least to their families, to gardening and shopping and decorating. Unobserved by me, they will visit theme parks, elderly relatives, and churches. And they will watch their children – or their grandchildren, or their nephews and nieces – participate in sporting events, including, no doubt, charitable fun runs such as ours.

They are all here, the mums and dads, the usual faces, a long crescent of summer-dressed parents sitting up on the grass bank that encloses the playing fields. In the hazy distance a roped circle of pennants, barely fluttering, marks out the circuit, and a great number of children, some on bicycles, are chasing each other round. I recognise Jack by his shirt, the back of his head. Under the awning of the adjudicator's marquee he jostles with some other boys to have his hand stamped, then sprints off to begin a new lap. But I can't locate Ben. Nor can I see Jan.

It is busy. Over by the temporary classrooms there's a beer tent, a barbecue, an ice-cream van. There are stalls selling home produce, 'ethnic' jewellery and scarves, school souvenirs. A young man in combat fatigues and spiked hair is sitting legs splayed, weaving a basket, I suppose for an audience, though presently no one is watching him.

Up here on the grass bank everyone knows everyone. The tannoy announces a teacher's name, the number of laps she's completed, and there's a cheer, a flurry of ironic applause. A few yards away are Gavin and Pauline, whose son Clinton some-times plays with Ben after school. They are sharing a blanket and picnic with a couple my wife calls the 'Regional-Radios'. He's a honey-voiced presenter; she's his producer. Arrayed about them are plates and bottles and freezer tubs containing rounds of French bread, olives, salads and cheeses, cooked chicken portions. They are drinking wine from paper cups. I notice a camera and a pair of binoculars, a *Sunday Times* and an *Observer*. All of which suggests a degree of preparedness and togetherness that is vaguely unsettling and demoralising, in a way that Sunday lifestyle supplements also often are. Several other people I recognise, and even know well, are sitting further along, and of course there's every reason to join them, and no problem, I hope, if I don't.

I hobble slowly away to where the slope levels out and cautiously get down on my knees on the grass, then onto my side, and ease myself onto my back. I lay my straw hat over my face. There's a prickling of sunlight through the weave, a smell of wicker and sweat, and I close my eyes, draw up my feet, and rest my hands on my belly – the recommended posture for easing the strain on my lumbar, though the pain continues to thrum in my back and my pelvis and down through my thighs. I breathe deeply, counting to five on each inhalation, seven as I exhale, and listen to the thinned-out yells of the children, the drone of the ice-cream van, the murmuring voices.

'We went through a conversion process five weeks ago,' someone says, walking nearby. 'We needed talent immediately, you know? People who'd add value and profile the minute we had them on board?'

An insect pesters my shin. The pain deepens, and I slip my hands under the arch of my spine, supporting myself on my fists. Which is more comfortable. The tannoy crackles, seeming somehow miles distant. A breeze disturbs the dry grass. And then I hear a voice I know well, close enough to give me a start. It is Will's wife, Anna, who phoned us last night to check that we would be here. 'Hello Jack-and-Ben's dad,' she says, sounding weary, fed-up, and I tilt back my hat, squint awkwardly upwards.

'Hello Nick-and-Nathan's mum,' I reply.

Her dark glasses are impenetrable. 'I saw you struggling along,' she says. 'I didn't realise it was so serious.'

'It isn't serious,' I say, and attempt to raise myself on my elbows, but a spasm defeats me and I sink back to the grass. 'Just sore,' I exhale.

She is smirking, trying not to. Often with Anna there is this grin, and sometimes the effort to hide it. She looks away to the school gates, her hands at her waist, her underarms shaved, and I gaze up at her dress, which is fuchsia-pink and patterned with splashes of yellow, one thin strap slipping over her shoulder. The cloth shimmers, seems expensive, and is stretched taut across the slight dome of her belly, the broad span of her hips. She is a handsome woman, dark and rangy, her sandalled feet planted securely. I notice a thickening vein snaking over one shin, a faint down just under her knees. I notice the frayed hem of her dress.

'So what happened?' she asks me.

'I turned forty,' I say.

Anna waits, her smile fading. She adjusts her shoulder strap. 'But seriously,' she says.

'Just that. I woke up, did some gardening, put my back out.' I rest my hands on my chest, close to my throat, as if holding a sheet there. 'That was my fortieth birthday,' I say.

'No more sleuthing for you then.'

'Seems not.'

Anna tucks her hair behind her ears, smoothes the front of her frock, and unexpectedly lowers herself to her knees, as though responding to something I said, some invitation from me. She lays a moist hand over mine. She is tipsy, I realise. 'I know a little poem about being forty,' she says, her breath yeasty and sweet. 'Would you like to hear it?'

'Go on then.'

'Depends if I can remember.'

She tilts her head sideways, her lips moving minutely. She is rehearsing. In the distance, beyond the school railings, the sun is flaring from the window of a parked car – a small white van in fact, the same age and make as my own, and perhaps at the wheel there is a man not unlike me, recording this scene – Anna kneeling at my side, her hand holding mine – though I myself would have avoided parking on the zigzags, anywhere quite so conspicuous.

'Let's see,' Anna says, silently tapping the words out with her fingers. '*It's the same for everyone. Our lives carry us till we are forty. And from forty we carry our lives.*' Then she nods, satisfied.

I look at her, smiling. 'Is that it?'

'That's it,' she confirms.

'It's not very long, Anna.'

'No,' she agrees.

'One of Will's, I suppose?'

'Oh please!' She shakes her head, as if affronted. 'No,' she says, 'he isn't that clever. I read it somewhere. Maybe it isn't a poem. It could be from a novel.' She twists her mouth. 'Can't remember. Sorry.'

'But you remember how it goes.'

'Yes.'

'Which is something,' I say, 'all things considered,' and feel her grip on my hand tighten. She leans suddenly closer, her mouth so tense I fear she is going to bite me. She is angry, and much more inebriated than I first thought.

'You know,' she says, 'you really shouldn't be so sarcastic, Mike. You really should give that one a rest. It's boring, you know. It really is.'

I say nothing, but carefully watch her. I can see my reflection in her dark glasses; I can just about make out her eyes. She is genuinely furious, it seems. Then the moment is gone and she slumps a little, lets out a long sigh. She pats my hand.

'Sorry,' she says.

'For what?' My tone is breezy, dismissive, and in fact I'd be quite happy if Anna chose not to answer me. I would be glad if she let go of my hand now and got up and went on her way. But she gives a small shake of her head, and bites her top lip, and looks over her shoulder. It seems she might be starting to cry. And though the melodrama in this annoys me, I do also feel I would like to embrace her, if that would be helpful. Except of course I am incapable, and these circumstances too public. Instead I ask conversationally, 'Didn't you have a coolbag back there, Anna? I thought I saw you with one.'

She stares a long time, as if weighing something up, the truth perhaps of what I've just said: she did bring a coolbag. Her garden in Benedict Avenue backs on to this playing field, and yet still she packed a picnic. She made those preparations, put herself to that inconvenience. 'Yes,' she concedes. 'There is a coolbag.'

'But no family?'

'Not currently.'

'Where are they?'

'Well, Nick is running.'

'And the other two?'

'My husband and Nathan are there,' she says, expressing little surprise. She nods towards the staff carpark, where my wife and Will have just come though the gates. They are walking slowly, their heads bowed, arms folded, evidently deep in conversation, and Ben and Nathan are dawdling behind them, sucking orange ice lollies. It seems they have been to the newsagents: there's a thickly rolled paper tucked under Will's arm. Anna briefly touches my cheek and cumbersomely she gets to her feet. Her legs have stiffened; I hear her knees creak. 'I'll get me a drink,' she says. 'Want one?'

'No,' I say, 'no thank you,' and watch as the white van pulls away from the kerb, a shimmer of gas from its exhaust, a brief shudder as it shifts gear.

My wife lifts her head then, looks over her shoulder. Perhaps it has just occurred to her that the van might be mine. Will shades his eyes with his newspaper and scans the couples on the grass bank. He tentatively waves in Anna's direction, but she has already turned for the beer tent, and before he can wave at me too I drop my head to the grass and pick up my hat and lay it back over my face.

4

You may or may not have heard of Will.

As a brand name, he once complained to me, 'William Brown' is far too easily forgotten, even by those who might actually have read him. On the other hand, the name is so nondescript, and so easily overlooked, that almost anyone might be persuaded they've encountered it somewhere: in a review perhaps, on the spine of a book in a friend's house. Which was my own position when I first met him, and it wasn't until he had itemised his novels for me – there were three of them then, and he told me their titles, described their covers, outlined the plot of the last one – that I finally conceded I knew nothing about him. His career was a blank to me, I apologised; his books had passed me by.

All of which was a lie. For two years at least – ever since our eldest sons had started in school – I had known *of* him, without having read a word he had written. And I was embarrassed to admit that, largely because my not having sought out his books was a conscious, mean-minded decision. Besides which, I *had* seen some reviews, and they hadn't encouraged me.

We were standing that evening in the yard of a recent

acquaintance of Jan's, a solicitor called Rosa, whose daughter attended the same playgroup as Ben and whose son played with Jack after school. Which is how we all tied up in those days, through the connections our kids made, though Rosa now is someone I rely on for bits and pieces of work, serving documents on debtors, reluctant witnesses, soon-to-be ex-spouses. Her own spouse was grilling kebabs in a shed at the end of their garden, and had been since we arrived. Half a dozen burnt-out barbecue trays littered the lawn, several crushed beer cans. A soft drizzle was falling and it seemed everyone but us had retreated indoors, including the children. It was getting dark; lights were coming on in the neighbouring houses. Will clutched a beer bottle close to his chest and angled his head, attempted to peer down its neck.

'I shouldn't worry though,' he shrugged. 'Maybe the fewer people know about me the better. Obscurity's probably a *good thing* for a writer.' He drained what remained of his beer, wiped his lips with his thumb. 'It's less corrupting of the important personal truths I have to share with you.' And then he smiled, very briefly.

'You're not *obscure* though, are you?' I said. 'There's three books out there. And they all have your name on.'

'Ye-es,' he said dubiously. 'Yes, that's *some*thing I suppose. I've leapt from obscurity to semi-obscurity. But it's not very helpful. You know? It's distracting.'

He rubbed agitatedly at the back of his neck, raked a hand through his hair. He was wiry, and dressed all in black, and he had very dark hair, very pale skin. There was eczema, I noticed, on his forehead, the side of his nose. When he frowned, his eyebrows formed a dark, continuous line. He was, I supposed, what my wife might call interestingly ugly.

'It's like, the work is what matters,' he said, 'but the minute you get published the work's compromised because either you think you've made it now – so you get complacent and write garbage, which I've seen happen – or else you start worrying all the time about what your editor, or your agent, or the next fucking *reviewer* is going to say. All these people you didn't have to bother with before. Which is me – I'm constantly looking over my shoulder, wondering *who's watching me, what are they thinking?*'

'Which can't be healthy,' I said.

'No,' he agreed. 'No, it's not.'

'And none of us knows.'

'What?'

'How tough it is being a writer.'

'No,' he said, deadpan, 'you have no idea. It is extremely hard being me.' And then he laughed, and quickly patted my arm. 'More drink!' he announced, and brandished his empty bottle, already narrowing his eyes at the light from the kitchen. He stumbled on the step, and the glimpse I caught then of his face wasn't remotely good-humoured, but scowling, tight-lipped. I didn't suppose he'd come back, and I wasn't sure if I cared. In a moment or two, I decided, I would find my jacket and go. We lived in the next street but one.

Yawning, I leaned into a drainpipe. I folded my arms and blearily gazed at a woman who'd just entered the bathroom, her stooping form in the frosted glass, the dark shape of her head, the red blur of her dress. I was by then fairly drunk, having lingered on the edge of far too many conversations that didn't include me, swallowing wine for something to do, and I hadn't intended to make Will's acquaintance. Another parent had introduced us – 'this is Will Brown, he writes books' – and then disappeared. She hadn't mentioned my name; she possibly hadn't known who I was. And nor had Will asked me.

The toilet flushed; the light clicked out. From one of the bedrooms there came screaming, several children at once, whether in play or distress I couldn't quite tell. The last I'd seen of Jack was over an hour ago, running through the house, hot and sweaty and impatient to get away from me. Ben had been asleep on Jan's lap in a front room. He was there still, I supposed, and if I were to leave I ought to take the boys with me. I ought to relieve Jan of that burden.

I glanced towards the side gate, which was padlocked, then noticed Rosa's husband ambling down from his shed, bearing a plate of grilled chicken, one hand hovering over it as if to keep off the drizzle. A cigarette wagged from the side of his mouth. 'You're doing very well,' I said, and pushed myself from the drainpipe. He glanced at me without recognition, without any suggestion of friendliness, and as I followed him into the warmth of the kitchen I realised how damp and cold I'd become, and how little I wished to talk further with anyone. But Will was edging back in my direction, easing away from the crowd round the drinks table. A woman looked up as he squeezed by her; she watched him intently.

I bent over a towel rail and patted my face. I hoped he'd continue on to the dining room, our conversation forgotten, but then heard the snap of a ring-pull. Froth spattered the floor, the scuffed toes of my shoes.

'Sorry!' he laughed, and passed me the can. There was another one under his arm, and he opened it cautiously, drank from it at once. 'So how about you?' he asked. 'What do you do?'

I wiped my can with the towel. I sipped a mouthful of beer. And because I'd been busy for most of that week on our house, and didn't want to encourage him, I said, 'I'm a painter and decorator.'

'Oh *really?*' he said. He swayed backwards. Music blared suddenly from the dining room, uncomfortably loud, and I saw two women cringe. They looked around in annoyance. Will was grinning, eyeing me sceptically. Some kind of reappraisal was taking place, some weighing-up of probabilities, and I allowed him to examine me, then splayed my fingers, showed him the gloss stains. Which seemed sufficient. He leaned closer, one hand pressed flat to the wall, and shouted into my ear, 'That's what my father used to do!'

'Did he?'

'It's what *I* should've done!' He touched himself on the chest with his can.

I waited. Rosa was lowering the volume; I heard her apologising. 'You think so?' I said.

'Yeah, definitely.' He nodded emphatically. 'Something practical, hands-on. Because that's another thing about writing – it's absolutely the least *physical* art form there is. If you think about it. There's music, sculpture, *dance* – whatever – your body's involved in some way, but with writing, it's the opposite, everything's clenched up.' And he demonstrated, scrunching his shoulders, clawing with his free hand.

'Which can't be healthy either,' I said.

'No,' he agreed. 'It's very *un*healthy.'

'So maybe you ought to get out more.'

'I ought to,' he nodded, and swigged from his can. A trickle of beer rolled down his chin; he wiped it with the back of his wrist. 'Because I'm sat there all day, you know? I rent this office in town – that new building just behind Rosa's? – and there's nothing in there but files and folders, and little yellow Post-its, and *stuff*, and it's like I'm banged up. It's like I'm in a prison. Solitary confinement. Day after day after day of solitary.' He squinted past me; something had caught his attention. Half-heartedly he said, 'But I should break out, you're right, do something more physical,' and then he extended an arm, and tapped my wife on the shoulder. 'Hi!' he said brightly.

'Oh. Hi.'

She was cradling Ben, apparently looking for me, and clearly quite tipsy. I placed my can on the tiled floor. I accepted our son from her arms. He was heavy with sleep, his mouth slack and drooling, and I smelled Jan's warm scent in his hair, his pear and apple shampoo. Briefly his eyes flickered open, and we watched him, all three of us. When he dropped his head to my shoulder, I quietly said, 'I was thinking of taking them home now. You'll make your own way?'

And Jan nodded, her cheeks and neck flushed, her eyes shiny with drink. 'Jack's ready,' she said.

'You've met Will?'

'Oh yes,' she said. The situation seemed to amuse her. 'He's Nick's dad. I told you.'

I glanced over my shoulder. In the darkened dining room some people were dancing. I heard Rosa cajoling her husband to join them. 'Did you?' I said.

'Yes,' she insisted, and softly struck me on my arm. 'When we came in!'

Will's face had settled on something close to a smile, though his gaze now was furtive, glancing between us. He pointed to Jan, then at himself. 'And I thought *you* told *me* that your husband was a private eye. Isn't that what you said? Two days ago?'

Jan bit her lip, assumed an expression of innocence. She looked to me, and clumsily I turned sideways to kiss her, one hand supporting Ben's bottom, the other the back of his head. 'I'm undercover,' I told Will, and slipped away then to find Jack, who was sitting at the foot of the stairs, his fists pressed to his cheeks, our jackets heaped up in his lap. He came without a word, and as I guided him out through the front door I craned to see as far back as the kitchen, and waved just in case Jan was still watching.

Among those people who know me, my occupation is clearly an oddity, a puzzle, and can make them uneasy. I am not the type, it seems; which is to say, not the type they would imagine. And in truth, it was never my goal to become what I am, a professional eavesdropper, a 'dick'. It is something I fell into, accepted. Other graduates my age – and perhaps you are one of them – drifted into local government, social work, accountancy or teaching, drawn there by the promise of security, a seemingly stable career. At Jan's insistence, I chose insurance, and worked for six years as a loss adjuster – assessing liabilities, investigating claims – until the firm that had trained me was sold to another, leaving me jobless. By which time I had made the acquaintance of several private detectives, their daily grind seemingly little different from mine. On occasions I'd employed them to work for me. Now I sought commissions from them in return, and I was often busy. Within a year I had set up on my own, and though I wouldn't say I've ever been entirely content with my lot, neither have I felt much desire to change it.

It's a job, like any other, and there is no particular 'type'. Temperaments vary. A policeman's disposition is useful, but empathy and intuition are as valuable as logic, detachment, a deadpan expression. Fearlessness doesn't come into it. You needn't be handsome, or able to handle a gun, or have a way with one-liners. You need only be patient, observant, polite. Niceness does get results, and a personable young woman with a diploma in sales can be as effective as any burly former detective inspector.

Or at least, this is the line I've become accustomed to taking, if I am pressed. To strangers of course my profession is 'interesting' – even 'fascinating' – and provokes many tiresome questions I would rather not answer. Amongst friends, as I say, there is often discomfort. In either case, I would prefer to remain 'undercover'. The habit of evasion is now ingrained, and whenever I can I will pretend to be what I no longer am, still pursuing a career in insurance, working as an 'independent claims specialist'.

It was only at Rosa's that I ever pretended to be a painter and decorator, or found myself so swiftly exposed. A fretful hangover followed, a nauseous regret at everything I'd said – though in fact I had said very little – and a creeping anxiety that Will must have seen through me. He must surely have known all along who I was – Jan's husband, the 'private eye' – and must have been aware that I was lying about my job, and lying when I claimed I hadn't heard of him. He'd allowed me to make a fool of myself, I decided, because I was 'material', something to write up in a notebook. And even if that wasn't the case, even if he had taken me at my word, his subsequent chat with my wife would have clarified one or two things – awkward for her at the time, and embarrassing for me the next morning.

But when finally I broached the subject with Jan she assured me that actually I had made a 'great impression'. Will had spoken of me 'quite warmly', and no, their conversation hadn't been at all tricky or uncomfortable, but 'silly', most of it. 'He was funny,' she said, 'once he stopped talking about himself.' And then she remembered a torn-off flap of pizza packaging on which he'd written the address and phone number of his office in town. It was in her trouser pocket in the washing pile. 'I think you've made a friend,' she grinned, handing it over, and told me I was invited to drop by his office if ever I happened to be passing. Will had suggested we might go for a beer.

And I was tempted, for a brief period, though in the end I did nothing. At one time, no doubt, I would have looked upon his offer as something more promising, a rare opportunity to form a new friendship, and perhaps be formed by it – a chance to become, I suppose, the person he imagined me to be. But I was thirty-six years old then, and a father of two, and I was, I decided, already too well known to myself and too little interested in others for there to be any scope for such developments. However much I might learn about Will through further acquaintance, it would only be so much additional information, more than I had the capacity or inclination to process. I wouldn't alter one jot, though I would have the unwelcome problem of adapting the person I 'actually' was to whatever demands his expectations might place on me.

Instead I resolved to avoid him – in so far as I could, given the hours our children spent in each other's company – and I have continued to steer well clear of his books, including a signed copy of his first novel, which he gave to me on my last birthday.

I read the inscription, then placed it on a shelf, and I haven't been back to it since. But while I cannot bring myself to read anything he has written – there are four novels now, and a collection of stories – I do look out for the reviews. I have sourced any number from the library in fact, and found a few others on the internet, and clipped and kept all the most recent ones, though I couldn't exactly say why, nor why I should hide them away – as I do – in an unlabelled drop-file at the back of a drawer in one of my filing cabinets upstairs.

'Semi-obscure', he may be, but William Brown is frequently reviewed, and usually favourably. He is, it seems, a writer much admired for his craftsmanship and the accuracy of his depiction of ordinary, unglamorous lives – lives such as his own, in other words; lives such as mine. With his 'unflinching eye for the ordinary', and his 'meticulous attention to detail', he is able, apparently, to 'root out and reveal the most elusive and surprising truths about love' and to portray – at least in his first book – 'the peculiar poignancy of life's quieter moments of triumph and regret'.

He is able to do this, but at a price: Will's books are not very exciting. His narratives verge on the 'slow', even the 'dangerously slow'. His subject matter is 'downbeat' and 'depressing'. And while his 'accumulation of minute particulars' does lend authenticity, it can also become 'so much clutter on the page, impeding the story'.

I am quoting the least sympathetic reviews, the ones I'll admit to most enjoying, but even his admirers take issue with the 'insularity' and 'uneventfulness' of the provincial world he depicts. 'Undeniably gifted,' says one – this was in the *Observer*, I think – he's in danger of becoming 'a prisoner to his own genius for the ordinary'. As are we all I suppose, genius or no.

That his books are slow and lack plot does not surprise me, however. Our lives around here are not the stuff of novels, or at least not of interesting novels, and I do feel I know a little about this, being a reader – which is rarer than you might think amongst so many graduates – and because I might once have been a writer. At one time that seemed a possibility, an option I might have pursued. Insurance is what happened instead; that and my marriage to Jan.

This of course is the last thing I would wish William Brown to discover about me, and is something I have forbidden my wife from ever mentioning, in any company, in case he should hear of it. But like Will, I also have a degree in English literature, and I also once completed a master's programme in 'creative' writing. These are not accomplishments I would ever advertise – and they might come as another surprise to most of our friends – but I am proud of them, privately, as evidence to myself that I am brighter than I might be taken for, and cleverer perhaps than I think I am.

Besides which, to mention either would, I'm sure, only raise the issue of why I haven't achieved more with my life than I have, and wouldn't make me appear any more admirable, but less. I wonder too if I might be suspected of making them up.

5

Write about what you know was the only advice ever given to me as a student, and for a while I stopped attempting to emulate, or imitate, whoever I happened to be reading then, and sought instead to describe what was happening immediately around me, producing a few pages a week of barely fictionalised conversation and incident that still somehow failed to ring true – however 'real' it was – for the obvious reason, I later concluded, that nothing any of us ever said or did at that time was quite genuine. It was all idiocy and pretension. We knew nothing, and I hadn't enough distance on it – or on myself – to realise that. And neither did Sarah, of course, who was the same age and no wiser. She often came to my room with a book as I typed and quietly sat on my mattress to read. She said she liked the clatter I made; it helped her to concentrate. She also liked to watch me at work, and liked to hear me read aloud what I'd written. Which was all the encouragement I ever needed.

There were six others in the house besides us, then several more who came and went, stayed for a while and moved on, and it was these people I tried to set down on the page. Our doors were never locked and our rules were communal, though not all of us were friends. There were factions and feuds, regular arguments, but still we abided by rotas, equal shares, weekly meetings. We took turns to bake the house bread and carry each other's clothes to the laundry. Our meals were vegetarian.

As a household we objected to most things, but especially money, possessions, careers. It was inconceivable that any of us might work in insurance. We didn't own suits, and I don't remember there being an iron, a tin of shoe polish, a clothes brush. We lived messily though austerely. There were tacit rules it seemed about everything, including what we could and could not enjoy. Enjoyment was suspect, too wasteful and frivolous, and we were earnest, committed, correct – some of us less so than the others, Sarah perhaps least of all. Her lapses were discussed in our meetings and rowed about later. The friction was constant.

Our housemates liked to call themselves anarchists, or 'true' socialists, or anarcho-syndicalists, and two of the girls claimed they'd become lesbians – 'dykes', they insisted – as a matter of principle. Prominent in our front room, and visible from the street, were posters supporting the miners, the printworkers, the Sandinistas. And though I did sometimes look upon all of this as play-acting, mere pretending, I never actually said so, except in private to Sarah. Nor did I attempt to satirise our lifestyle in my stories; I hadn't that temperament. I still turned out for the protests, the pickets. I did what was expected, and you may even have seen me – distributing leaflets in the town centre, hawking newspapers, rattling buckets – and kept well away. I wouldn't now blame you, and I cringe to remember all of this. I was twenty-one years old then, and I wouldn't want to go back there.

The house itself was shabby, built on four floors, and smelled fungal, as did our clothes. It was draughty and dilapidated, with old electrics, old plumbing, and it always seemed dark. From my desk I looked out on a garden untended in years, knotted with brambles and weeds. Sarah's room was directly beneath mine. Her French windows opened to a tangle of bicycles, a junk-covered patio, our bins. She said my typing unsettled the dust on her ceiling, and sometimes at night I would hear noises – the creak of her bedframe, a giggle – and press my ear to the floor, listening for her gasps, her boyfriend's eventual groan. Afterwards they would talk, their voices too low to decipher, quieter than the pulse in my ear. And later, much closer to morning, I might wake to the thump of the front door as he left. He rarely lingered for breakfast. His name was Anthony, and he wasn't one of us; he didn't have our approval.

We called him Tony the Tory, though he always denied he was any such thing. He laughed and said we'd misjudged him. His real views, he hinted, might just surprise us, but he never would say what they were, and I doubt there was much to reveal. Politics, I'm sure, pretty much bored him. The severity of ours must have been quite perplexing.

Tall and broad-shouldered, he had the bearing, the presence, of someone at ease with himself, public school educated, accustomed to money. His father, I knew, was a company chairman, his mother a university lecturer. Anthony himself organised music events – not the sweaty fundraisers in pubs that we were used to, but commercial ventures with sponsorship, regional media coverage, national names. There was a locally-televised 'Battle of the Bands' competition, a Friday night jazz club in the conference room of a hotel, and many 'special promotions' elsewhere.

A few years older than we were, he dressed older still, in Harris Tweed jackets, beige corduroy trousers, polished brown brogues. His cheeks had the flush of outdoors. He drove a fast car, and his smile when he breezed into our kitchen – his keys looped round one finger – suggested he found us amusing, a little ridiculous, but he was always polite, even when he was being insulted. And the girls who hung around in our house – the girls especially – often insulted him. They also needled Sarah about him, goaded her constantly, and she accepted whatever they said. She never tried to defend him. It seemed she required disapproval, from everyone except me.

Sarah wasn't my girlfriend, though we spent many hours together, alone in my room, or hers, drinking wine in the park, playing pool, trailing from café to café in town. Sometimes, walking home from a pub after dark, she would tuck her arm under mine; sometimes we held hands. Lounging about on my mattress, our housemates downstairs in the kitchen or attending some meeting – and there was always some meeting – I would pillow my head on her lap; she might ask me to massage her back. We were close, closer I'm sure than she was to Anthony, though it was Anthony of course that she slept with. And without Anthony I doubt there could have been a Sarah and me.

Endlessly we discussed him, Tony the Tory, like two children, conspiratorially whispering. She was trapped, imprisoned, she led me to think. Their relationship was not healthy. It brought her nothing but misery. But she was addicted to misery, we agreed. She could think only bad of herself, and needed, we decided, someone older and steadier than her, from whom she could hide and keep secrets, unsuitable habits and friends. She needed someone to kick against, antagonise, lie to, someone as complacent as Anthony.

They had much in common, far more than I did with Sarah. Their backgrounds were similar. Their mothers were in some way connected. But they were quite different types. Anthony hadn't Sarah's self-absorption, her moods or self-doubt. He was energetic, gregarious, and wherever they went, Sarah complained, their twosome quickly became a three, then a four or a five, until she wondered what she was there for, why he had brought her. She felt neglected, redundant, and never knew what to say to his friends. Which was a feeling we both had in company. We were socially ill-adapted, we agreed. The person we felt most at home with, and could talk to most easily, was each other. And we talked about everything. I knew far more than I needed to know about their sex life, his appetites. I knew he liked to be scratched, bitten hard. I knew he liked her on top of him, her hands gripping his wrists, her nails digging in. Often he came too soon, and Sarah made him start over. She enjoyed his clenched desperation as he tried to come again. He was comical then, she said. They had met at a mutual friend's wedding the previous summer: both very drunk, they'd crept from the marquee and had sex in a field. It was her idea. Afterwards he had thrown up.

Sarah told me these things, and also confided to me what little he confided to her – his secret self, his fears and insecurities – which she usually, in my company, derided, though I suspect it was just these confessions that she most wanted to hear, to have him share with her.

In the main Anthony kept himself guarded; she called him 'remote'. He might criticise her behaviour, her dress-sense or lifestyle, but she never could provoke him to arguing. She didn't know how to hurt him. Other than sex, she wasn't sure how to please him. Whatever her mood, Anthony's stayed much the same. He was imperturbable, as emotionally distant, she said, as her own father. Which of course we discussed, examined from every angle. They both made her feel foolish, immature and demanding; they made her feel like a burden.

And perhaps she was all of these things, though I could never see it myself, not at that time. I was glad to be burdened. Often unhappy, she came to me as a cat might, to curl up at my side, and sometimes she wept. Her tears were like no others I've seen – she made no noise at all, and her face did not alter. There was no trembling chin, no grimacing. The tears welled and spilled over, rolled fatly down. I stopped them on the tip of a finger, wiped them away. And when I tried to write about this, I found that I couldn't; I didn't know how or where to begin.

6

It is evening, the last day in May. The blue-grey clouds of a damp afternoon are folding and drifting. The wind blows in gusts. The student's bedroom is empty and her window left open. A white curtain flaps against the outside wall. A giant paper globe sways in the draught, glows faintly orange. Soon there'll be darkness. I drop my empty can to the wastebasket and switch on the light. The stopped clock, which I ought to rewind, shows ten minutes past two. I wait a few moments longer, looking up to her window, then turn and go back to our living room, where Jan is now curled in an armchair, a glass of red wine at her side. Her legs are tucked underneath her. She's wearing her spectacles and the gas fire is on low. Her marking for tomorrow is done, stacked on the floor. The wet weather, she told me, has put her off yoga.

'What are you reading?'

She doesn't remove her gaze from the page, but lifts the book from her lap and angles it slightly, so the cover is visible: it is Will's first novel, the copy he gave me.

'Any good?'

She licks a thumb and prepares to turn over the page. 'Mmh . . .' she says, noncommittal.

A door slams up the street. I recognise the sound of it. Most doors, listened to closely, have their own signature: the impact of the door on its frame is modulated by the snugness of the fit, the tightness of the hinges, the weight of the knocker, the proportion of wood to glass, any looseness in the letterbox or resistance in the Yale. And this door *thuds*, dully, without resonance, many times every day.

I finger a gap in our net curtains and see a girl with blonde braids, platform shoes, green- and purple-striped tights. She is clumping down the hill from number 73, which is five doors up on the right and once occupied by a family like ours but rented now to a group of young men who may well be students or in the drift of days and months that often comes after. Visitors are frequent, including this girl, and though two of the boys are readily identifiable – one a pale boy with dreadlocks, bone-thin and dressed as if for the beach, the other burly and bearded – the rest are indistinguishable. Until midday they are usually quiet, presumably sleeping. From then on there's music, bawled conversations, sudden shouts, laughter and arguments, the thud of this door. It seems they cannot live quietly. It seems to me their lives are lived to no particular purpose – there are no campaign posters on their walls, only pictures of girls and skateboards and young men like themselves – and I doubt they're much aware of the people around them or the annoyance they cause.

I am older than I once was, of course, and less tolerant. And this evening I am restless, as lacking in purpose as they are. Upstairs, Jack is also unsettled, shifting things about in his bedroom, as he frequently does. I let the curtains fall and turn to face Jan. Her glasses have slid to the bridge of her nose and she's frowning a little, one lip sucked under the other. Her forehead is freckled and wide. Sighing, I say, 'I'm going out for a walk.'

She looks at me kindly. 'Okay,' she says, and tilts her head, smiling. 'Don't forget your keys.'

I set off down the hill and turn left. Dusk is now falling and the last lamps have been lit though many curtains and blinds have still to be drawn on the day. The damp in the air carries the scent of wet soil, fresh leaves, and the breeze comes from behind me, warmer than I expected. I walk with shoulders squared, supporting each stride with my stick, and gaze in on the decor and domestic lives of our neighbours, confident they will see little more than their reflections should they glance up, perhaps my own face thinly glimpsed and unrecognised.

Most are looking at televisions; some are eating off trays. One elderly woman is busy at a bureau, stapling and folding. Another, two doors along and much younger, sits in a dining chair, where I frequently see her, talking on a red telephone. Everything here is familiar. In several windows, upstairs and downstairs, there are students staring at computers or hunched over notebooks, revising perhaps for their exams, and soon many of them will be leaving, their belongings loaded into hired vans or parents' estate cars, a few to return in the autumn, the rest to move on.

And even when vacant, these houses-for-rent will remain

obvious by their shabbiness, the cheapness of the furnishings, the presence of wardrobes and beds in the living rooms, and by the notices taped in the windows, directing visitors to come in by the back door. One sheet of A4 says: *Entry Up Rear Passage Preferred*. Another: *It's a back alley THANG*. They are fading now, and some – pinned outside and exposed to the elements – are almost completely erased. But in August or September the next occupants will put up their own signs, and I will continue to read them, each time I walk my children to or from school, whenever I trail down to the off-licence for my beers.

More regularly changed is the signboard outside the church, which this month proclaims:

> *No one is too bad to come in.*
> *No one is too good not to.*
> *Everyone is welcome.*
> *Come. Listen. Decide.*

No doubt a new message will be posted for June, something more topical perhaps, and punning, designed to amuse. They usually are, and usually, like jokes, I quickly forget them.

A little further along is the glass-fronted foyer of the church hall and here I pause to read the times of a jumble sale this weekend and a crafts fair in July. There are notices too for an under-fives playgroup, which meets in a room at the back, and a new youth club – the Wacky Wednesday Wonders – which is planned for the holidays. A Senior Citizens' lunch club is held here on Mondays and Thursdays. The Women's Fellowship hosts 'informal gatherings' on Fridays. The St Luke's Players put on three productions a year.

All of which makes my heart sink, for reasons I cannot quite fathom, and when I hear footsteps approaching, and glimpse in the window the reflection of a man with a dog, I turn and move on rather than have to bid him *Good evening*.

The road is clear in both directions. I cross at the next junction and enter a street of three- and four-storey houses with basements where the pavements are pink with rotting blossom and the tarmac is fissured and humped by the roots of the trees. It is darker here, the streetlamps partly obscured by the foliage, and most of the windows are curtained, the gaps too narrow to see through. Green plastic boxes sit by the front gates, each filled with bottles and papers neatly assembled for collection tomorrow. A light comes on in a bedroom. I look up and see a woman I recognise, another parent from the school playground, and for an instant it seems she is staring straight at me, but then yawns and stretches and begins sorting some clothes. She flaps a towel and folds it, and as I walk slowly on I continue to watch her, looking over my shoulder, and stub my foot on a box of glass jars left out for recycling.

The noise startles a cat from a porch and sets a dog barking. There's a brief jolt of pain in my back. Someone is peeking, I notice, through a gap in their blinds, and I proceed then with head bowed to the corner of Benedict Avenue, where the

Sommers now live, across the street from Anna and Will, and where I decide to go now.

In the film *Rear Window*, which is one of my favourites, the evening temperature edges into the eighties and very few curtains are closed until the actual moment of bedtime, if even then. Jimmy Stewart, a photographer confined to his apartment with his leg in a cast, looks out on a square of New York tenement buildings whose backs are obligingly laid open to scrutiny, the private lives of his neighbours negligently exposed to his lens as they dance, argue, drink, and murder their wives.

There's a 'Miss Lonelyhearts', I remember, who sets a table for two and acts out the arrival of an imaginary guest. There's a 'Miss Torso', a ballet dancer of sorts, who performs callisthenics in her panties and bra and entertains suitors most evenings. On the top floor a middle-aged husband and wife go to sleep on their balcony. In a flat to the photographer's left a couple of newlyweds keep their shades lowered, while in the studio apartment to his right a heavy-drinking songwriter sweeps the floor in his underpants and plays disconsolately on a piano. And then there's 'The Salesman', who dismembers the remains of his wife with a butcher's knife and a saw.

No doubt you'll have seen it. The film was repeated the week before last and what struck me this time was its obviousness. The set is so clearly a film set and the characters so simply summed up, so plainly what Stewart supposes they are. There is suspense – the film is by Hitchcock – but no mystery. Each of the private worlds the photographer peers into contains a recognisable story, complete in itself, and he is able to observe them all from a single panoramic perspective, without ever leaving his station or – until the climax – being noticed himself.

There's much about the film I enjoy – the pastel colours for instance, Thelma Ritter's wisecracks, Grace Kelly – but it's this scenario, the unobstructed surveillance of other people's domestic existence, that appeals to me most, though of course it's untruthful. In all the years I have worked as a professional snoop, and all the hours I've spent observing strangers from cars, watching windows from other windows, exits and entrances from street corners, I've rarely seen anything so tidily framed, so readily interpreted, and the scant few scenes I've witnessed that are in any way memorable have almost all been incidental.

One afternoon, for example, in a neighbourhood of doctors and bankers and lawyers, I stood in the quiet of a bedroom and watched a man masturbating in his back garden. My job was to capture on film the activities of a different neighbour, an elderly lady suspected of poisoning my client's three cats, and as I stood alone at the window, surveying the scene and considering the best location for installing a camera, I glimpsed a naked man to my left.

Sheltered by the blind wall of the next house along, the trees in his own garden and the frame of a pergola, he was hidden from every angle, I realised, but mine. Balding, thick-set, he was perhaps the age I am today – this would be eight or nine years ago, and I thought of him then as 'middle-aged'. The day was hot, his patio fierce with bright sunshine. He stood for a while on his back doorstep, lazily stroking himself, slowly becoming erect, and when at last he was firm he stepped fully into the light and tossed himself off, casually, in no hurry at all, as though holding a hose to his lawn. Once finished, he shook some semen from his hand and went back indoors and shortly afterwards re-emerged with a glass of white wine, still naked, though flaccid, and wearing a pair of blue flip-flops.

He appeared to look up at me then. I stared back and his gaze drifted away. I assumed he couldn't have seen me – no window is truly transparent, at least not from both sides – but when I described this scene to Jan in the evening she wasn't so sure. He must have known I was watching, she said. And she wasn't amused, as I'd hoped she would be, but disapproving – both of the man for what he had done, and of me for spectating. If I hadn't provided the audience, he wouldn't have behaved as he did.

Which was a possibility, and one I later worked into the anecdote I made of the incident. It became for a while a staple story, another tale I could tell whenever I found myself receding into anonymity in company, or the opposite – called upon to participate, to account for myself or describe what I did for a living. And while my listeners never failed to be interested, and were usually amused, sometimes even shocked in an exaggerated, drop-jawed kind of way, always I would sense some other, more private assessments being made – questions asked about me, queries set against my name, as if what I did was immoral, or perverse; as if I was not to be trusted. And so now I don't bother; my job, as I say, is something I would prefer not to discuss.

The story was anyway misleading of course, in what it implied about me and what it revealed of my work. Most of the time I see only fragments – glimpses and snatches, parts of pictures, parts of stories. Like the photos I take and the footage I gather, my view of the world is a view of its shadows, its corners and margins. It's a grainy, partial view, and mine is not a vivid existence – professionally or privately – but one that requires a great deal of patience, diligence and caution. Always there's some 'mystery' – some small question to answer – but hardly ever suspense, and it's rare that I experience anything approaching excitement, or act in any way that might put me in jeopardy.

And yet, as I come now towards the house where Anna and Will live, I find my heart thumping. There's a taste of something urgent on my tongue, a giddy feeling of lightness, and though it wasn't my intention when I stepped out this evening, or even when I turned into this street, I take a quick glance behind me, half expecting to see one of the Sommers, and then slip down the alley that leads to the rear of Anna and Will's.

At once I am confronted by darkness. And silence. The noise of the breeze in the trees suddenly ceases. The passage is narrow, a tall windowless gap between two 'handsome' Edwardian terraces, and I hold out my stick, sweep it slowly before me. The ground is pliant, unsurfaced, and my footsteps make barely a sound. I pat the wall for guidance, and look back over my shoulder. The street shows as a column of sodium-lit colour, orange and purple. No one is following, and I'm certain there is no one ahead, but still, I try to walk sideways, attempt to see in both directions at once.

The houses are long – three rooms deep, I remember – and where they give way to their gardens the passage becomes like a tunnel, roofed over by hedges, a thick tangle of branches.

Here I hesitate, tempted to stop and turn back. The dark is less uniform, the shapes more suggestive. I grip my stick by the wrong end and hold it poised like a club. I tread softly forwards. A trailing stalk brushes the side of my face and I hunch my shoulders. I crook my free arm above me. I flex my stick. But this is ridiculous. My fear is not that I might be assaulted, but that someone will see me, step out and ask what I think I am doing.

In most situations I would have a plausible story prepared. Lately, on certain kinds of surveillance, I have taken to wearing a reflective vest and a hard-hat and making notes on a clip-board. If anyone should ask – which they haven't – I could claim to be a council-contracted surveyor examining traffic flows. Paradoxically, I'm sure, the high-visibility vest makes me less noticeable, because less suspicious. But here I'm not on surveillance, and nothing could be more questionable than being alone in this passage at this time of the evening.

The tunnel emerges to another, much wider passage that

disappears left and right along the rear of the houses, and when I reach it I straighten. I arch my back and inhale a smell of damp undergrowth, night-scented flowers. I have been out here before, on a couple of occasions, playing hide-and-seek with the boys. The Browns' garden is three along to my left, and somewhere in the dark beyond that – ten or twelve houses further – there's an entrance to the school playing fields, its black iron gate now permanently bolted.

The chain-link fence that encloses the grounds runs alongside me, and is rusting, I remember, in many places collapsing. A long line of sycamores and beech trees rises behind it; the shoots of hedges and nettles poke through. And perhaps if someone were to challenge me now I could pretend to be looking for this shortcut in to the fields, though that in itself might raise further questions, and wouldn't stand up if the 'someone' should be Anna or Will.

A rustle travels through the tops of the trees. I keep close in to the wall and edge along to their gate. Carefully I lift up the latch. From this point onwards, of course, I can have no excuse. The gate opens only so far – just sufficient to squeeze through – and then jars against a rise in the ground. I slip inside and stand for some moments quite still. I hear an emptying cistern, a muffled clump from indoors. I am, I know, surrounded by clutter. There's a mess of planks and old bicycles, discarded furniture, piles of concrete and bricks. But I can see nothing, only gradations of blackness. I hold my breath, alert to every sound, and gradually at the edge of my vision I begin to distinguish the spokes of a wheel, a tower of plant pots, a water butt. My heart is pounding. And what I am feeling, I realise, is not fear but excitement, a tingling in my kidneys that reminds me of childhood, a trembling sense of adventure.

At this end of the garden I am shielded by bushes and trees. Directly before me there should be an old shed. I shuffle towards it, testing the ground with my stick. I reach out a hand, splaying my fingers, and touch its rear wall. The wood is rotten, spongy with damp. I feel my way to the corner, then down the narrow gap at its side, and in the shadows at the foot of the lawn I kneel and stare up to the house, and what I see then is Anna and Will in their kitchen. I find a tableau as tidily framed as any observed by James Stewart.

The kitchen is large, twice as long as it once was, and spacious enough now to accommodate the refectory table at which Will sits reading some sheets of A4, wearing spectacles I wasn't aware that he needed. Nearer to me, Anna is searching the cupboards. Lazily she opens one after the other, as though uncertain what she is looking for. The units are metallic, reflective, in a style called 'soft statement aluminium', and were fitted last spring when this glazed extension was added to the end of their kitchen, the work paid for not by Will's books but with money inherited from Anna's great aunt or great uncle. Though big, their house is shabby throughout and they frequently say they are penniless.

Anna lets her arms drop. She is barefoot, and dressed in a pair of saggy pink trackpants, a washed-out oversized T-shirt. Her hair is tied in a short ponytail. She says something to Will, then ambles towards him, tapping her fingers along the length of the worktop, the back of each chair. He doesn't look up but peels off the top sheet of A4 and slides it under the pile. He squares the pages, continues to read, and Anna stands close behind him. She places a hand on each of his shoulders. She seems to be examining the back of his head. Lethargically, she begins to massage his neck.

I do know her fingers, the feel of them. At Jan's insistence last year I had my hair close cropped in a style – a 'number four' crewcut – which she then decided was wrong for my 'shape of head'. It did not suit me, but the cool on my neck and ears, which made me shiver at first, was briefly invigorating. And briefly – at a party given by Anna and Will to celebrate this kitchen – I enjoyed the attention my stubble attracted. Many people wanted to stroke it. Anna, drunk from the outset, was amongst them, and I remember the jolt when she bumped into the back of my chair, and the shock when she began to caress me.

She stroked backwards, one hand passing repeatedly over the other, in a way that was altogether too lingering, too self-consciously 'sensual'. Embarrassed, I looked down at the table. I pushed some olive stones around on a saucer and waited for her to stop. I stretched across to my left for a bottle of wine, and to my right for a glass, but still she continued. Then Will passed by us, on his way out to the garden with Rosa. 'Oh leave the poor chap alone, Anna,' he said, and that was the end of it. Her hands left me, and swaying, she began to follow him out, then stopped and sat down. I poured my drink and got up and went through to the living room. I stood beside Jan. 'You're looking very flustered,' she told me.

Will is speaking now, slumped back in his chair. His lips are soundlessly moving. He frowns at his sheaf of A4. He taps a finger on the edge of the table. Anna stoops and embraces him. She folds her arms over his chest and looks up at the windows, at the glazed double doors to their garden, as though posing for somebody's camera. Her chin is resting on Will's shoulder, her cheek is pressed against his, and she appears to be staring straight at me. Her eyeline is level with mine, and though I know she will see nothing but their reflection, I find I can't hold her gaze. I shrink back. I lean close in to the side of the shed and watch as she kisses his cheek and releases him and walks from the room. Will returns to his reading, doesn't acknowledge her leaving.

A pale light shows in the bathroom window; a line of bottles appears in silhouette. She will be climbing the stairs now. In a moment or two she may come into a bedroom, and really I ought not to be here; it is time I went home. But still I linger. I shuffle forward on my knees and survey the rest of the garden; I consider changing my position.

The light in the bathroom goes out. A sudden wind thrashes the trees. Seeds pitter on the roof of the shed, and then I hear the sharp scrape of Will's chair. He stands and stretches and takes off his glasses. He turns towards the hall door, apparently listening to something. His head is bowed. I scan the windows upstairs. Nothing is there, nothing is moving. Will folds his glasses into their case and takes a long look round the kitchen. He turns out the lights.

I suppose he too will be going to bed now, and slowly, supporting myself on my stick, I begin to get to my feet. My back has stiffened. I brace my hands on my thighs and cautiously ease myself upright, and when at last I lift up my head I glimpse a movement indoors. Will is still there in the dark. He is approaching this end of the kitchen. Stealthily he keeps close in to the units; he walks sideways on. I dare not move. I try not to breathe. The shed is one short stride behind me; the shadow of a honeysuckle is falling across me. Will cups both hands round his face and presses his forehead to the glass of the door. He looks out. Then gently he lowers the handle and leans his shoulder into the frame, and when the door gives – a soft release of air as the seal breaks – I feel as though I too am released. Quickly I abandon the scene; I terminate this evening's surveillance before the subject detects me.

7

The house next door to ours has been empty for just over a year, ever since the elderly spinster who lived there – its original occupant – went suddenly senile and died in what seemed a matter of days.

One wet afternoon she wandered out in her nightgown and attempted to catch a bus into town; we heard this from friends. Soon after that she was taken away in an ambulance – which we watched from an upstairs window, and decided was none of our business – and the next we knew her nephew, her only surviving relative – a crabby, corpulent man from somewhere out in the country – was emptying the house of her things. He told us she'd already been buried; he didn't say where.

Her name was Mrs Calder and she left behind her a property unaltered in fifty-odd years, every 'original feature' intact, including the kitchen linoleum. But these were the original features of post-war rebuilding – her former house and four others were bombed out in the war – and of course the presently sought-after features are Victorian, Edwardian, Art Deco. Any new owner would have had the choice of living in a charmless – currently considered charmless – relic of 1950s interior design or suffering the expense and upheaval of a major upgrading: plumbing, electrics and heating, floor coverings, windows and door styles.

The estate agent's board beside the front gate changed three times before the house went to auction, where finally it was bought by a developer who directed its gutting and refitting over a period of seven or eight months beginning last autumn. A new board has since appeared, and according to the details, which I printed out from the Internet, the house now 'benefits' from UPVC windows with country-style leadings, a Shaker-style kitchen with built-in appliances, a conservatory with feature stained glass, a fully insulated loft, gas central heating, Victorian-style fire surrounds, traditionally panelled interior and exterior doors, and is back on the market at more than twice the price we paid for our six years ago.

But still there's no clamour, and yesterday I watched from my attic as an estate agent – a young man of twenty or so – pulled up in a blue Volvo, behind him a red soft-top Mercedes. A couple got out, possibly our age though dressed a lot younger. She was slim, blonde and lipsticked, and wearing a tasselled jacket and boots in matching fawn calfskin, a pair of tight-fitting jeans. He was tall and broad-shouldered, dark-stubbled, and dressed in black leather. They were not like us. They followed the agent indoors, eyes dutifully raised to survey the exterior, arms sceptically crossed, and re-emerged maybe two minutes later.

'So what value *would* you give it?' called the agent, sorting his car keys.

'I wouldn't want to upset you!' replied the man, strapping himself in at his wheel.

Unsmiling, the woman examined her face in a mirror, flicked back her hair, and stared at the terrace of houses opposite ours, as though wondering at the plight of anyone with no choice but to live here. Moments later they drove off, pursuing the Volvo, in search of somewhere more suitable, an 'executive' apartment perhaps, with twin garages, a city centre location, 'convenience-living appeal'.

There have been a few others to view, but none quite so glamorous, or unsuited. The only ones I remember in fact were a couple very much 'like us', who arrived on foot with their three children, spent a long while looking round, conversed in murmurs in the garden, considered the house from across the street, and eventually parted from the agent with loud promises on both sides to 'be in touch very soon'. I recognised them from the school run and they would have made useful neighbours, I thought: their kids and ours could have been friends; I might have enjoyed watching the mother come and go. But it seems they have chosen instead to buy a Victorian end-of-terrace a few streets along, where the gable wall is seriously cracked and every windowframe needs replacing, but where, I assume, the ceiling roses are intact and there's a cast-iron fireplace in one of the bedrooms.

Which is why next-door is so unpopular. In this neighbourhood we don't care for the ersatz 'feature', the fake period detail, but seek genuine character, the authentic sag and wrinkle of a life that's actually been lived – always providing that life is pre-war. There are similar, though smaller, houses in other parts of the town – many far better preserved, and considerably cheaper – but they are located in enclaves more menaced by factories and council estates and the major arterials, which is where most of us began as first-time buyers still happy to be childless ten and twelve and fifteen years ago, our sights set from the start on somewhere like here.

'Desirable' is the word most often used about this area in the estate agents' windows, and naturally it's becoming more desirable – though not to the likes of the couple in the Mercedes – as it becomes less affordable, more the exclusive preserve of the middlingly successful. The truly successful live elsewhere and we don't know them. Nor would we want to.

There are exceptions, but 'character' is what we seek in our homes, and 'character' – more perhaps even than money – is what we would most like to possess, or be thought to possess. We wish to be interesting, to be the kind of people who suggest hidden depths, unusual quirks of thinking, principled noncon-formity, possibly even some past acquaintance with addiction or depression or self-destructiveness. And yet we also wish to be comfortable.

You might call us bourgeois-bohemian, which is to say we are neither. We're too bourgeois, too complacent or cautious, and we give too much thought to our mortgages and pensions, our ISAs, shares and insurance policies, to be truly bohemian. But our homes are colourful and cluttered and we often dress shabbily and consider ourselves creative, relaxed, still open to circumstance, the spontaneous moment, and I'm sure if you were to collect your child from Jack and Ben's school this home-time you would find any number of individuals in paint-spattered jeans in the playground, many of them listed in the local authority-funded 'Open Studios' catalogue, our annual guide to the home addresses of two or three hundred painters, potters and printmakers, all within a twenty-mile radius. Some are genuine of course – 'real' artists – but many are not, and most of those that I know of would seem to depend on the support of a professionally-salaried spouse, or an early inheritance, or the proceeds of a London house sale, and only 'work' when it suits them, when the mood is right and the weather conducive to their muse.

We have no equivalent directory of local authors, though doubtless there are many in the playground who would be happy to hear themselves referred to as writers. I'm aware of several academics and freelance journalists amongst us, for instance, *bone fide* authors of educational textbooks, scientific papers, consumer advice guides. And there is also, I know – because I've eavesdropped on the conversations – one woman who describes herself as a playwright on the basis of a drama for children performed by the St Luke's Players last Easter, and another who promotes herself as a poet on the back of a pamphlet produced by a local and now defunct 'partnership' publishing venture, coincidentally run by her husband. There will be others who are writing novels or memoirs, I'm sure – the academics and journalists included – and I do sometimes wonder if they regard Will as yet another of their kind, a 'wordsmith' like them, diligently 'scribbling away', and no more deserving of attention than they themselves are. Which is to assume they have actually heard of him, and would know what he looks like. He doesn't often come up to the school.

Anna I frequently bump into – two, perhaps three times a week, on the approach to the school in the mornings, waiting in the playground at home-time. Her boys come to our house to play; ours go to hers. Jack and Nick are in the same trampoline class. Occasionally we will meet by chance in the park, or down at the shops. And when we're not filling these moments with whatever cheerful inanities will suffice, there might be some mildly ironical acknowledgement of our dissatisfactions, a shared admission that life is hard and full of tripwires and snares. Or perhaps it's the case that I initiate such admissions; it's my habit to probe after them, because very often Anna will then complain – however mildly – about Will. She'll compare him unfavourably with me.

Of course the hours I work are flexible, which is to say unpredictable, even erratic. An observation period may stretch to twelve or fifteen hours; a simple enquiry can keep me busy all week; many jobs will take me from home. But days of idleness do also occur, and even when my schedule is full my time can still be my own, to apportion as I see fit, and I can often manage to make room for my boys. Escorting them to and from school is one job I enjoy – and feel I should do – but is something that Will, apparently, loathes. And yet he is here this afternoon, standing alone by the caretaker's hut and staring straight at me. He jerks his chin in acknowledgement and realigns his body as if to make room for me. It seems I have no choice but to join him.

'Clocked off early?' I ask, more chirpy than sounds natural, and he tugs at his nose, scratches his stubble. He allows the flicker of a smile. My heart, I realise, is racing.

'Didn't clock on,' he says.

'No?'

'Not today.'

I brace myself against my stick and we stand shoulder to shoulder, facing across to the classrooms. There's a sound of chairs scraping, desk lids dropping. A female teacher shouts over the noise: pretty Miss Dorning, who once taught our eldest and now teaches Ben. Will's arms are folded. He sways gently forwards and back, apparently restless, though silent. 'Anything up?' I ask.

'Up?'

'Anna okay?'

'Anna? Yeah. She's fine.'

I hesitate, nod. 'How come you're off work?'

Will inhales a long thin breath through his nose. He slowly exhales. 'Not much point in being there?' he offers.

'No?'

He shakes his head. 'Not at the moment.'

A soft luminous cloud passes above us. The light momentarily dims, our shadows fade and return, and I look at him quickly, then look away. It is, I suspect, a peculiarity of the English, or of English men in particular, that conversation is easiest when both are facing directly ahead. In cars we can talk, or walking side by side down the street, or admiring our gardens. But Will is a difficult one. Any conversation with Will, unless he is drunk, is very often like this, a question followed by silence, an eventual reply, another question. And though today I would much rather stand and say nothing, fearful of where a conversation might lead us, still I find myself asking, 'Any particular reason, Will?'

'For what?'

'Why there's no point?'

'Nothing to write about,' he shrugs.

'I see,' I say, nodding.

The asphalt around us is steadily crowding with parents, most of them mothers, and I gaze across at the feet of a woman nearby. She is wearing black clogs. There are blue plasters over her heels where the straps of some other shoes must have cut into her, and she's talking animatedly – and easily – to another woman, who's wearing espadrilles so threadbare her toes are exposed. They stand together most days, though most days, when I'm here, I would be watching them from the other side of the playground, where Anna usually waits by the flowerbeds. They are both eye-catching women.

'Or else,' Will continues, 'there *are* things to write about – the usual things – only I can't seem to get them down on the page.' He makes a half-hearted jabbing motion, as though attempting to spear a pea on a plate. 'It's becoming a problem,' he says. 'A bit of a worry.'

'So you're blocked?' I say.

Will looks at me sideways. He bobs his head left and right, a gesture which means, I would guess, 'You *could* put it that way.' And then he glimpses something far off, the first burst of children to emerge from the Reception Year cloakrooms. He stretches his neck, lifts himself on the balls of his feet, and tentatively raises a hand, ready to wave.

'Ours'll probably come from the other door,' I say, pointing across him. And in fact his son Nathan is already out, lugging his burden of schoolbags towards the spot where he expects his mother to be. He stops some way short and looks round, then dumps the bags and just stands, dark-browed and curly – the image of Will – and placidly waits to be found. His father has plainly not seen him.

'How about you?' he asks then. 'Getting about more easily now?'

'Not exactly,' I say. I waggle my stick. 'Improving, I suppose. Getting there.'

Many other children are fanning into the playground, including my youngest, bright-faced and dishevelled and beetling towards us. A football arcs through the air, clatters a netball hoop; two boys on bicycles narrowly miss him. 'But you're back at the spying?' says Will.

I hesitate. 'Sorry?'

'You're back at work.'

84

'Soon,' I say cautiously. 'Not quite yet.' I brace myself for my son. Giggling, he thrusts his bags at my midriff – a practice we've already 'discussed' – and when I refuse to accept them he cheerfully persists, forcing the straps over my wrist and onto my arm.

'Right,' says Will, as if none of this is occurring. 'That's good. I was hoping to ask you about that.'

'About my work?' I say, glad of the distraction of Ben. He's excited and clearly there's no point in resisting. I bend down – as much as I'm able – and allow him to hook the bags onto my shoulder. I point with my stick and speak into his ear. 'Go and tell Nathan his dad's here. Quickly.'

Will watches my son as he runs off, his 'giddy-up' gait and splayed feet, and finally then he notices Nathan. He waves with both hands to attract his attention. 'Yes,' he says, smiling, and lowers his arms. 'I was wondering if maybe I could shadow you for a week or so? Tag along when you go out on surveillance, that sort of thing? See what you get up to.' He makes eye contact. I glance away. 'Depends how you feel, obviously,' he says. 'I haven't thought it through yet, how we'd arrange it, what sort of fee and so on.'

'This is for research?'

'Yes.'

'For a book?'

'The one I'm stuck on, yes.'

'Right,' I say, nodding, and notice our playwright is staring straight at him, though not – I suspect – because she has been listening, or knows who he 'is', but because here is a man she hasn't previously seen, a 'stranger' amongst us, and it's her instinct, or reflex, to register his height, build, distinguishing characteristics. I would do the same, and I haven't the slightest doubt that every one of our children, girls as well as boys, could safely make their own way home in a neighbourhood as vigilant as ours is. Jack in fact has a key to our front door, and is trusted to accompany Ben when I cannot meet them. It isn't a long walk – six or seven minutes at most – and every road they must cross has lately been 'calmed'. Jan's school is nearby and she's usually home before they've thought to kick off their shoes.

'You're not keen then?' Will asks, accepting Nathan's bags, absently ruffling his hair. Nathan pulls away and confers on something with Ben. He cups his hand round my son's ear.

'I'm not sure,' I admit. 'It's a difficult one, Will.' Clusters of parents are beginning to disperse. Over by the gates Nick and Jack are waiting to leave, hanging onto the railings, and dismally it strikes me that I could have avoided this situation, and the prospect of a week in Will's company, if I'd only resisted the lure of a few minutes' conversation with Anna, which, I now realise, was my main motivation in coming up here today, and possibly has been for some time.

I nudge Will's foot with the tip of my stick and point across to our sons. As we start walking to meet them I say, 'The trouble is, I can't really see what you'd get out of it, Will. Most of what I do is pretty humdrum, you know? It's nothing like what happens in the films, or in books. It's not like Sam Spade, or Hitchcock or whatever. Even the adulteries – I can't remember the last time I was asked to bug a bedroom, or anything like that. It's mostly just chasing up husbands for non-payment of maintenance, checking they're as strapped as they say they are. Making phonecalls, knocking on doors, running credit checks. It's pretty dull,' I say, pausing by the school gates. 'I think you'd get bored.'

But Will is not to be deterred. 'Dull's fine,' he insists. 'I don't mind dull.'

Children and their parents are parting around us, steering buggies and prams, bicycles, scooters. Several other mothers glance curiously at Will. Some scowl at me. We are getting in their way and I shift a little to my right, then back to my left. 'Well for instance,' I say, smiling apologetically to the woman with the clogs, 'you mentioned surveillance, okay? These are the jobs I turned down last week.' I count them out on my fingers. 'There was a scene-of-accident report, which would've meant an hour or so measuring and notetaking and taking photos of road junctions. I had three process servings, which is basically all proper procedures – it's a rigmarole, dotting i's and swearing oaths. And there was one missing person – a debtor gone AWOL, nothing remotely interesting.' I close my hand, hold up my thumb. 'And the only one that came anywhere near to surveillance? The council asked me to investigate some dogs. They were causing a nuisance, barking all hours.' Nathan and Nick, I notice, have already set off for home and the attentions of Anna. 'Do you see what I mean?

You might just as well make it up, Will. It wouldn't take that much imagination.'

'Imagination's the problem though,' he smiles. 'I've got none.'

'Not even for barking dogs?' I say. But there is no need to pursue this; I believe I know what he means. I feel afflicted in much the same way, and as I watch my sons crossing over the road – Jack holding Ben's hand – I realise I have no real objections to Will's proposal, or none that would persuade him. He is, I'm sure, genuine: he would like to know what I know, and has no cause to distrust me. 'Look,' I concede at last, 'I'd better be going. But let me think about it, okay? I'll see what I can come up with. Yes?'

And patting his arm, I walk quickly on, my stick barely touching the pavement as I lengthen my stride to catch up with my boys.

8

As I come into our bedroom from my shower, warm and drowsy, a threadbare towel tucked round my middle, I smell Jan's cleansers and moisturisers, a fragrance – according to the labels – of juniper, liquorice and 'moonflower'. It is, as they say, reviving – 'a tonic' – and I breathe deeply, though there is also a taint of soiled clothing or mould or stale air in the room, an underlying fustiness that is often in here and which we can't seem to locate or get rid of. It survives airings, bed changes, polishings. It recurred soon after we redecorated. 'There's that smell again,' I say, and drape my towel along the radiator.

'Yes,' replies my wife. She is sitting up against her pillows, an A4 desk diary opened out on her lap. 'I know,' she says, and sucks on the end of her biro.

I stretch and yawn and pad naked round our room, stiffly collecting stray socks, folding discarded T-shirts. I leave a trail of talcum powder footprints, and if Jan once looks in my direction she does so discreetly, without my noticing. I open a window, inhale the night air. I leave the curtains slightly apart and carefully lower myself to our bed and ease myself under the sheets. I caress Jan's leg, and guardedly I glance at her, but my back is already aching, my left eyelid twitching with tiredness, and she is clearly not interested. I gaze up at the ceiling. The house is silent. The time is half past ten.

Quietly I say, 'I'll make some phonecalls tomorrow.'

Jan taps her chin with her pen. 'If you think you're ready,' she says.

Three and a half weeks have now passed since I last went to work, and the inactivity is making me weary, more prone to tiredness than ever I was when fully employed. I yawn at all hours, drift in and out of daydreams, catnap most afternoons. Some crucial fibre has slackened, it seems. I can no longer stay up late, for instance, and have taken to retiring at much the same time as Jan, which she does not like. I have become familiar again with her nightly routines, the sequence of toilet, hand wash and teeth, the rapid undressing, the lengthy hair-brushing, the application of her oils and lotions, then the ten or twenty minutes she devotes to her diary.

Unlike me, Jan has always kept journals, diligently written each evening as she sits up in bed. She bites her top lip as she writes, gnaws on her pen when she pauses for thought. She resembles a schoolgirl, much as I imagine she must once have looked, and there's something girlish too in her handwriting, each letter so rounded and clear, and I'm sure if I were to dig out the earliest of those journals – she began them when she was fourteen and has kept every one; they're stacked willy-nilly in the wooden chest on which our television rests – I would find much the same style. The letters would be formed in similar fashion, perhaps even the syntax, the way she expresses her thoughts, though I imagine at school she would have drawn circles instead of dotting her '*i*'s and would have used many more exclamation marks.

But the fact is I haven't bothered to look, and neither, I think, has Jan. She buys the diaries half-price in February or March, a new one each year, and ignores the pre-printed datelines and feints, preferring instead to cover every square inch of paper from first page to last. A large scratchy asterisk indicates the end of an entry; the day and the date – no abbreviations – is underlined at the start of the next. She briskly commits to the page as much as she needs to, then closes the book and dumps it on the floor until morning. By day it sits in her bedside cabinet, and when it is finished, completely covered in ink, it goes downstairs to the trunk. Her purpose is not to remember, to file her life for future reference, but merely to place a full-stop on each day. Once written, that day is gone; she can sleep and wake to the next.

And if I know as much about this as I do, it is because I have on other occasions come to bed early and lain here beside her – waiting, perhaps, to make love, or for the light to go out – half-interestedly watching the point of her pen as she has spelled out her sentences, sometimes offering suggestions if the name of a person or place should escape her. Even when she's been critical of me – *M wrapped up in himself*; *M no help at all* – she has made little effort to hide it, and I haven't objected to her grievances, inwardly or openly. She is welcome. It's her diary, her thoughts, and the fact that she is happy for me to look if I want to, and leaves the diaries always in a place where I can find them, ought to be as much guarantee as I need that there's nothing happening in her life or her heart, nothing private or secret, that I need be alarmed about or hurt to discover.

Not that I am worried.

'Will Brown left a message,' she says with a yawn, and closes the book, her pen tucked inside it.

I close my eyes. I link my fingers over my midriff. 'What about?'

'Listen to it,' she says, and drops the book to the side of the bed. She twists about to reorder her pillows, fiddles to switch off her lamp. 'Maybe he wants to be your new best friend,' she says, and in the darkness I smile.

At the dinner table this evening Ben looked up from his plate and asked me, 'Who's your best friend, Daddy?'

'I don't have one,' I told him. 'Only Mummy, she's my best friend.'

Beside him, Jack disguised a smile. 'Sad,' he said, and shook his head slowly. 'Very sad.'

Ben took a moment to consider. He turned to Jan. 'Who's your best friend, Mummy?'

'Not telling,' she said, and both boys glanced at me, then again at their mother.

'But *who*?' Ben insisted.

'Not telling,' she repeated.

'*Mu-um!*' he whined. 'You've got to.'

Jan heaved a long sigh, pretended reluctance. 'All right,' she said heavily, 'Daddy, then.'

Jack tutted, resumed eating. His brother sat holding his knife and fork, dreamily gazing at me, then out of the window. Quietly Jan got to her feet, began clearing up.

'Really?' Ben asked her at last.

'Really,' she said without inflection, and he nodded, pushed his plate across the table towards her. He was, I sensed, disappointed. And in some way, I suspect, so too was my wife.

I would not blame her. Ours is above all a companionable marriage, and though it isn't exactly the case that we take each other for granted, or are indifferent to each other, or uninterested, or bored, there are certainly periods when that is the case, and now is perhaps one of them. In due course no doubt – based on past experience and the pattern of our years together – this detachment will give way to some stronger force, some more pressing energy – a sexually-charged renewal of affection perhaps, or a short-lived return to the bitterness and fury that occasionally, bewilderingly explodes from beneath us – but for now there is wedlock, and routine, and the familiar facts of our daily existence.

Having said which, it might also be the case that my wife's journals are a blind, a diversion, the surest way of preserving her privacy. Perhaps what goes down on the page is what doesn't much matter – the useless clutter of her day – and with that out of the way she is then free to contemplate what really concerns her. And if so, I am glad, for the truth at this point in our marriage is this: I wish my wife to lead a life independent of me, of my involvement or attention, so that I too may be free to inhabit my own private self, my own private thoughts. Which, for three and a half weeks now, have circled round Sarah. Despite the presence of Jan, and the nagging distraction of Anna, it is Sarah I think of most often, and as I settle to sleep at Jan's side this evening I do wonder if through the years Sarah has made as many visits to me as I have to her, if I stalk the back of her mind as she does mine. I wonder if she also dreams about me.

That period in my life lasted for little more than a year – a year and two months – though I suspect I am making it seem a lot longer. Certainly it feels a long while to me now, an era I lived through, and perhaps still haven't grown out of.

Sarah was someone I already knew, though vaguely, from our time as undergraduates together. She was in the year below me. We'd attended some of the same lectures, seminars, parties. And it was Sarah, drunk at a party, who invited me to move into that house. I was about to begin my master's degree; she had just dropped out of her course. She told me they had a spare room: it had belonged to a boyfriend who'd left to become an aid worker somewhere. She herself was unemployed and intended to remain so.

Before Anthony, Sarah had had many 'boyfriends', most of them short-lived – a night or two maybe, sometimes a week. The aid worker had lasted three months. She claimed she couldn't remember them all, but there must have been dozens. I wasn't quite so experienced. Until I met Jan in the spring I'd had only four other girlfriends, and slept with just two of them. Of course I described each one in detail to Sarah. She said she was jealous, but seemed to want to know everything; she never stopped asking questions. 'What about Wendy?' she asked me.

'What about her?'

We were lying fully clothed on my bed, and the wall was behind me. Sarah had me cornered, trapped, and I was comfortable with that. Sunlight poured across the floor. The house was noisy with people – talking in the kitchen, stomping up and down stairs. Dinner was being cooked, a smell of onions and garlic. Someone was humming, softly splashing in the bathroom.

'Were you in love with her?'

'Not really. I think I *thought* I loved her, sometimes – she had nice eyes.' Which were like Sarah's, looking at me then, the green flecked with amber, her dark lashes curling out at the corners. 'I was just horny really.'

'Did you tell her you loved her?'

'Yes,' I smiled. 'She asked me to say it – it made her horny too.'

Our postures were almost identical: foetal, facing each other. Sarah's cheek was pillowed on her hands; my head was resting in the crook of my arm. Our knees were touching. She nudged my toes with hers. 'What about Lauren?' she asked me.

'I told her as well.'

'And Arianne?'

'Yes.'

'And she *still* wouldn't have sex with you?'

'No. But neither would Eva, and I told her all the time.'

To say the words had been chancy, exciting, and not exactly a lie. I'd had no designs when I'd said them, but needed to hear how they sounded, test what they felt like. Once spoken, perhaps the words would come true; perhaps then I would know what they meant. But with Sarah I already knew. With her I was certain, though it seemed impossible that I should say so. We were intimate and shared everything, everything but that. I tested the phrase in my mind, shadowed our real conversations with imaginary ones. I persuaded her to leave Anthony, that house, the life we were leading. I practised saying these things even after I'd begun seeing Jan.

'Do you love Janette?' she asked me weeks later. We were sitting in a corner of Anthony's jazz club, her leg pressed against mine, our table cluttered with ashtrays and bottles and glasses. It was the first time I'd been there and I wasn't impressed. The music was taped and the venue starkly functional, no more than a place for students to drink after hours. Anthony's chair had been empty for over an hour; he was circulating. Jan was ordering drinks at the bar, dressed in clothes she said she'd bought especially for that evening. I kept my eyes on her as I talked.

'It's early days.'

'Have you told her, though?'

'Sarah!'

'Have you?'

'No.'

'Do you think you will?'

'Maybe, it depends how things go.'

'So how's it feel now, what's it like when you're with her?'

'Comfortable.'

'More than with me?'

'It's different, Sarah.'

This was in the very beginning, when Jan was still strange to me and I was happy enough to share what I knew of her: that she was training to be a teacher, and lived on the university campus; that she returned to her parents most weekends, who lived twenty miles out in the country; that she had no interest in politics.

All of which made her unusual, as different from us as Anthony was. And uniquely, among the people I knew then – and possibly now – she had no gripe about her upbringing. While we were all angry, in some way at odds in ourselves, and needed the outlet – the tension and drama – of our constant rows in that house, Jan was always equable, stable, and had a tolerant, even indifferent attitude towards the neuroses and crises of others. She didn't pass judgement, but didn't appear to care or understand either. Like Anthony, she kept some part of herself to herself, and she too, when she called at our house, seemed incongruous, out of place, though she hadn't quite his self-assurance or knack of talking to strangers, not then. Jan said very little in fact. On the first occasion she ate in our kitchen I remember the other girls asking in detail about the clothes she was wearing, barely disguising their cattiness, their disapproval, and Jan answering them plainly. She bought her clothes on the high street, whereas they all dressed from jumble sales, charity shops, market stalls, and this, among other things, was an 'issue'. Only Sarah was ever friendly towards her, that evening or later, though carefully friendly, just as Jan was in return. They were never intimate. And until I moved out of that house I never would tell Jan that I loved her.

Love meant the intimacy I shared with Sarah, and my dependence on that. It was the yearning when she wasn't around, and the excitement when she appeared, but also the hurt. Sarah knew how to hurt me, as I knew how to hurt her. There were periods – days on end – when we did not talk, but baited and riled each other. The cause would be trivial, and quickly forgotten; it seemed we needed little excuse. We were cruel, vindictive, and meant it. Perhaps we sensed that worse could be said and the situation still be retrieved. I suppose we enjoyed it.

But Sarah was cruel in other ways too, in ways I didn't think I could respond to. My mattress, as she knew, lay just the other side of the wall from the bathtub she sometimes got into with Anthony. And as I lay reading, or trying to sleep, I would hear their giggles, their silences, the soft rhythmic lapping of water, the chink of their wine glasses on the enamel. She must have known too that I heard the sounds that came from her bedroom, though not that I pressed my ear to the floor and tried to imagine myself in Anthony's place. Once, disturbed by their lovemaking, I crept downstairs to an empty kitchen and took a carton of milk from the fridge, and as I stood drinking by the sink in the darkness I gazed out at our patio, then across to Sarah's French windows, and glimpsed the skin tones in the gap between her curtains and the backlit shapes on the fabric. I lingered until she switched off her light, and when in the morning I told her what I'd seen she made a show of being outraged, pretending to hit me, softly pummelling my arm. And yet, the next time I came down, a week or so later, I noticed that the gap in the curtains was wider.

It seemed she wanted to be seen, and overheard, just as later it seemed she was quite prepared to be discovered when at last we made love.

Our sex was infrequent and didn't begin until shortly after I'd started sleeping with Jan, though of course I didn't make that connection, not then. It happened, and seemed natural, and I was too naive to think otherwise. I remember the first time especially, the newness of Sarah, the details – the texture of her skin and the smell of her hair, the feel of her breasts on my chest, the span of my hands on her buttocks. It was mid-morning, and the house, I assumed, was empty – I'd spent the previous night in Jan's room on campus. And though Sarah was unresponding when I whispered her name, and didn't mewl or cry out, or make any of the noises I would hear when she was with Anthony, her curtains remained open to the garden, her bedroom door was ajar, and when we heard footsteps on the stairs she did not panic – as I did – but rolled on to her side and calmly waited to see what would occur.

I scrabbled about for my clothes in the mess that customarily covered her floor and hurriedly attempted to dress in a corner, half-concealed by her wardrobe. The footsteps continued on to the kitchen and Sarah looked across at me and giggled. She draped herself in her dressing gown and blithely swept from the room, leaving the door wide open behind her. I crept upstairs later, unnoticed.

For the rest of that day I found no other opportunity to be alone with her, and when we next talked it was not about us, or of what had occurred, but again about her boyfriend, her feelings for Anthony. She confided then not only what she most hated about him, but also what she most liked. She complained that none of us appreciated his qualities. Anthony was 'sweeter' than we realised, she said, and considerate and generous, and he made her feel special. He found her beautiful, she said. As I did of course; as everyone did, everyone except Sarah herself. And because I loved her I allowed myself to be used in this way. Sharing these confidences was as close as we could get to each other without making love – and perhaps closer, for those half-dozen times when we made love again would be preceded and followed by further discussion of Anthony, more intimacies, more whispered speculations about him.

9

There is this about Will's conversation, even his passing re-
marks: a sense that most things he says have been tested first on
the page, that nothing is quite off-the-cuff, but recited, re-
hearsed. His anecdotes have the feel of well-honed routines,
and in fact there are stories and opinions, I know I have heard
more than once. Anna must have heard them many times over,
and is to be applauded I suppose for not heckling or yawning –
for instance when he starts in on the subject of children, 'family
life', parenthood. His only real achievement, he once told me,
was to father his children; his sole purpose in life is to do the best
he can for his boys. In company, and especially if he's been
drinking, he will proclaim that parenting is what makes us most
human, that children are what give point to existence. He'll
confide that he personally would like to have more – three
would be his minimum, five his ideal – and that he regrets not
yet having girls.

As for Anna, I assume she must daydream through all of this,
or choose not to be listening, because in fact his involvement in
the life of his children appears to be minimal. From what I've
observed and what others have said – and from what Anna

herself has revealed – it seems he 'participates' far less than he would have us believe. She does almost everything. Mealtimes usually happen without him, and it's a rare treat for Nathan and Nick if he reads to them at bedtime. He doesn't run baths, cook breakfasts, or kick a ball about in the park with them. He excuses himself from carol concerts, class assemblies and most other school-related activities. And now, it seems, he has taken to working on Sundays, apparently panicked by the lack of progress on the book he is writing.

'He left about ten,' Anna says, leading Ben and me down their long hallway, her sandals clacking on the bare boards. Her hair is gathered again in a ponytail; her jeans are ripped just beneath her backside. 'He did *say* he wouldn't be ages . . .'

Shouldering my walking stick, I usher my son in ahead of me and we squeeze past an old wardrobe lying on its side at the foot of the stairs, then a couple of bicycles propped against the wall, and a scatter of shoes, some bright plastic toys, and follow her into the kitchen, where there's a smell not of food but disinfectant. A mop is standing in the sink. Some of the floor tiles are wet. Stooping, Anna points my son in the direction of Nathan, who is squatting in the garden with a jar and a spoon, purposefully digging a small hole in the lawn.

'I expected him back, oh . . .' She looks to the clock on the wall. 'Half a fucking day ago.' She smiles at me broadly, a big pasted-on smile I'm not meant to take literally, that disappears in an instant. Then sighing, she says, 'So . . . what can I get you? Tea? Coffee?'

'I'm fine,' I say, 'really. I won't hang about. But you're sure about Ben? Nathan can always come round to ours.'

'Or there's a bottle of wine open. I can offer you wine.'

'I'm driving,' I say.

Anna briskly rinses a couple of glasses. 'Ben can stay as long as he likes, Mike. I'm happy to have him. And Nat's happy. So there's no problem. Are you sure you won't have a drink? You're not driving far.'

She twists the stopper from a bottle, hunching a little, and I notice the sharpness of her shoulder blades, and how thin are her arms. She is wearing a black vest, and beneath it – the straps and edges just visible – a cherry-coloured bra. As she pours her own drink, a thick hank of hair slips forward and covers one eye, dangling near to her mouth. She blows at it and frowns. She tosses her head and some more hair comes loose.

'Yes, no?' she says, the bottle held in one hand, an empty glass in the other, her dark hair dishevelled.

I hook my stick on the back of a chair. 'Okay, then,' I say, 'a small one,' and sit sideways on to the table, facing out to the boys, conscious to keep my back straight and my posture aligned, my feet flat to the floor. Nathan has his arm around Ben and they are peering down the gap at the side of the shed. Nathan's jam jar lies abandoned in the grass. 'So where's Nick?' I ask her. 'Gone to work with his dad?'

'No,' she says, and places a full glass at my elbow, another nearby. 'Nick has not gone to work with his dad.' She slides into a chair and rakes back her hair, then swiftly regathers it. She tugs her ponytail through a red band. There is black stubble under her arms. I reach for my glass. Outside the boys are wading through weeds as high as their knees, disappearing from view. Anna pinches her glass by its stem and slowly revolves it, her lips pursed, then abruptly looks up, as if I've just spoken. Her gaze is direct, but she says nothing.

'So where is he?' I ask.

'Sorry?'

'Nick.'

'Oh, Nick is out,' she says. 'Nick is somewhere about. The park, I hope.'

'You *hope*?'

'Think. Believe.' She shrugs, and there's a hint of a smile, a slight tuck at the side of her mouth. 'He is ten, Mike. Boys need to be allowed these adventures, don't they? They need to go off and explore. You can't mummy them forever.' She slumps back in her chair, one arm fully extended, still touching her glass. Her other arm hangs down at her side. 'Though actually, saying that, I can't see Jan letting go of yours, not before they start shaving.' She looks up at me. 'If then.'

I raise an eyebrow and faintly she smirks. The edge in her voice is surprising, and strikes me as unfair. My wife especially is someone who feels sorry for Anna, her situation, and often worries that she might be unhappy, frazzled by childcare, bored and frustrated, possibly 'desperate'. I would need to look it up in a dictionary but 'febrile' is the word I would apply to her, if it means what I think it means – nervy, intense, highly strung, somewhat needy. None of which makes me feel sorry for her, not quite. Nor does it suggest that I might be wise to avoid her.

'Well no,' I say carefully, 'we do let them out, Anna. Just so long as they stick together, and we know where they are. And they come back when we tell them.'

'Good,' she nods, sipping. 'Good, I'm glad to hear it. And what about you, Mike? Do you have to say where you're going and when you'll be back?'

'I don't *have* to,' I answer, forcing a smile. 'I *choose* to. It's voluntary.'

Anna looks at me steadily. Her gaze is unnerving, and I reach for my glass. Small in the distance I can hear the boys' voices. Quietly beside me Anna says, 'And do you have adventures, Mike?'

There is a circle of moisture on the table. I place my glass precisely over it. 'Depends how you mean,' I say. 'But no, I wouldn't say so, not really.'

'I "mean" professionally.'

'No, not professionally.' I let out a laugh, louder than I intended. 'Especially not professionally,' I say.

'So why is my husband the writer so interested in becoming your sidekick?'

'I don't know, Anna. I have no idea. I've already told him, he'd be better off making it up.'

'Privately then.'

'What?'

'*Adventures*.' Her tone is teasing – what I suppose she hopes will sound teasing.

'No,' I say flatly.

'What about Jan?'

'What about her?'

'Does she?'

Annoyed, frowning, I don't immediately answer, but look across to the clock on the wall, which shows five minutes past four, then softly I say, 'I very much doubt it, Anna.'

The clock is a train station timepiece – the words *GWR, Paddington* on its yellowing face – and beneath it, standing on its side on the floor, is a metal signboard for *Westward Ho* tobacco, rust-bitten and dented. Formerly, before the Browns had their kitchen converted, this board was displayed with a collection of plaques – *First Class, Second Class*, the various acronyms of the rail companies – and another, far rustier board advertising *Ovaltine, The World's Best Night-Cap*. A string-net luggage rack served as a shelf for their vegetables. And there were other things too, railway artefacts, all of them original, bought up from boot sales, junk shops, auctions. Despite the disorder in the Browns' house, they had given some consideration to the decor, and Anna's kitchen especially was themed, a place of arrivals, departures, brief encounters. Which is a thought that suddenly makes me uneasy.

'I'd better get going,' I say, and finish the last of my drink. My chair screeches on the tiles as I stand. 'What time shall I come back for Ben?'

Sighing, her expression clouding, Anna sits forward. She pushes an index finger through a small spillage of wine on the table. She traces the shape of a letter, a capital *A*, and then says, looking up, 'You do realise my husband is in love with your wife?'

'Excuse me?'

Anna takes a breath, momentarily holds it. 'I said, you do realise my husband is in love with your wife.'

'In what way?'

'The usual.' She tilts her head at me. She suddenly laughs. ' "In what way?" Mike! How many ways are there?'

I stare at her. I realise I am glaring.

'Don't worry,' she says. 'I don't mean he's fucking her.' She finishes her drink in one swallow, pinches her face at the taste. 'Or not yet, not that I know of.'

'What are you talking about, Anna?' I shake my head at her, and slowly she stands. She presses her hands to the small of her back and arches her spine. She looks away to the garden, where Nathan has emerged from the side of the shed. The broken shaft of a spade is tilted over his shoulder. Ben is behind him, struggling under the weight of a car tyre. They stand together in the shade of the honeysuckle, where I myself stood a few evenings ago, and stare back at us.

'I'm sorry, Mike,' she says then, and lets her arms drop. She sighs heavily. 'It's been a long, aggravating day and I'm tired, I shouldn't have said that, forget it.'

'Forget it?'

'Ignore it then, discount it. I don't know what I'm talking about.'

'Anna!' I complain. 'What do you mean your husband is in love with my wife?'

'Nothing,' she insists, and lightly she slaps herself on the back of her thighs, a gesture I suppose of self-motivation, a reminder that she ought to get on, that there are things to be done. 'It's just how he operates, Mike. It's how he functions in life.' Suddenly she moves towards the dishwasher and yanks down the door. But whatever she was hoping to find there, she is disappointed. She slams the door shut with a force that surprises me. 'There always has to be someone, Mike. Do you understand? With Will, there always has to be someone. So really, I wouldn't worry about it. I'm sure *she* has no idea, and I'm sure nothing will ever come of it.'

I take our two empty glasses to the sink, in which a filthy mop head is draining. 'So what you mean is, he has a crush on her?'

But already it seems Anna is bored with this conversation, and distractedly she says, 'If you like, yes . . . you could call it a crush.' She sweeps some breadcrumbs from a worktop to her hand, drops them into a pedal bin. She touches the mop handle, then leaves it. 'So!' she says. 'What shall I tell him when he gets in? Would you like me to pass on a message?'

I hesitate, puzzled. 'About . . .?'

'You wanted to discuss a job?'

'Right,' I nod, and gaze absently around us, at our muted reflections in the sheen of the units, at the open double doors to the garden, and at our children, who are kneeling now within earshot. Nathan is showing Ben a spare house key, hidden beneath a glazed plant pot.

'Mike?'

'Yes,' I say, and watch as Nathan replaces the pot in its saucer. 'But we'll need to discuss it. Maybe when I collect Ben – will he be back then?'

'Or you can phone,' she says.

'I'll need to fetch Ben.'

'Yes,' she says. 'Sorry.'

'So?'

'*I* don't know,' she says, exasperated, as if it ought to be obvious. 'Six, half-six . . .?'

'Okay,' I say, and for a long moment then there is silence, as though neither of us is quite sure what ought to come next.

Anna lets out a sigh. She smiles. 'It was nice to see you anyway,' she says simply, sincerely, touching my arm, and I am, I know, intended to hear the sincerity, the simplicity. She does mean it, and she would be glad to see me again.

'And you,' I say, holding her gaze, and slowly her smile becomes quizzical. There is the ghost of a frown, but still she is smiling. I try not to look away. Like several other women we know, Anna is someone who laments that she has become 'invisible' as she's grown older, that men don't seem to notice her as they once did. But I certainly notice Anna. She is not invisible to me. And standing here in her kitchen, in the rising stench of the mop in her sink, I feel again as I did at the fun run, that I would be very glad to embrace her. And perhaps she realises this. Possibly this is something she would welcome, but our children have now come in to join us. They are scavenging for food in her fridge. Nathan is crouching on the floor just behind her, Ben is reaching across him, and it looks as though they've been crawling through hedges: bits of the garden are stuck to their clothes and their hair – twigs and seedlings and leaves. Ben stuffs something into his pocket and glances furtively up at me. Grinning, he turns back to the fridge.

Anna says, 'I'll walk you to the door.'

'No. It's okay,' I say, more relieved than frustrated. 'I think I can find it.' And planting a kiss on my fingers, I touch my son's head and turn for the hallway, one hand vaguely raised in farewell, leaving my stick still hooked over the back of a chair, unmissed until I get out to my van.

10

Dressed this afternoon in our suits, Will and I are wider than we are used to. His padded shoulder nudges mine as we cross over the road, and again as we turn into Stevenage Drive. 'Sorry,' he murmurs, and touches his tie, tugs on his collar. He hasn't worn this suit, he told me earlier, in nearly a year, not since his father was buried. My own jacket and trousers have been on the hanger a mere month, but the weight and shape of them feel as odd to me now as the scent of my deodorant, the tight fit of these shoes, or the fact that I'm walking so briskly, my stick discarded at last. Will gives a slight shuffle and quickens his pace to match mine. I would be happier if he dropped back a stride and followed behind me; I realise I should have brought the van closer and saved us this walk.

We have driven fourteen miles today to serve some documents – a divorce petition, in fact – on a woman named Helen Slater, and Will's purpose is merely to be here and watch. Any unpleasantness need not include him, and his nervousness now is becoming distracting. I reach inside my jacket for the papers and glance again at the address. The houses on this side are odds, and up in the hundreds. We are looking for number sixteen.

'We want the other side,' I say.

Will pauses at the kerb, doesn't step down until I do. It is half past four and the pavements are almost deserted, even of children. Many of the houses are boarded up. Quietly he says, 'It's funny, I grew up in a street just like this.'

'Lots of people did,' I say.

'Exactly like it, I mean. Same layout, same kind of houses. Same curve in the road.' He gestures behind us. 'Those flats. We used to face a block just like that – you see those blue balconies, with the washing out? That's what I saw every morning when I got up. There was a woman over there used to shove her kids out, then go shopping or whatever, and they'd just hang over the railing gobbing at people until she got back. I used to watch them from my bedroom window. I had that room just over the porch there.'

He points to one of the houses, grey-rendered and semi-detached, the front lawn unenclosed. The porch is a slab of grey concrete, supported by a pole. The white paint on the pole is blistering and the concrete is furry with moss.

'It was handy,' he says. 'Whenever I heard my dad coming after me with his belt I could climb out that window and drop to the porch, then slide down the pole and run across to the flats. I used to hide in the bin sheds round the back. My sisters had to come and find me once he'd gone out. Or passed out – sometimes he just fell asleep and forgot about it.'

He gives a small shake of his head, a sad, wry little smile, and vaguely I remember having heard this story before. Besides sharing his thoughts on the subject of parenthood, Will is fond of recounting grim tales such as this one, unhappy anecdotes about the harshness of his upbringing, and I suppose we're all meant to admire him for his fortitude or great good luck in coming through it. Not unscathed we're led to surmise, but through it all the same, to the point where these days he can smile – wryly and sadly, but forgivingly – on the disadvantages he has had to surmount, given the enviable success he has made of himself.

The only surprise is that he has said quite so much without the aid of a drink. And I suspect if I were to encourage him now he would tell me more about his father, a lot more. But I have a job to attend to, and besides, I was born in a similar street, to a similar childhood, and though my father wasn't a drinker, or a bully, he too could be frightening and he also disciplined his sons with his belt or his slipper or the back of his hand. Many men did then.

And of course it persists, though not so much among people like us, liberal fathers determined to be friends to our children, more trusted than feared, more loved, I suppose, than obeyed. Certainly the papers I've come to serve on Mrs Slater today would more commonly be sent out by a wife to her husband, and frequently his violence would be cited as the main cause for their divorce. The next document I must deliver, in fact – tomorrow morning, and with Will once more in tow – is an injunction forbidding a father from further assaulting his wife and their two sons. It does go on, and many others besides me will know of it professionally – the social workers and teachers, doctors and probation workers whose children attend the same school as my own.

As for Mrs Slater, she has made no accusations, and her husband does not appear to be violent, though he has done as much as he can to provoke her into a divorce, to the extent of cohabiting now with his 'paramour' – who is pregnant – in the Slater's former family home. He wishes to remarry of course, but Mrs Slater won't release him. She won't give him that satisfaction. For the past two years – more or less since she learned of his adultery – she has lived out here with Beatrice, their only child, and though she does accept the maintenance he voluntarily sends her, she refuses to acknowledge his letters and phone calls and she won't allow him proper access to his daughter, who's twelve.

This much I know from our friend Rosa, the solicitor, who is acting on his behalf. And I know, from the papers bulking my pocket, that he is seeking a divorce on the grounds of her 'desertion'. It was she who left him, after all. Or so Rosa will argue.

Also in my pocket is a from D8A, proposing new arrangements for Beatrice and disclosing that Mrs Slater rents her house not from the council but a private landlord and works part-time as a classroom assistant and that Beatrice is a dyslexic. The husband, Graham, is a lab technician at the university, and in form D89 – written in his clumsy hand, and not for Mrs Slater's attention – there is a description of her as *short & skinny, buck teeth, dyed hair (all colours)*, most of which is confirmed by the photograph he's supplied to us and which I palm from my trouser pocket as we come nearer the house.

I examine it briefly and what strikes me now, just as when I first saw it, is how familiar she seems, how unlike a stranger. Not that we are acquainted.

I said I was a reader, and one book I began during my convalescence, but could not finish, was by Tolstoy. *Anna Karenina*. It proved too heavy on my arms for reading lying down, which is why I had to stop. But it's famous and you will recognise the opening: *All happy families resemble one another, each unhappy family is unhappy in its own way*. And perhaps John and Helen are the proof of this. The circumstances of their separation are unlike any I have come across before, but this photograph – taken when times were good and they were happy – is almost identical to several we have at home, and which most other families will have, in an album somewhere, maybe hanging on a wall.

A parent – in this case Mrs Slater – is pictured with a child. Looking upwards, she is squinting slightly in the sunshine, but her smile, and the animation in her face, reach out beyond the lens to the person with the camera, who is no doubt talking to her, no doubt smiling too. It's a snapshot, nothing formal in the composition, a private moment captured, and as I look at it I feel I too could fall for Mrs Slater, goofy as she is; I could be the man behind the lens, whom she obviously loves. Her happiness includes me; this face invites me closer.

Which could not be said of the woman who is staring at me now. Arms folded, Helen Slater watches our approach from her living room window and though she is unmistakably herself – the pronounced overbite, the spiky red-dyed hair – she is clearly older, and more careworn, less friendly.

I murmur to Will, 'I think we're expected,' and he glances up, looks quickly away. The street is on an incline here and there are five or six steps to reach her front door. I take them slowly, gripping the handrail, and feel the tightness in my back, the sharp pinch of my shoes. I knock firmly and remove the fold of papers from my pocket. Will waits at the pavement, gazing back the way we've come, as if to suggest that he is not with me.

There are footsteps, a door-chain jangling, and Helen Slater holds the door half-open. 'Yes?' she says.

'Helen Slater?' I ask, and she nods, says nothing. I have done this often enough before and believe I can judge in this instant how our transaction will now proceed. Here, I suspect, I need only be businesslike, observe the formalities, and Mrs Slater will cooperate, however grudgingly. 'I'm sorry to disturb you,' I say, 'but I've been instructed to serve you with these documents. There's a petition for divorce and a statement of arrangements for children, and a form for acknowledgement of service.'

I present the papers to her and she allows her hand to receive them. She doesn't look down, doesn't actively take them, but merely makes one limp hand available. Her gaze flits to Will, then back to me, and I detect the flicker of a smile then, something close to a smirk. In bare feet and jeans she is as her husband describes her – short and skinny – but there is also, I notice, some slight resemblance to Anna, who is taller and somehow more 'substantial', but who also regards me with just such an expression, both defensive and mocking – even derisive – and this fleeting reminder of Anna is momentarily unnerving: my concentration deserts me.

Behind Mrs Slater the door to the living room is open and I can see Beatrice, still in her school sweatshirt and trousers, staring at the television. She has hooked one leg over the arm of the sofa and her sock is trailing loose from her foot. 'I take it that's Beatrice,' I say, and smile in a way I hope is encouraging, but Mrs Slater does not reply. I am free to leave now, and really I ought to, but still I hesitate, conscious of Will's presence behind me, a prickling of sweat on my neck, a sense of some obligation unmet, and when at last I say, 'Look, I am sorry about this,' Mrs Slater calmly releases the papers, lets them spill from her hand, and wearily closes the door on me.

I leave them splayed on the step and descend, my duty discharged. The fact is, the merest contact of respondent and papers will in most cases suffice. I stated clearly what they were, and she heard me, and if she chooses now to litter her porch with them that is no more my concern than the mess she has made of her life, though I do at heart feel sorry for that. Tomorrow lunchtime I will swear an affidavit in Rosa's office that process was served, and that will be all, my small part in Mrs Slater's life played out, however cack-handedly.

I glance at Will as we cross over the road and regret that he had to see me perform so unprofessionally. He has now un-buttoned his jacket, loosened his tie, and is walking with head bowed, his hands pushed deep in his pockets. He is, it seems, as embarrassed as I am.

'So there you are,' I say finally. 'That is how you end a marriage.'

He nods. 'That easy,' he says.

'Usually easier,' I admit. 'But you take my point? It's not a wildly exciting job, Will. Some weeks this is all I do, hand over documents. I'm like some glorified postie.'

'Except you can't just push the stuff through the letterbox.'

'No.'

'And you're better paid.'

'Marginally,' I say.

In fact, of course, there are many legal niceties to observe, precautions to take, 'eventualities' to respond to: there is a great deal more to my work than I have yet told him. And because he doesn't speak again, but merely keeps pace with me, his gaze fixed to the pavement, I find myself talking more than I would wish to; now the job has been done, it seems I cannot stay silent.

'I have had trickier ones,' I say. 'Usually blokes. A lot of them refuse to accept whatever it is – they just fold their arms and try to stare you out, or try to shut the door on you. Which isn't exactly a problem – so long as you touch them with the papers, any bit of them, then you can say the spiel and back off, before they start to come after you. Some of them get angry. Not many, one or two. I remember there was one guy who got me by the lapels and started grinding his forehead into mine. We were eyeball to eyeball, and he had really bad breath – that was the worst of it. And there was another one who tried to kick me. But most of them, it's all threats. Or they just want to cry on your shoulder – *Come in and have a cuppa and I'll tell you what a bitch she was*, sort of thing. This is the divorces obviously . . .'

We glance left and right, cross over the road. A young woman walks by us, pushing a buggy. Her eyes flit towards Will.

'But the debtors and bankrupts, a lot of them seem to know you're coming and make themselves scarce. Or else, if you do manage to catch them, they pretend they're not who you know they are – *Oh he moved away months ago*. Or, *He's just this minute popped out and I've no idea when he'll be back*. Or sometimes you'll get the ones who claim they *are* so-and-so, when actually they're not. So you serve them with the summons or whatever, only to find out later they *aren't* so-and-so, they were protecting so-and-so, and because so-and-so didn't per-sonally receive the summons, so-and-so is under no legal ob-ligation to turn up at court. Which I've had happen to me.'

Will does not appear to be listening. Furrowing his brow, he looks down at his watch. 'Do you think you could drop me at my office, Mike,' he says. 'When we get back?'

I look at him. 'Won't Anna be expecting you?' I ask. But he shrugs, does not answer, and we walk the remaining distance in silence. My van is parked up on a verge and as we draw near it I notice an elderly man standing out on his porch, dressed in a vest and pyjama bottoms, a pair of red leather slippers. 'Afternoon,' I say. He jerks his head in acknowledgement, and sucks on a cigarette. Will leans against the bonnet of the van and gazes back the way we've come. I pause for breath, slowly separate out my keys. 'So, was that any use to you?' I ask him.

'What you've just been saying?'

'Well, that. But Mrs Slater. Process serving.'

Will considers a moment, drums his fingers on the side of the van. 'Her husband was having an affair, did you say?'

'Yes.'

'How'd she find out?'

'I'm not sure,' I shrug. The door lock is stiff and I'm afraid the key will bend if I force it. 'Sometimes you just do, don't you? You guess things. Though from what I've been told, he was maybe the type to taunt her with it. I think he just came out and told her one day, to see how she'd react.' I shake my head. 'This lock's jammed,' I say, and remove my key to examine it.

Will stretches his arms and stands. He turns to face me. 'I'll tell you what would be really useful,' he confides then, lowering his voice as though afraid the old man might hear him. 'I'm wondering how a suspicious wife would uncover an affair if the husband *didn't* want to own up to it.'

I stare at him.

'Or vice versa,' he says. 'Suppose the wife is having an affair, and the husband is suspicious about her. Could he tap her phone? Is that a case where you'd bug the bedroom? Say it was you, Mike – I'm wondering what sorts of things you could do to find out what your wife was up to. Maybe what gadgets you'd use.'

'*My* wife?'

'Hypothetically. Not *your* wife, obviously. Not Janette.'

'Janette,' I repeat, vaguely disturbed by this use of her name. Except to her parents, and sometimes myself, she is known to everyone as 'Jan'.

Will doesn't respond, perhaps doesn't see any cause to.

'This is for your book?' I ask him.

'Yes,' he smiles, seeming surprised, 'for my book.' He slips out of his jacket and tugs off his tie. 'It's fiction,' he grins, and rolls up his sleeves, unbuttons his collar.

I gaze at him a moment, at the dark hairs on his chest, which fan up to his throat, and the thick hair on his arms, the backs of his hands, even his fingers, and find myself wondering if this is something Anna likes or dislikes, or is simply resigned to; I wonder if this is something she would want to escape from. Behind him the old man responds to a call from indoors and chucks his cigarette aside, wipes his feet on the doormat. He winks at me before he goes in.

'And it's the husband who suspects the wife?' I say, thinking of Anna, the claims she made in her kitchen.

'Yes,' confirms Will.

'So he goes to an investigator?'

'He could do.'

'I see,' I say, and carefully guide my key back into the slot. This time there is no resistance; the lock yields, the mechanism clunks open, and as I contemplate Will's question I gaze down at my reflection in the side door – my sober tie and unbuttoned jacket, my paunch – and what comes most clearly to mind then is the image of Helen Slater standing at her living room window, watching the approach of two men in dark suits, the arrival of the next piece of bad news in her life, and looking up I say, 'To be honest with you, if it *was* me, Will, and I did have my suspicions, I'm not sure I *would* want to do anything about it. I might just leave well alone. Possibly at this point in my life, I might just do that.' I open my door and prepare to manoeuvre myself into my seat. I smile at him. 'Wouldn't you?' I say.

I I

I have a lazy interest in electronics, the technical specifications of the devices I use. I understand the operational issues involved in choosing between 'free oscillating' and 'crystal controlled' frequencies, 'hardwire' and 'transmitter' phone taps, 'parallel' and 'series' intercepts. I could install the cables for a camera in a suspended ceiling, or mount a pinhole microphone through a tube in a wall, or strip a telephone wire to attach a headset and recorder. I know how to balance high and low impedance inputs and outputs for maximum clarity of signal. None of this is too far removed from the DIY that occupies me at home, and like the DIY, if I should require any more specialised kit there's a place I know of just down by the river, a 'security systems' suppliers that deals in covert surveillance equipment, much of it American and East European, surplus from the Cold War.

The business is run by two brothers, Sanjeev and Kuldip, and occupies the same breezeblock building as the tool-hire shop that loaned me my chainsaw. Sanjeev is the salesman, Kuldip the technician, and while Sanjeev invariably calls me Mr Hannah or 'sir', Kuldip addresses me always as 'Michael', an ironical inflection to his pronunciation, the suggestion of a joke shared between us. We are, he seems to be saying, respectable men engaged in an unsavoury business. And I don't doubt his decency, though I rarely feel so seedy myself as when I visit his workshop.

In a flux-smelling, airless back room Kuldip sits hunched over a workbench cluttered with circuit boards and tiny components, his T-shirt frayed and discoloured, patchy with sweat, and drinks endless mugs of dark coffee as he painstakingly 're-engineers' all manner of everyday objects – clocks, calculators, retractable pens – for use as cameras, recorders and radio transmitters. Haphazardly stacked on the grey metal shelves all around him are boxes of proprietary products – state-of-the-art, ultra-miniaturised, guaranteed for two years – which Sanjeev sells by mail order. There is a website, and business, they say, is 'not bad'.

Among the boxed items are gadgets for listening through windows and walls, video cameras concealed in smoke detectors, tiepins and sunglasses, and telephone adapters that can make a male voice appear to be female, or vice versa. There are tape recorders hidden in cigarette packs, 'quick deployment' microphones disguised as credit cards, and micro-cameras built into wristwatches. And there are counter-surveillance devices to detect or defeat each one of these items.

None of which comes cheaply of course, though everything they sell is effective. Their goods are reliable. A miniature transmitter obtained from the Singhs and inserted into a standard telephone socket could broadcast a signal from as far away as Will's house, for example, to a receiver and cassette recorder located in my office upstairs. Distortion would be minimal, the running time of the 'unit' indefinite. But while such an apparatus would be quite legal – and in my case tax deductible – it would be a criminal act for me to trespass on the Browns' property to install it, or to draw on their electricity to power it, or to intercept the public telecoms system to eavesdrop on what they are saying. I would require the permission of the property owner, the electricity account holder, the telecoms subscriber.

In other words, I would need to be invited, and in fact most of the work I do in this line – phone tapping, room bugging – is at the request of a spouse with suspicions, such as Will says he is writing about in his book.

Of course in my own home the issues of trespass and theft would not arise, and in answer to Will's 'hypothetical' question, I could very easily spy on my wife. I could monitor her every word, record all her movements on film. I have the expertise and the technology. In legal terms I do have the licence. But other scruples must also apply: no marriage could survive such close scrutiny, such absence of trust. My wife lives her life, thinks her thoughts; things happen to her and are recorded in her journal or lodged in her mind or confided to friends, and always I have felt it is right – prudent and 'proper' – that I should keep my distance from this. The prospects for any long-lasting marriage, I'm sure, depend as much on what is withheld as what is revealed. However much a couple might share, it's what little they don't know about each other that will lend their life interest.

Or at least, this has been my opinion for as long as I've been certain of my wife's faithfulness to me. And even now, as I come into our bedroom this evening – the boys finally settled to sleep and Jan at the theatre – I don't truly believe I have any cause to distrust her, or that I'm behaving out of suspicion, any pressing need to uncover her secrets. It's the inevitability of finding nothing that excuses my actions. I am not seeking proof of her guilt but confirmation of her innocence and the last thing I intend is the kind of aggressive 'intelligence' gathering that Will has in mind. No electronic devices are being deployed here; nothing could be less 'invasive'.

My side of the bed is nearest the door. Jan's cabinet, in which she keeps her cosmetics and hairdryer and diary, is in the opposite corner and as I make my way round there I notice her only pair of high heels lying askew on the floor, and the loop of a bra strap hanging from a half-open drawer. A clump of panties and tights has been dumped on the bed and there's a scatter of jewellery in front of the mirror. The wardrobe door is wide open and a pair of her trousers is about to fall from its hanger. A tube of lipstick has rolled across to the skirting.

Such disarray is unlike her, but Jan's preparations this evening were unusually rushed. An argument with Jack about homework delayed her, then a lengthy call on her mobile, and when I came from drying Ben in the bathroom, I found her presenting her backside to the mirror, lifting the flap of her jacket and swearing. Already late, and flustered, she quickly kicked off her shoes and dropped her trousers and knickers, and then emptied the contents of her underwear drawer on to the bed. She needed, she said, a pair of pants that wouldn't show through the trousers, and would be comfortable to sit in, and weren't full of holes. She needed a new pair of trousers. She needed, she complained, 'a whole new fucking wardrobe'.

But neither Jan nor I has much enthusiasm for shopping, and especially not shopping for clothes. We no longer feel at ease – which is to say, I suppose, we are no longer the right age – and are content now to select our clothing from catalogues, or from department stores in the sales, and will buy two and sometimes three of the same item if we find that it suits us. Our underwear especially is sober, snug-fitting, supportive: that is, definitely not bought for titillation or 'fun'. And while Jan does own two pairs of lycra-mix stockings, 'nearly black', with lace-trim elasticated hold-ups, the fact is I bought these myself from the Clearance shelf in the supermarket one light-headed afternoon three or four years ago and she is reluctant to wear them.

They are tangled up now with her tights on the bed, and as I stand gazing down at them, and at the worn-through panties that she is so tired of, I find I am oddly disturbed, and puzzled, by their allure. I am aroused, as on occasions I will feel aroused when left alone in a client's house on assignment, and it's when I catch sight of my face in Jan's mirror that I have a first inkling that a boundary is being breached here, that something in our marriage is about to be sullied. I am intruding. This too could be the room of a stranger. The feminine clutter around me could belong to any man's wife.

And realising this, I do what only my own wife's husband would trouble to do: I begin to tidy our bedroom, the mess she left behind her.

I scoop her underwear from the bed and drop it back in its drawer and I push that drawer properly closed, along with all the other drawers. I remove her trousers from the hanger and tuck them under my chin and re-align the creases and return them neatly folded to the wardrobe, which I fasten fully shut. I divide her jewellery into rings and earrings, brooches and bracelets, and return these in careful handfuls to their trays. I pair up her discarded shoes and slide them toes-first beneath the bed, and while I'm on my knees I line up all her other shoes, squaring them neatly side by side, and retrieve her lipstick and stand it prominently on the dressing table. Then I straighten our bedclothes, and plump up our pillows, and looking all around me I give a small nod – as if, I'll admit, for the benefit of somebody watching, an imaginary camera – and finally, as though performing the obvious next act in this sequence of chores, I crouch and take Jan's diary from its cabinet and sit down on her side of the mattress and quietly I gaze for a while at a scuff mark on its cover as I wait for my breathing to steady.

I glance behind me at the door, which is closed, and then look at the curtains, the wardrobe, the mirror. There is no camera. I am alone, unobserved, in our bedroom. My wife is out for the evening, my children are asleep, and I am about to commit a betrayal, however minor, after which many other betrayals may become possible. But even as I recognise this, I let the thought go. With an inward shrug I allow the book to fall open; I lick my thumb and turn to the first entry.

The volume begins with a heavy snowfall in April last year, which I had forgotten about, followed by a week in which I was absent from home, working in Wales and then Durham, which Jan merely notes without comment. I read her account of that week, and the one after – my return briefly described as *M with us again, v distant & broody, and picking on Ben, who's hyper* – and then run a swift finger down each of the subsequent pages, scanning for names.

And what I find is more or less what I might have expected. I merit about as many mentions as the boys, and though the tone of Jan's complaining about me has an edge which is new, my appearances are brief and take their place among the usual catalogue of ailments, staffroom gossip, appointments kept, the boys' activities, worries about the house – the damp patch in the back bedroom, the whining of the boiler pump – and she says very little here that I don't already know. On one occasion when I was working away she had a visit from her headmaster, Chris Bates, whose marriage was failing, and talked to him all evening – offered him advice over a bottle of wine – but the account in her diary hardly differs from the one that she gave me. Chris occurs on several other pages in that same period, a sad figure, and Will too is mentioned, though rarely – a few banalities noted in passing, revealing nothing – and with growing impatience I flip ahead to find what she wrote on my birthday:

M's 40th, v low-key. Got him 2 shirts (one each from the boys), bottle of whisky, and a watch with his name & birth date inscribed. He seemed OK about these but what to get someone who doesn't have 'interests'? He claims 40 is no big deal but woke me twice last night tossing & turning & moaning in his sleep and then went mad today chopping down trees in the garden and ended up putting his back out, which was almost funny, tho seems serious & a massive mess to clear up now which it looks like I'll have to do. Jack went v quiet. Ben bless him wanted to be 'helpful' and did the washing-up for me – cold water! School the usual. Tiring evening but paid some bills etc and feeling pretty good now though not sure why, puffed up like a balloon & period due.

There is no mention here of the phonecall she took in our kitchen that evening. And skimming ahead, no account either of the time she spent with Will at the fun run, or any acknowledgement that she recently read one of his novels, and possibly these omissions are significant; if I was paranoid I suppose they might seem so.

I flick forward to the blank sheets at the end of the book, and then, as I work half-heartedly backwards, slowly turning the pages, I remember a similar diary, a red accounts ledger as densely written as this one, shown to me by a young man – a recent husband – two or three years ago.

'Look closely,' he said, and I did, but could see nothing. 'No, look again. Look closely,' he insisted, and something did then catch my eye, like a fleck of dandruff on a dress, or a crumb on a table: a tiny cryptic entry slipped beneath the underline of a date heading. In fact there were many such crumbs, microscopically small notations, impossible to ignore once the first had been seen: *N3pm, Nam, 2hrsN* and even, once, *N!*.

'N stands for Nick,' he said, grimly triumphant. 'She's got a bloke called Nick.' Which she didn't – *N* stood for a pet name I can't now remember – though there was certainly a 'someone'; an affair was being recorded.

In my wife's diary however there's nothing, and as a last gesture I scan quickly for other evenings when she went out to the theatre. She's a member of both the main playhouses in town and sees every production, always at the start of the run, again at the end if it's good. And though sometimes she'll attend with a friend – another teacher perhaps; twice that I know of with Will – more often than not she will go on her own. She says she doesn't mind having no one to talk to; in fact she prefers it. The social aspect doesn't concern her. She's content to remain in her seat in the interval, doesn't want to discuss her impressions, or listen to anyone else's, and she likes to walk home as soon as the curtain has fallen. This is what she tells me, and what her journal appears to confirm: in every instance she notes the name of the play and the lead actors, perhaps also the director, but offers next to no comment. The weather gets more attention.

And laying the book in my lap, my hands squarely gripping

the edges, what I feel most of all is let down. My wife, on this evidence, is blameless, just as I set out to confirm, and yet I am disappointed. Which perhaps ought not to surprise me. My reaction is not so perverse or unusual; I have seen it often enough in my work. In matrimonial cases, satisfaction is rarely straightforward.

Peace of Mind at Affordable Rates is the strapline under which I advertise my business in the *Yellow Pages*, and like the name of my agency – *Spotlight Investigations* – the wording isn't original. If you were to look for *Detective Agencies* in a *Yellow Pages* anywhere, you would find other, bigger operations with the same or a comparable name, and similar panels offering similar services:

> *Home Buyer Reports*
> *Surveillance*
> *De-bugging*
> *Process Serving*
> *Missing Persons*
> *Insurance Fraud*
> *Matrimonial*

Many other agencies will also promise 'peace of mind', or something just like it. And this is, I believe, the main 'product' we sell. More even than information, it is what our customers require from us.

I mentioned the man masturbating in his back garden. Clearly he was unusual, but that particular 'locale' is one I've since come to know well, a belt of high-income housing where I am regularly employed to install covert cameras to spy on successive au pairs and nannies, and though I've yet to uncover a single case of laziness or dishonesty, bad temper or rough treatment of a child, what I have done instead is settle parental nerves, put minds at rest, provide reassurance.

Likewise, I've established a portfolio of small- and medium-sized companies locally who will engage me to sweep their premises for room bugs and phone taps, and though in ten years I've only twice unearthed evidence of eavesdropping, this is no admission of failure: the removal of doubt is what my customers have sought from me. Their premises were either 'sterile' or 'contaminated', and they needed to know for certain either way.

With matrimonials however, the motives and hopes of the parties are often more tangled. To the suspicious husband or wife, proof of a partner's innocence may come as a blow, confirmation of their guilt a relief. The aggrieved party may feel frustrated not to have their suspicions confirmed, or elated to have evidence at last of wrongdoing. Behind which, no doubt, there will lurk many months of accusations and denials, counter-accusations, self-questionings, many months of 'not knowing'. And for the guilty party, too, exposure may bring more relief than distress. Having tired of the burden of keeping secrets and telling lies, all the complications of conducting an affair – and possibly lacking the courage to make an open admission, and anyway wishing to share his or her new-found joy with the world – the adulterer may well be glad of a chance at last to 'come clean'.

These are among the simpler scenarios. The motivations behind others are more obscure. I am thinking for instance of a woman called Caroline Clarke, who refused to believe in her husband's fidelity however often my reports insisted she had no cause to distrust him.

Middle-aged and dependent on benefits, Caroline repeatedly borrowed from her elderly mother to hire me. The mother was bed-bound, and lived with the Clarkes, and kept a close tally of the money she loaned. Both she and the daughter were dour, taciturn types, not easy to warm to. The husband however was cheerful – it seemed perpetually so – and would quickly find company wherever he happened to be. He enjoyed drinking, the usual banter, and evidently liked flirting, but though he was frequently drunk, and sometimes boisterous, I never once saw him make a move on any of the women he talked to. Always friendly, he chatted and looked but took it no further. And yet still his wife would want to employ me. Weeks after we had agreed that she should stop wasting her mother's money, she would again be on the telephone, determined that this time we should 'nail' him.

Everyone has something to hide; this is my professional and personal opinion, but often, I'm sure, that 'something' is the core of who they are, which cannot be seen or eavesdropped upon; it can't be set down in words, or captured on film. It isn't a 'story'. And clearly, no amount of surveillance could have brought Mrs Clarke closer to the source of her husband's happiness, or helped her understand her own lack of it. Nor should I expect to locate in Jan's diaries the solution to my own dissatisfactions. The prospect of a 'complication' in my life, which might once have seemed so disruptive and threatening, does now present itself to me as something attractive, but it would appear I haven't the courage to act without Jan's permission, without her acting first. And that permission, I now see, is not to be found in these pages.

I return the book to its cabinet, aligned as I found it, and stretch out on the bed. I push off my trainers and look up to the ceiling, my arms crooked above me, and as I gaze at the trembling shadow cast by the lampshade I begin to pursue in my mind a familiar sequence of pictures: Anna kneeling beside me, her hand over mine; Sarah resting her head on my shoulder; Anna touching my arm; Sarah foetally curled up on my mattress, pillowing her cheek on her hands, her eyes heavy-lidded and wide. And then, as I have done countless times lately – Jan usually fast asleep at my side – I follow these thoughts to another, imaginary world in which I am no longer married, and yet still have this house, these days, my children, our ongoing life.

I imagine myself widowed. And though I know there is much to be ashamed of in this – it's a cowardly fantasy, in which I am blameless, my freedom acquired without the complicating guilt and pain of divorce – what is more shameful perhaps, a sorrier fact to admit, is that the scenarios I invent for myself should all involve women I already know, never straying too far from the plausible or the familiar. This is my private world, in which I am free to do whatever I choose, go anywhere, and with whomever I fancy, and yet always I find that what I fancy is what I already know. It seems I haven't the imagination to stray further than Anna or Sarah. It seems I may not have the gumption to stray even there.

12

Jan steps into the hall from the living room just as I enter the house. She's still dressed as she was after work: a grey skirt and grey cardigan, her red hair loosely plaited and pinned. Her expression is serious. She shuts the door quietly behind her but doesn't let go of the doorknob. There is silence inside; the TV is off. The boys, I suppose, will be doing their homework, lying flat on the floor on their bellies. The time is twenty to eight.

'Hi,' I say, frowning, 'what's up?'

She doesn't reply, but waits for me to pass, inclining her head to the kitchen. She follows me through and leans back on the door, and again she keeps hold of the handle, as if to prevent me from leaving. Her manner is urgent and she speaks in an undertone, too low for the boys to pick up. 'Have you been talking to Will Brown?' she says.

'What? Now?'

'Lately.'

'Was I supposed to?'

'No, but have you?'

In fact I have just returned from the scene of a car accident very near to his office, taking photos and measurements, drawing a sketch plan of the scene. I was there this afternoon too, and might have called in on him, but didn't. As I empty my pockets I say, 'Not for a couple of days.'

'But recently?'

'Yes,' I say, annoyed by her tone, reluctant to help her. I shrug the reflective vest from my shoulders. 'We spoke a couple of days ago.'

'And?'

'Jan!' I complain. She is agitated, unlike herself. Her neck is flushed; the pores in her face seem larger, inflamed. I turn my back on her. I switch on the kettle. 'What's the big excitement?' I say, and look for a teabag, a cup.

'He's left Anna,' she tells me, and her voice dips, as if confiding news of an illness, a death.

'Right,' I say carefully. 'Okay.'

'You didn't know?'

'No,' I say, 'I didn't know.'

Jan shakes her head, wraps herself tight in her cardigan. Bleakly she stares at the floor, then sighs and looks up.

'Who's he left her *for*?' I say.

'No one,' she shrugs, and gestures away from herself. 'He's just moved out.'

'Right,' I say, and look across to the window. A scatter of raindrops sparkles in the air. The weather all day has been just like this, blue skies and dark clouds, sunshine and showers together. The light slowly dims now, the temperature percept-ibly drops, and suddenly there comes a volley of hailstones, bouncing from the window ledge, the bricks in the yard. The noise is thunderous, then eases, and stops. At the top of the garden my mound of branches is peppered with white; in a minute or two the hail will have melted. Beside me the kettle is starting to steam. We hear the creak of the living room door.

'Mu-um!' calls Ben.

'So, when did this happen?' I ask.

'Last night,' says Jan. 'I've just got Anna off the phone. She thought you might know something.'

'Me?'

'Yes,' she says, and steps aside as Ben charges into the kitchen. He throws his arms round her thighs, presses his face to her belly. He looks up at me slyly. He is grinning, and fleetingly I think of Anna last Sunday, standing beside me as Nathan and Ben rummaged about in her fridge. And then I find I am laughing.

'What's so funny?' Jan says.

'I was supposed to be meeting him tomorrow. In his office. He wanted to know about tracing someone, how you track down a missing person . . .'

'He's not missing,' she says. 'He's living in his office.'

'His office!' I laugh.

'Yes,' she exhales, and pushes weakly on Ben's shoulders. 'Let go of me, please,' she says. 'You're hurting.'

'So what happened?'

'Ben!' she snaps, and reluctantly he does as he's told. 'Nothing. Apparently nothing happened. He came home from work yesterday. He had his dinner. He made his announcement. He packed his things and walked out. Gone.'

'Who's gone, Mummy?'

'A stupid, stupid man,' she says, and grabs for the kettle as it starts to boil over. She empties it into the washing-up bowl, though there is nothing needs cleaning, not even a teaspoon. '*Fuck!*' she says then, and Ben turns towards me, wide-eyed, elated. Jan does not normally swear. Nor does she behave so erratically.

'I don't see why you're so bothered about it,' I say.

'Well I am,' she replies, and tips the water away, upends the plastic bowl into the sink. She turns round to face me. For several beats she says nothing. 'And you've no idea what he's playing at?'

'No,' I confirm. 'I've no idea. Why would I?'

'Because you're his friend,' she says testily.

'Hardly,' I sigh. 'That would be you, Jan. He talks to you more than he does me. Why do you think his wife phoned you?'

'She didn't,' she says simply. 'She asked for you, Mike.'

There is a phrase about friendships I once came across in a newspaper when I was in my mid-twenties, that struck a particular chord and stayed with me for years. The article would have been in the *Guardian*, a 'women's page' feature – possibly one in a series – on the nature of long-lasting female attachments. I remember the accompanying photograph of two women in dark casual clothes sitting facing each other on a white sofa, their postures caught somewhere between animation and relaxed, settled intimacy. They were perhaps the age I have reached now, and I know I felt a vague sexual yearning for both which surprised me, a feeling that I would have liked to have been as intimate with either of them as they were with each other.

This was at a time when I was becoming broodingly nostalgic for the intensity of the friendships I had known at university, itself a time – and here is more or less the phrase in the article – when I hadn't so much made friends as I had been made by them. That is how the two women described the beginnings of their relationship, and it seemed equally to explain my own most valued connections, all of them with people – excepting my wife – who had moved many miles away, dispersed into jobs and lives I knew only from letters, phonecalls, the occasional short visit. Every letter I received was precious to me then, even the briefest of postcards, and I kept them all in an embossed-leather suitcase that had once belonged to my grandfather, the only memento I had of him and itself a treasured item.

That suitcase now sits beneath Jack's bed, though what he keeps in there I wouldn't know. The letters I weeded when we began work on our attic, by which time I'd already lost contact with nearly everyone I had known in those years, including my own former self, and of course Sarah. Jan again would be the exception; she is a constant. But I have few other close friends now, and especially not male friends, though I can't say I regret this. Always my most intimate friendships have been with women, and I do still feel more comfortable with our female friends than with their husbands, just as Jan appears more at home with the men than their wives.

I've been told I'm a 'good listener'. Like Jan, it seems I am someone who inspires or encourages confidences from others, and perhaps that's because I'm as physically unpredatory as a priest, though clearly not all women will trust or admire this. 'You're a real truth merchant, aren't you?' said one, a friend of Jan's at a party, and I could see it wasn't, in her eyes, a virtue. It was boring, and no doubt there are countless other women who will recoil from any man who appears as 'earnest' as I do, as 'honest' and 'sincere' and 'straightforward'. Too much 'open-ness' too soon is one sure way of closing off possibility, after all, and leaves little room for conjecture, supposing, anticipation; it leaves little scope for surprises or 'fun'.

The company of men is of course different. It's an axiom of my profession that the 'enquiry agent's' main asset is his address book, his circle of contacts, and though I'm not a naturally gregarious person I have in the past taken care to be sociable, to cultivate acquaintances and establish 'connections'. Increasingly now I don't bother. Those few friends I've retained are mostly local, and occasionally I will join them in the pub on a Friday, or midweek for the football, but I am vague about what many of them actually do for a living – and so how they might be useful to me – though I do know it might be something in local government or social services or scientific research or the law. One is a schoolteacher, and a few are self-employed, offering computing and editorial and consultancy services of one kind or another.

The fact is, it isn't our professions that define or connect us, that make us known to ourselves or each other. It is our neighbourhood, the 'lifestyle choices' we share, and perhaps also a sense of dissatisfaction or disillusionment, having arrived at a point in our lives – a more-or-less mid-point – from which we'd previously always hoped or imagined we'd be able to pause and look back and congratulate ourselves on how far we had managed to come. Instead we've none of us come quite far enough, and while the habit of looking ahead, planning for a better tomorrow, remains with us, we are less hopeful now, less blithely sure of our prospects. We live our lives without applause, and trust that contentment will eventually be our reward, however elusive it might seem in the meantime.

Not that we will often discuss this. For the most part confession, self-revelation, any sharing of confidences, is something we will try to avoid, depending of course on how much we've been drinking, and who remains in the pub at the end of the evening. As a rule we will argue for argument's sake, defend opinions we don't hold. We will vent our feelings on topics of absolutely no consequence, and swap stories that are plainly exaggerated, falsified, twisted. It is play, boisterous and foolish, and though play – like 'fun' – is one thing amongst many that I don't feel entirely at ease with, far less amenable are those evenings when we will find ourselves distracted by a barmaid, or a student playing pool with her boyfriend, or a group of young women at a table nearby, and a kind of desperation will creep over us, a man-to-man sharing of resigned hopeless arousal, and I will want nothing more than to go home and curl up with my wife.

This evening however it is my wife who suggests that I ought to go out, irritated no doubt by my restlessness, and impatient it seems to be left on her own. She is tucked into an armchair, a cushion clutched to her belly. The bottle of red wine by her side is already half-empty and she is watching the television, indiscriminately watching whatever there is. She sips from a glass that is full to the brim.

'Shouldn't you go easy on that?' I say, idling across to the window, standing by the gap in the curtains. 'You've got school in the morning.'

'I'm fine,' she says, and briefly lifts her gaze from the screen. 'I thought you were going to phone Will . . .'

Outside a drizzle is falling. The sky is murky and the street-lamps have yet to come on. It is almost midsummer, but chilly and dark, and as I look out at the rain I try to picture Will in his office, lazily swivelling from his desk to answer the phone. I see him framed by the window, contemplating this same dreary evening as he replies to my questions, but though I can picture him clearly – his face and his posture, even the clothes he is wearing – I cannot imagine him further; I have no idea of his mood, or what he is thinking. Nor can I imagine our conversation, what exactly I'd ask him or how he would reply.

He has gone from us now, and though I do want to know why – I want to know all there is – I am not sure I want to hear it from him. And shaking my head, I say, 'No, he wouldn't welcome it, Jan. Can you see him wanting to unburden himself to me?'

'You won't know unless you phone him,' she says.

I shrug. 'Maybe.'

'I think you ought to,' she says. 'Tell him what an idiot he's being.'

A taxi descends the hill slowly. In the passing glow of its headlights I see a shimmering line of wet plastic, a procession of black binbags dumped outside the houses over the road. There are three or four at every gate. It is a Tuesday and this evening there will be bags and wheelie-bins obstructing the pavements of all the streets in our neighbourhood. The lorry comes early tomorrow. On a Wednesday morning that is what wakes us – the racket of tumbling rubbish, hydraulics, men shouting – and as I follow the taxi's red tail-lights to the foot of the hill, where the driver beeps his horn and pulls up, I picture Anna coming from her porch to her front gate, a heavy binbag in each hand, the hallway dark and empty behind her.

She will heave the bags through the half-open gate and drop them onto the pavement, and then scurry quickly back in to her house, her shoulders hunched against the rain and her arms folded over her chest. Shivering, she will close the front door with her foot and make a noise of relief and disgust – the kind of noise that a wife will make for her husband – and then she will listen a moment in case she has disturbed her two boys, who ought to be sleeping. There won't be a sound, and she will wander through to her kitchen and stand for a while staring at the glazed double doors to the garden. She will see her reflection, and the dining table beside her, and the empty chair on which her hand rests, and if the phone were to ring now I doubt she would answer it. I imagine she too would look for a bottle of wine, a corkscrew, a glass. She would leave the phone ringing and turn out the lights and go and sit on her own in her front room, the curtains drawn against the miserable weather and the gas fire on 'low', the television showing the exact same pictures to her as to my wife.

'No,' I say then, 'there's things I have to do anyway, Jan. There's a house I should be watching.'

'Oh?' She looks at me briefly. 'You didn't say.'

I close the gap in the curtains. 'No. It's just something . . . I should've done it already.'

Jan uses the remote to change channels. She flicks through them all and arrives back where she started. Sighing, she says, 'Well phone him from the van, then. You'll have nothing better to do.'

'Yes,' I say, 'maybe. We'll see. Depends how long it takes.'

'Hi, it's Mike.'

For a second or two he doesn't reply. Perhaps he is putting something aside, or gathering his thoughts; possibly he is gesturing to someone. I imagine he must be surprised, but his voice when he speaks is measured, controlled; there's no hint of the tightness or nervousness I might have expected. 'Hello, Mike.'

'You're working late,' I say.

'Yes,' he replies.

'I'm not interrupting?'

'No,' he says, and sounds as if he is stretching. 'It's nothing I can't go back to.'

He is, I'm sure, on his own. And here of course is my opportunity to ask if he would like to come out for a drink. But my intention for now is merely to confirm that he's still in his office, that he hasn't already returned to his wife.

I lean towards the passenger door of my van and scan the windows on the other side of the street. 'I just thought I'd check we were still okay for tomorrow.'

'Tomorrow . . .?'

Every curtain is closed, and the nearest streetlamp appears not to be working. The rain has eased off, but the clouds have yet to disperse. There's no moon, and no stars. It is very dark.

'You wanted me to show you that CD . . . the electoral roll?'

'Sure,' he says vaguely. 'Okay.'

'I was thinking early-afternoon sort of time?'

'Yes. I suppose . . . Though – could we make it the day after tomorrow? Or better still, Friday?'

'If you like, that's fine by me.' Gently I unlock my door. 'It's just that I thought I'd better check . . . I understand your domestic arrangements have altered somewhat.'

He laughs. 'Somewhat,' he says.

I wait a moment, but Will isn't about to volunteer any more. 'So. About one-thirty?' I say. 'On Friday. I'll come to your office?'

'Yes,' he says, 'I'll be here.'

'Okay then,' I say.

He is silent.

'Bye then.'

Will doesn't reply but hangs up, and exhaling heavily, I sit back in my seat. I scrutinise my wing mirrors and the upstairs windows of the houses to either side of me. I look over my shoulder.

In most residential areas there will be someone as vigilant I am, as alert to every sound, every passing car and pedestrian, and who will phone the police if a van such as mine should linger too long, if the driver should still be at the wheel each time they look out. I understand the type and can usually pre-empt them. If I were to notify the police now of my presence, describing myself and my vehicle, and giving some plausible account of my business, the officer on duty would doubtless provide me with an incident number and vouch for me should the neighbour phone in. But tonight I am sure there's no need. I don't intend to remain, and no one appears yet to have noticed me.

I slip out of my van, leaving the door unlocked, fractionally open, and then walk in the direction of Anna's, surreptitiously scanning her windows and those of her neighbours, and though I'm certain that nobody is watching I continue on to the very end of the street, where I pat my pockets and give a big sigh and turn back.

There are in fact three bags at her gate, one stacked on top of two others, and the whole house is in darkness. Perhaps she has gone to bed, or is taking a bath; perhaps she is sitting alone in her kitchen. The pavements are deserted, and as I pass by her gate again I casually reach for the top bag, barely breaking stride as I lift it away. I grip it tightly by the knot she has tied. There's a chink of bottles, some settling of contents, but it weighs surprisingly little. I hold it comfortably away from my body and quicken my pace. Soundlessly I pull open the door of my van and swing it across to the passenger side. I get in at the wheel and reach for my strap. My heart is thumping now, and I sit for some moments observing the windows, my mirrors, the pavements, but no one appears, nothing moves, and finally I slam my door properly shut and switch on the engine, my headlights, and it's then I glimpse a movement, the sudden flash of someone running by, briefly there at my shoulder.

It is Mr Sommer, jogging. He cuts between the two cars parked ahead of me, and as he looks back, checking for traffic, I recognise him clearly. Our eyes in fact meet, though I trust he does not realise this. He won't, I'm sure, have been able to see through my windscreen. But when he arrives at his gate, five or six doors further down on the left, he stops and bends over, his hands on his knees, and lifts his head to gaze in my direction. Panting, he waits, and I have no choice but to drive past him. I pull out, and accelerate smoothly, fixing my eyes on the road, and when I come to the junction I look to my mirrors and find he's still there, still watching, his hands on his hips now, performing some kind of flexion. And possibly – it is hard to be sure as I turn into the next street – he raises a hand in acknowledgement.

13

Perhaps, like Jan, you are someone who enjoyed a happy childhood; possibly you have also stayed close to your parents. Amongst the people we know, this would make you unusual. At our social gatherings, once the talk of childcare and schooling, house prices and home improvements has been exhausted, and as the drink begins to tell, the conversation always, inevitably, turns to where we have come from, to our upbringing and the damage it's caused us, perhaps even continues to cause us. Often it seems the end-point of any journey towards intimacy amongst us is an admission of time spent in therapy, a confession of how unhappy we once were and of how bad we too were becoming as parents. Everyone, it seems, is carrying the burden of some more or less dysfunctional past, which they are hoping to remedy now in the lives of their own children.

Everyone, that is, except for Jan and myself. My wife is the most 'well-adjusted' person I know – self-contained and dependable, usually cheerful – and on the whole, these words aside, I have never been much given to introspection or self-questioning and so couldn't tell you about the time I spent in counselling – as our friends can – or the insights I gained there, for the simple reason that I have never been, and would not wish to.

My own family was above all things functional. There was little in the way of upheaval, crisis or distress; there were no raised voices, heavy silences, tears. My parents had their roles, their duties to perform, and they did so uncomplainingly. My father was the provider, my mother the housekeeper. He was the disciplinarian, she was the organiser. They were undemonstrative, stable, entirely predictable, and they lived their lives quietly.

In his lighter moments my father, with chirpy irony, would sometimes address my mother as 'Mrs Hannah', and she, with no irony at all, nearly always addressed him as 'Dad'. But there were no great displays of affection, and they did not argue, at least not in front of us boys, my brother and me. Any intimacy between them, whether physical or emotional, was kept hidden from us, and if I picture them now it is as they would be after tea on a Sunday, sitting either side of the fireplace, the clock on the mantelpiece chiming every quarter of an hour. My father would be reading the newspaper; my mother would be sewing or knitting. At a certain point they would switch on the television and we would be allowed to put our homework aside.

I do realise how conventional – and old-fashioned – an image this is. But that *is* how they were in my childhood, and how they remained until they died. She lived to be seventy-nine, my father eighty-three, and they were cremated within a few months of each other. She died of cancer of the colon. He then suffered a stroke, apparently unable to manage on his own. This was just over two years ago.

They had been late to get married – my father was the age I am now, my mother thirty-six – which I believe was unusual then, for people of their generation and class. For years they had both worked for the Gas Board, my father as a fitter, my mother as a telephonist, and I suppose at some stage they must each have resigned themselves to bachelorhood and spinsterhood, and perhaps that air of resignation had become ingrained. Stoicism seemed to define them.

The parents of my schoolfriends were all a lot younger and livelier, and of course I would sometimes be asked if these two greying, oddly formal people were my grandparents, or if perhaps I'd been adopted. Once or twice I said yes. It seemed plausible.

My brother was four years older than me and physically quite different and in some ways our relationship mirrored our parents'. We played together when we were small, and occasionally we fought, but if I ever hero-worshipped him, I don't remember that now. We occupied the same house, observed the same emotional code, called the same two people 'Mum' and 'Dad', but were never particularly close. We were neither rivals nor friends, and are practically strangers today. He called me Michael, I called him Christopher, and it was a surprise the first time I heard someone refer to him as 'Chris'.

Far more of a surprise was the sight of his grief at our father's cremation. I looked around and saw his wife comforting him –

this stooped, sobbing man – and eventually I offered my handkerchief, as if that might staunch his tears, the noise he was making. She accepted it from me, but my brother shook his head. He already had one, bunched up in his fist, and briefly he looked at me, apparently puzzled, or in some way annoyed – whether by my presence there, or by my composure, or by his own distress, I could not tell. But he did become a little quieter then, and afterwards, once he'd regained his self-control, neither of us seemed quite sure what to say, or how we ought to behave, and the guilt of that – possibly also the regret – has no doubt widened the distance between us. I think we shook hands when we parted. I may have patted his arm. I do remember his wife standing just behind him, gazing at me with soft, sorrowful eyes – her hands clasped in front of her, her head sympathetically tilted – and when I went to kiss her cheek she stepped forward with alacrity and embraced me, as if she'd been waiting just for that opportunity.

But what I recall most of all is the blankness I felt, the sense of disengagement from everything around me, and it is this – the blankness, at both of my parents' funerals – rather than any trauma or 'unresolved' hurt, that I suspect I might find if ever I chose to examine or 'revisit' my childhood.

All of which may or may not give a clue as to who I am now and where I now find myself. Certainly, if the dinner party conversations I have had to endure are any indication, the key to my character must lie in my upbringing; it is there that the culprits are to be found, where the blame will be apportioned.

This is also the message of the magazines my wife likes to read. And of course it's in the nature of my occupation to look for patterns, connections, stories, clear lines of cause and effect. But in fact I believe that most of life, including my own, is really quite random, somewhat plotless, accidental.

As a boy, it is true, I would sometimes sneak into my parents' bedroom when they were busy elsewhere and sit alone on the edge of their bed, quietly absorbing the strangeness of them and their separateness from me, which seemed in some way connected with the yellow of the flowers on their wallpaper, and the dark sheen of their furniture, and the slightly musty smell that lingered in their absence. Occasionally I would stand with my ear pressed to a wall or the floor or a door, listening to their voices, their private conversations, which of course were rarely as interesting as the fact that I was listening. And later, when I was old enough to be left at home on my own, I did make several painstaking examinations of their belongings, their wardrobe and drawers, every conceivable hiding place – including our attic and my father's garage – looking for evidence of their secret selves and the life that came before me, anything 'personal' about them. I was similarly thorough in my searches of my brother's room, and found nothing there either.

But I would not offer this as any 'explanation' for the way I've become. I am not a private detective because I once spied on my family, or because my childhood was so uneventful, so lacking in incident. These were not 'formative' experiences. The prying part of myself, the patience that verges on inertia, the inner blankness of the spectator, these I'm sure were there from the start, and though I do recognise that it isn't the 'normal' behaviour of a grown man – a responsible citizen and conscientious father and husband – to steal a binbag of rubbish from another person's front gate, or to smuggle it into his own home, this does still strike me as more or less in tune with who I am, and who I've always been.

I do not feel uncomfortable to be up here in my attic, wearing these rubber gloves, as my family sleeps below me. It does not disturb me, as possibly it ought to, that I am about to pick through our friends' kitchen peelings and tissues and plastics. Nor, I should add, do I find the prospect especially appealing.

I have already opened a window, and left the attic door ajar for the draught, but the smell when I rip open the bag is still quite revolting. Downstairs Jan has started to snore, as she always does when she's been drinking. I don't suppose she will wake now before the early hours, when she will stumble through to the toilet and groggily return and immediately fall back to sleep. Tomorrow she will be ill, and regretful, and if she actually remembers that I went out this evening in my van, she probably won't think it worthwhile to ask where.

In the Browns' rubbish there are three bottles, which I'm sure I could let roll down the stairs without my wife stirring, but still, I lift them out carefully and gently transfer them to a fresh binbag laid out at my side. One of the bottles is for vodka, the other two for wheat beer, and there are half a dozen crushed lager cans too. I pick these out next. The Browns, it seems, are not nearly as diligent at recycling as we are, and evidently don't compost all their peelings and leavings. There are far more of these than I anticipated, and as I winnow them out I note in particular the ones that are strange, the foods that we would not eat – the avocado and aubergine, pineapple, lemongrass, and what looks like the remains of a steak. I find any number of transparent packagings for foodstuffs and batteries, cotton buds, pan scourers. There's the moulded tray from a geometry set – repeatedly pierced with a compass – and a stiff, torn cone that might have secured the cap of a medicine bottle. Other plastics are coloured: fromage frais tubs, shampoo and bubble bath bottles, a scattering of concertina-jointed drinking straws. There are toilet roll tubes, sweet wrappers, soup tins, a blister pack for paracetamol, and several wispy mats of fluff and dark hair. And there are tissues. None of which is much different from what I would have expected to find, in this or any other of our neighbours' rubbish bags.

What keeps me interested are the things I haven't yet re-moved, and which I've been saving. There are several items of what looks like old underwear, and several shaped pieces of card – the packaging, I presume, for whatever articles have been bought to replace them. There's a medical information leaflet, on which I think I glimpsed a diagram of a woman's lower half. And there's a stapled pad of scrap paper with a list in someone's handwriting and some typing on the reverse.

But as the binbag empties and these items become less obscure

I realise that I'm about to be disappointed. I pinch an edge of cloth and lift out a pair of men's briefs, 'cotton rich' and worn through, once a dark blue but now faded. The others are black, and grey, and all of them Will's. Some are pocked with holes, some stained with age. There is nothing of Anna's, and the illustrations on the pieces of card depict yet more pairs of men's briefs, all in the same style, the same colours. He takes a 'regular' fit. And though the purchase of new undergarments is one common indicator of a man who is having, or contemplating having, an extramarital affair – the kind of 'giveaway sign' bullet-pointed in some of the articles Jan reads in her magazines – an equally likely explanation, for which the evidence is here on the floor, is that his old pants are now too shabby to wear, even in front of his wife, even to sleep in.

Anna meanwhile would appear to have had a fungal infection, a recent problem with thrush. The leaflet illustrates the correct procedure for inserting a pessary into the vagina. Which isn't remotely what I would have been hoping to find, and is in fact somewhat dispiriting, as sobering as any other intimate piece of medical news, and brings on a belated feeling of grubbiness, an uncomfortable recognition of the seediness of what I am doing. I scrunch the leaflet into a ball, impatient now to be done with all this, and toss it into the other bag, along with Will's pants. In a moment or two I will knot that bag and take it down to our gate for collection tomorrow.

I shiver in the draught from the window and shift my position. Only the notepad remains. It is damp and food-stained and appears to have been made from several sheets of A4, torn in half and stapled together. I lay it on my desk and stiffly get to my feet. I close the window and peel off my gloves. On the top page there's a list in Anna's handwriting, the items as banal as any chalked up on the board in our kitchen: *milk/bread/stamps, change beds, phone bank, chase up P*. The other pages are blank. I turn the pad over and look at the typing on the reverse, and I sit down.

I switch on my desklamp. What I have, it would seem, is a collection of sentences and paragraphs for one of Will's novels, presumably the latest one. They appear to be notes for a person called Harry. Many are scored through in crayon, or amended in pen; some are ripped across the middle. The font I recognise as Times New Roman, twelve-point plain – the same typeface as I use to write up my reports. I quickly skim through the pages, then re-read them more slowly, and what strikes me is that these are lines I myself might have written; if I were to attempt a novel, this is very close to how it might sound. And though I am certain that Will must have drawn on his own situation – on what he himself knows – for much of what he says about 'Harry', I do also wonder if any of this is supposed to describe me, if this is the result of our four years' acquaintance, or more particularly of the time he's spent lately as my 'shadow' at work.

I lean back in my chair. I allow my posture to slacken, and as I listen to Jan's soft snoring below, another, more troubling possibility also occurs to me – that Will's main source was not in fact me but my wife, that he hasn't actually been scrutinising me, but merely talking in private to her. Perhaps I needn't have searched through her diaries for evidence of a betrayal; perhaps the evidence is here in these notes. Possibly she has betrayed me by revealing to Will far more about me than I would ever have wished him to know.

I would like to go down and ask her. I would like to shake her awake now and demand her attention, but of course I couldn't show her this pad without also having to explain how I came by it. I couldn't wake her without having to reveal what I have been doing while she has been sleeping. And so I sit up, and begin reading again, and attempt this time to reassure myself that any resemblance to me is 'purely coincidental', as unintentional as the note in Will's novel will doubtless claim it to be.

Sometimes when the light was right and his wife and children were happy Harry would take a moment to survey all he had and a big bubble of excitement would rise up in him, a big choking ball of elation, and it would thrill and surprise him. These tears came from just the same place and were just as mysterious. Harry was always surprised to find himself host to such happiness. He was equally surprised now to discover he could harbour such sadness.

– Harry loves the wife but thinks of this as a melancholy/ sentimental thing – it's fellow sympathy for someone as trapped by a habit as he is. Sometimes he feels sorry for her because she's married to him and often he feels sorry for

himself. He hasn't really altered since they got married – his needs have stayed constant. Hers have changed – she's developed & she's bored with him now.

'I think you prefer habit to happiness,' his wife said. 'Well, I don't any more.'

Harry had progressed as far along the road of self-discovery as felt safe to him. He knew as much as he needed to and not a lot of it was good. The best refuge now was indoors. Home was where the heart was best protected. That was where it was least exposed to harm or temptation, or so

– Harry has his secret life but his wife also has hers. She's v distant these days – she carries her own incommunicable burdens. They've become more & more unknown to each other as the years have gone on. He's basically incurious about her. She's fed up with him. They don't have sex and neither misses it – or Harry thinks neither misses it . . . (?)

– sense of time running out or catching up – physically he's falling to bits or thinks he is. Arthritic pains in knuckles & thumbs, creaky knees, fallen arches, bad back, eczema, worries about prostate, heart palpitations, chest pains, eyesight etc . . .

Life, Harry considered, was like a car. At the age of six it was doing 6 mph and you noticed everything. You could step out and pick the buttercups. You hadn't travelled far. Your parents were still close by. At twenty the car was doing 20 mph and you were still noticing things. You felt a sense of exhilaration in the acceleration. You felt you would like to go faster. Collisions wouldn't be fatal. Any damage could be repaired and forgotten. But gradually the car picked up speed and you noticed much less. After forty you had much less time to take in the scenery. You concentrated all your efforts on staying in control of the vehicle which now felt dangerous. You felt vulnerable in your vehicle. Any collision would be fatal. You were aware of the distance you had travelled and you knew you were going too fast to jump out. You were hurtling towards your inevitable

Harry was a private detective. He was also a private, secretive person. 'Furtive' was a word he might have used about himself. It was a word that connoted cunning and slyness, he knew, but the meanings he personally preferred were caution and shyness. He thought of himself as more fieldmouse than fox. He was more anxious than thievish. A sense of shame had always been with him and he was above all furtive in the ways he sought to evade that. He hid from himself. Harry slunk away from too close a confrontation with the truths of his life. The irony was that he should feel he had so much to hide and that his life was so utterly empty, so hollow and lacking in substance.

– Harry's never been a person who relates easily to others. He doesn't show much excitement, he's never frivolous or impul-

sive and he's not easily angered – he's above all steady. He's aware this doesn't make him very good company. He hasn't much of a gift for conversation. He can only observe. Sometimes he looks in the mirror and feels he's facing a stranger.

Loneliness stalked him. It always had done. He was more prepared now to admit that.

– recently he's got into the habit of archiving. Constantly making inventories of his life. He's become intolerant of loose ends and he loathes clutter and mess.

Harry was endeavouring to resist the tendency of any life towards entropy, especially family life. With so many children in the house there was a lot of untidiness, a great deal of disorganisation.

– some things will have to go, so first he destroys his private notebooks. Harry has always kept a detailed account of his day-to-day life.

Professionally Harry sometimes surprised himself with the things he had learned. But if he could trade this knowledge for an equal measure of expertise in some other field it would be for a greater insight into literature and writing. Harry had always dreamed of becoming a writer.

He destroyed his notebooks and then he began on his private correspondence. Some letters and cards he kept, others he burned. He went through his photograph albums. He threw some photos away, others he rearranged. He re-examined every file in his office. Everything he owned he questioned. He was being overcautious. He knew this. He was acting out of guilt, a heightened sense of paranoia. He was seeking to cover his tracks, to eliminate the incriminating. Yet there was more to it than that. In going as far back as he could, in putting the facts of his life in order, Harry was determined to go cleanly, with his life begun, lived and ended as one tidy package. Why he should be thinking in these terms, with such attention to the idea of no longer being here, Harry could not say. He did not know.

Harry trusted no one, himself least of all.

14

Words have never come easily to me. I may be a 'good listener', but I wouldn't claim to be a good talker, and in truth I was never particularly fluent at writing. All through my university course – the nine or ten months in which I was encouraged to think of myself as an 'author' – I produced no more than the minimum wordage required, and struggled to achieve even that. Always I agonised over what to put down, and immediately distrusted whatever it was, convinced the words I had placed on the page must be flawed in some way, incorrectly punctuated, ungrammatically organised, their true meanings other than what I imagined them to be.

The more I pored over them, the less sense they would make. And yet I wanted my work to be faultless, beyond reproach, and so I would type and re-type every page. Correction fluid was no use to me. Even the smallest error would mean a clean sheet, a fresh start. My desk was an old dining table with fold-down extensions and rickety legs, my typewriter a reconditioned Olivetti with several stiff keys, and as I punched out the letters the table flaps would rock into the legs and the clatter would resound through the wood. It was a noisy activity, which sounded purposeful, but for much of the time I didn't know what I was doing, what I wanted to say. I could type, but that didn't mean I could write, and the longer I remained in that house the more exhausting the effort became.

The more unsettled I came to feel, also. To my housemates there was always something 'suspect' about my writing. My literary aspirations were viewed as an indulgence, 'contributing' nothing, and when one of the girls accused me of 'bourgeois individualism' I wasn't surprised. That was how we spoke to each other then, and in my defence I described the hours I would labour to produce a single page and equated this with the political struggles that we all endorsed. I had grown up in a home without books, I said, in a town where there wasn't a bookshop, and where the public library had been burned to the ground. My parents were not readers, and neither were the parents of anyone I knew. Everything in my background had conspired against me, and so, when I tried to write, it was always a struggle because the words I used were already owned, inaccessible, the property of the already cultured, the wealthy and powerful. I wasn't indulging myself, I said in all seriousness, but battling against privilege.

And though this was clearly the worst kind of special pleading, assuming the mantle of victimhood to which we all aspired at that time, it did seem to persuade her, and for a while it half convinced me.

But in fact I had very few genuine convictions – about politics, writing, who I was in myself – and if it wasn't for Sarah I'm sure

I would have moved out of that house a lot sooner. She alone had faith in my writing – or in the idea of me as a writer – and however much of a charlatan I felt otherwise, my feelings for her at least appeared to be 'true'. They were 'real'. And yet they were also what caused me the most anguish to place on the page. Many times I attempted to write about her – about what I thought I knew of her – but the sentences soon became tangled. I could not write plainly, or express myself accurately. I was in love, and hopelessly so, but Sarah also made me unhappy, and sometimes I was sure that I hated her. She was sweet and affectionate, and easily hurt, but her affections were promiscuous, not mine to depend on, and despite the intimacy we shared and the secrets she told me, I never did feel I could 'read' her; she was always unfathomable, and became even more so once I began seeing Jan.

I had moved into that house towards the end of September, just as my MA was starting, and it was some time around Christmas before I first spoke to Jan. Although our courses were separate we knew several of the same people. We went to the same cafes and parties and pubs, and it was late one night in a pub that I finally asked what her name was, and what she was studying, and if her hair was genuinely that ginger. By the following April I'd come to think of her as my girlfriend. We met more or less daily on campus. We shared a bed two or three nights a week. But she was still more unknown than known to me; Jan was still to be learned, as a language needs to be learned, and when Sarah took me into her bed for the first time it didn't strike me as wrong, as any kind of betrayal. I wasn't thinking of Jan. She was gone from my mind then.

Other occasions with Sarah would follow – not many: five or six, maybe seven – and each time I would be eager, my conscience untroubled. To me it was 'natural', the obvious next thing for us to be doing. But in fact it led nowhere. The sex did not bring us closer. For Sarah, it seemed, sex was a physical comfort, something private and consoling, and possibly, too, it was how she took her secret revenge on Anthony for his remoteness, and on me for the time I spent with Jan. She gave me what I thought I most wanted, but was mute and unresponsive throughout, and at her least approachable, her least affectionate afterwards. It wasn't attention she sought from me in bed. It wasn't my understanding, my sympathy, a listening ear or a shoulder to cry on. These she could have at any time. Nor was it anything deeper, an intimacy we could not achieve through mere talking. Mostly in bed she just wanted sex. Which for me was never enough. I never just wanted sex. And possibly she understood this. Possibly she knew that I was in love with her, and perhaps she also loved me. Sometimes I thought so, and once, for a brief moment, I even felt certain. But that, I soon realised, was the end for us.

My course had by then finished, and Jan had begun her first teaching assignment. It was late summer, another September, and as I sat at my desk, disconsolately re-reading the work I'd produced in the year and trying to think what to do with it next, I heard Sarah's soft tread on the landing. We were alone in the house. For most of that morning I'd been aware of her movements downstairs. Now she came into my room and stood for a while at my back, massaging my shoulders. I laid my papers face down. She didn't say much. After some minutes I swivelled slowly around in my chair and held her, my face pressed to her breasts. She wasn't wearing a bra; it was rare that she did. I lowered my hands to the back of her legs and drew them up under her skirt to her knickers. Her skin was cool. She tugged her T-shirt from her waistband, pulled it over her head, and soon we were both standing, unhurriedly discarding our clothes. Naked and silent we climbed under my sheets in the sunshine, and what I recall then, as she guided me into her, was the steadiness of her gaze, her wide clear eyes holding mine.

Previously, those other few times, her eyes had been closed, or focused elsewhere, and it was this, her openness now, her lack of any defences, that made me believe that she loved me. And all at once I ejaculated. As she lay beneath me, her legs splayed and her eyes fixed on mine, I came all in a rush, elatedly kissing her forehead, her eyebrows, her nose. I breathed her name, and whispered I loved her, and with a trembling last thrust I subsided, inhaling the scent of sweat and shampoo in her hair, the milky warm smell at her neck. Smiling, I lay over her, and stroked the side of her face. And then Sarah snorted. She suddenly started to laugh.

I withered. I rolled onto my back. Seconds passed. I turned my face to our clothes, dumped on the floor by my desk. I looked up at my typewriter, at the blank sheet of A4 curled round the roller, and then at the Post-its and postcards and photos that littered my wall, and dismally I asked her, 'What's so funny, Sarah?'

She waited a moment. 'Not you,' she sighed.

'What then?'

'Just men, when they come.'

'I'm not "just men",' I objected.

'No.'

'Is Anthony?'

'No,' she said, her voice small and reluctant, seemingly already wearied by this. 'No, he isn't either.'

'But he *is* comical, Sarah. You've told me.'

She didn't reply.

'Sarah?' I persisted, and looked at her profile, the sorrowful cast of her face as she stared at the ceiling. 'Am I as funny as he is? Shall we talk about it? Who do you think is the funniest, Sarah?'

A plump tear welled from her eye, dripped down, and of course I pitied her then. I breathed her name and embraced her. I cupped a hand to her face and gently turned it towards me. 'Sorry,' I murmured, and kissed the tip of her nose. I searched her moist eyes, but though she accepted my gaze, unflinchingly returned it for as long as my hand remained on her cheek, there was nothing there; she was as far removed from me then as she had ever been. I lowered my hand to her shoulder and she turned her face again to the ceiling.

For several long minutes we lay uncomfortably close, my right leg across hers, my limp penis pressed to her hip. I watched her nostrils widen and pinch as she breathed. I stroked the length of her arm, rested my hand at the top of her thigh. She did not move. I laid my hand over her groin, her thick mat of hair, and she let me caress her. Pliant, or indifferent, she closed her eyes, parted her legs, and I continued even though I knew it was futile; I continued until the ache in my fingers and wrist gave me a reason to stop.

Her eyes remained closed. Her breathing was steady. I raised myself onto one elbow and looked at her. For a long while I just looked at her. This, I sensed, would be our last time. I smoothed my hand over her belly and up to her breasts. I lowered my mouth to her nipple, bit gently, and she did not resist me. I manoeuvred myself over her and eased her legs wider. I pressed myself into her, and then, like Anthony, I tried to come again. Desperate and sweating, I made myself 'comical', but however quickly or slowly I pounded I could not ejaculate, and she would not assist me. She did not stir and at last I gave up. I withdrew and lay by her side.

She opened her eyes. 'Sarah?' I said, and carefully she stood up on the mattress, balanced herself with a hand on the wall, and stepped over me. She gathered her clothes and went from my room to the bathroom. I heard her fasten the latch on the door. I listened as she filled up the bath. Half an hour later I crossed to my desk and gathered my papers. I dropped them into a boxfile. Then I began to take down the pictures and notes on my wall.

For some weeks after that we hardly spoke to each other. Sarah remained polite and friendly towards Jan, and was more than usually affectionate with Anthony. She was relaxed and talkative in the company of others, and appeared 'interested' in our house meetings, but with me she was sullen. If I spoke she would pretend not to have heard me. If I came into a room, she would wait a few moments then leave. It seemed she could not bear to be near me. And though this was familiar enough – there had been periods of estrangement before – the depth of her hostility now was unnerving. It was upsetting, but also infuriating, and the longer it went on the more convinced I became that I loathed her. I would listen out for her voice, then despise it. The words I overheard seemed to me stupid, her laughter affected. Everything she did I found fault with, and without her as my ally I resolved to move out of that house as soon as I could. I began to take my meals separately; I stopped 'participating', kept to my room, and when finally – one damp night in October – she knocked and looked round my door, I did not welcome her but stared and said nothing.

'Can I come in?' she asked, hesitating.

I was sitting on my mattress, reading a book. I shrugged and leant back on the wall.

'Peace offering?' she said, and held out a bottle of whisky.

I shook my head and returned to my book. Sarah sat in the

typing chair at my desk. She swivelled slowly to and fro, the bottle clasped at her knees, and when it was clear that patience alone would not make me acknowledge her, she came across to my mattress and knelt down by my side. She said she thought we should talk. Our housemates had begun to discuss me; there was a lot of ill-feeling. And she was worried about me. I didn't seem happy. She realised this was partly her fault, that she wasn't being fair to me. And she did want us to stay friends. She thought we should make a start on the whisky and then go out to a pub.

But even when she unscrewed the cap on the bottle and sat close beside me – her back to the wall and her shoulder snug against mine – I refused to talk, refused the drink, and continued to look down at my book. There was nothing I wished to say, I now realised, except that I loved her. I wanted her to leave Anthony, that house, the life we were leading. I wanted her to run away with me.

I wanted that desperately, but of course none of this could be said because I was afraid of the answer. Either she would decline, and so make clear her attachment to Anthony, or else she'd agree, and I wouldn't then know what to do, for though I desired it, I also feared it was hopeless. Without an Anthony we wouldn't know how to be close. I wouldn't be able to delve into her feelings, her secret life, because whatever hurts and grievances she then harboured would all be about me. I would become her new 'Anthony' in fact, and soon she would need to find some other intimate to confide in. Without an Anthony to conspire against, we two could not survive.

And perhaps this was the end of ambition for me, the moment at which I accepted that all things were not possible. It's a commonplace notion, I'm sure, that many lives exist for us, and even continue in some way in our absence. Certainly the person I was at that time was the person I imagined Sarah wished me to be. That version of myself belonged to her, and you might say she still 'owns' it. But that evening I relinquished it. I realised there could not be a future in which I was a writer and Sarah was central. Such things could not happen for me because I hadn't the belief, the courage or self-confidence to bring them about.

Nor had I the words. I could not ask Sarah to leave with me. I could not even speak to her, and when finally, her patience exhausted that evening, she gave me the bottle and got up from my bed and went from my room, I felt something close to relief, a momentary sense of release.

Grief would soon follow, but in those first few hours I retrieved my stories and notes from their boxfile and calmly tore them in two. I dropped them into my waste bin and tipped away everything else I could find that related in any way to my MA, including some of the novels I had read in that year – the ones I had attempted to imitate – and then, sitting alone with the whisky, I pushed my typewriter aside and began to draft in longhand a letter in which I disclosed to the page for the last time all the things I thought I wanted to say to her.

None of which she would ever read, though I suspect that Jan may have. I suspect it was always my hope that Jan would.

All through this period Jan had been working in a school somewhere near to the village where she had grown up and where her parents still lived. She slept in her old bedroom most weekdays, and came back into town at the weekend. There wasn't a phone in our house and so I never quite knew when to expect her. Sometimes she'd arrive on the Friday, sometimes the next morning, and if I should be out then she'd come straight up to my room and wait for me. She might sit at my desk with her marking, or lie on my bed on her belly and read. Once I found her asleep. Two days after I'd written my letter I found her sitting in my swivel chair, slowly turning to and fro, as Sarah had. Her hands were clasped at her knees, her gaze was fixed on my mattress, and she hadn't yet unbuttoned her coat.

I kissed her forehead. 'You okay?'

'Yes,' she said distantly. 'Just thinking.'

'But not staying?' I touched the collar of her coat and for a second or two she didn't seem certain, then began to unfasten the buttons. Behind her on my desk was her overnight bag, and beside that my notepad, the loosened leaves of my letter face down beside it. 'Just got here?' I asked.

'Not quite.'

'You'll want a cup of tea.'

'No.'

'Anything?'

Jan shook her head. 'I'm fine,' she sighed, and walked across to my wardrobe. She draped her coat on a hanger. Twisting, she raised one foot and then the other and tugged off her shoes. She placed them on a low shelf, their polished toes facing outwards. She loosened the waistband on her skirt, unravelled her hair from its clips. And then in her stockinged feet, suddenly homely, her hips seemingly wider, she sat on my mattress and tucked her legs underneath her. Warily she smiled at me; she was now ready. 'So,' she said. 'What have you got to tell me?'

And what I felt then was something like gratitude. I sat down in my chair – the seat still warm from Jan – and though it may not have been her intention, I began to confess everything that had passed between Sarah and me, not just recently but from the very start, and not simply the facts but the overheated hopes I'd entertained for us. After which, I supposed, Jan could decide whether or not to persist with me. The decision would be hers. And perhaps I was hoping that she would leave me, if only temporarily; I did believe I deserved that. Certainly I expected her to be angry.

Instead of which – for a very long while – she was silent, staring across at my window, the dark October sky. When eventually I approached her – just as Sarah had approached me – she flinched at my touch, and then shrugged and said she had guessed as much anyway; she wasn't surprised. If anything she was sad for me. It was a sad situation. And she would take that cup of tea now.

'Sorry?'

'Tea.'

I stood up. Uncertainly I turned for the door.

'Mike?' she said.

'Yes?'

'Did you really say you'd chucked away your stories?'

I looked down at my desk. 'Yes,' I said, and gathered up my notepad, my letter, my biro. I dropped them into the drawer; I would decide what to do with them later. 'Why?'

Jan shook her head. 'Nothing,' she said, and drew up her legs, wrapped her arms around them. She rested her chin on her knees and turned her face again to the window. 'We'll need to think what you're going to do next,' she said.

15

Assuming you troubled to look, you would not find me in the phonebook. In the residential directory we are listed under Jan's surname, Fordham, which she held on to when we got married. In the *Yellow Pages* there's a listing for *Spotlight Investigations* rather than my actual name, and a postbox number rather than my address. Once – years ago and not for long – I did lease an office in town, but even with that 'shopfront' most of my dealings with clients took place on the phone and most of our meetings still happened elsewhere – usually in their own homes or where they worked. I could not justify the expense of the office, and I have since wondered how Will – who often claims to be poor, but whose house and mortgage are much larger than ours – can manage to live with the monthly payments on his.

The building in which he works is small and nondescript, a modern functional block incongruously tucked away amongst the wynds and alleys of the old town. It's in an area I know well, and know to be costly. The renovated guildhall where Rosa has her legal practice stands immediately in front of it. Another solicitor's I work for is in the next cobbled lane, and a little further along is an advertising agency that sometimes employs me to sweep its conference room for phone taps and bugs. The last time I went down there in fact was in the middle of March, when they were competing for the account of a national road haulage company, and I remember afterwards walking over to Will's. It was a lunchtime, and sunny, and I was free for the rest of the day. I located his name on the door-entry console and lifted a finger to the buzzer, but I could not make myself press it. I turned away, relieved, and as I stand here today, my left ear inclined towards the intercom, I do feel a similar reluctance to meet him. Always with Will there is this ambivalence.

Yet still, when his voice crackles 'Hello?' I pipe out my name and push straight through on the buzz. The door slams behind me and I proceed left through a fire door and up an echoing glass-sided stairwell to the third and top storey, where I half expect he will be waiting. He isn't. The corridor is dim-lit and carpeted and smells of cleaning agents, synthetically floral. The only sound is my own quickened breathing. I scan the name-plates as I pass by them – *Dogfish Design Studios, Financial Futures, SoftTek Solutions, Kirkpatrick Dress Hire* – until I arrive at a door which is unmarked and slightly ajar. I tap twice, and as I tentatively enter I hear the chink of a spoon on a cup, a kettle just starting to steam.

'Coffee?' asks Will, glancing over his shoulder. He is standing in a small side-room where there's a sink and some beige-fronted units and a view through the windows of the old city wall, a multi-storey carpark, the pyramidal glass roof of the new shopping mall. Peering in, I notice a toilet behind a partition.

'Thanks,' I say, 'no sugar,' and push my hands in my pockets.

Will drums his fingertips on the edge of the worktop. 'Won't be a minute,' he says.

'Right,' I say and take a few steps into his office and pause and gaze around me. The decor is blue-grey, the furniture and fittings mock-teak, and there is none of the imprisoning clutter I've often heard him complain of, and which I was hoping to find.

I look quickly towards him. He opens a small fridge and reaches for a carton of milk. I have a minute at most, perhaps only half that. The device in my pocket is no larger than a pen cap, little bigger than the battery it contains. I take it out and whip my wrist to uncoil the antenna. Hurriedly I select the nearest tall cupboard and stretch up and wipe a small area for dust. I place the bug on top of it. The strip of adhesive fixes at once, as Kuldip said that it would. The aerial – eighteen inches of wire – hangs down at the rear. It cannot be seen.

I clean my finger on the inside of my pocket and stand in the centre of the room. Behind a chrome and leather armchair there's a pile of pillows and sheets and neatly folded blankets. In the space between two filing cabinets I notice a suitcase and a zipped tartan holdall, one stacked on top of the other. The rolled-up mat in the corner is presumably Will's bed. But these items apart, there is little to indicate a man who has left his family and is now squatting at work.

Nor is there much to indicate a professional writer. On one windowless wall he has pinned a solitary chart, an academic year planner. On another, nearer his desk, there's a cork pinboard, covered not with lists or notes but a selection of his sons' drawings. Very few books are on display – certainly none of his own – and there are no labels on any of the boxfiles and folders lined up on the shelves. His desk is virtually empty and the lid of his laptop is lowered. All of which suggests a degree of preparation for my visit today; he has, I suspect, hidden away as much of himself as he can.

'Spartan,' I say.

Will hands me my coffee. 'Tidy,' he replies, and pushes the door shut with his foot. He isn't wearing any shoes and his socks are threadbare at the heels. Whatever other precautions he's taken, they haven't extended to his appearance and fleetingly I do feel sorry for him, the situation he's in. His tracksuit bottoms and T-shirt are crumpled, his hair uncombed, and his complexion, I notice, is blotchy, his eczema inflamed. I loosen my tie, unbutton my jacket.

'Do you sleep all right here?' I ask.

He shrugs, and sits at his desk. 'It's okay. Rosa's building is floodlit at night, which comes in through my blinds. Plus those corridor lights never go out, and that door doesn't quite meet the carpet – you can see – so the light gets in under there as well . . .'

I look to the door. 'You'll feel the draught,' I say.

Will laughs. For some reason this is amusing. 'Yes,' he says.

'There are draughts, and it gets very dusty. But it's the light really that bothers me. And the noise from the carpark.'

I lower myself into his armchair. The tubular frame yields a little under my weight and the leather seat-cushion slips forward. I don't suppose it is good for his back – my own tightens at once – and I do wonder that he should keep it. In Benedict Avenue, I know – because he himself once showed me – most of the furniture is upright, supportive. I blow on my coffee and say, 'Wouldn't you rather be at home?'

'You've seen our house,' he says.

'Yes.'

'It's full of stuff. I'm a tidy person. Anna isn't.'

I meet his gaze, frowning, half smiling. 'And that's why you've moved out? Because your house is untidy.'

'In part,' he insists, looking down at me. 'It's Anna's mess, not mine.'

'Not the boys'?'

'They're tidier than she is.'

'Right,' I say and nod and look away. I sip my coffee. I glance at his cupboard. 'Doesn't seem much of a reason for ending a marriage, Will.'

'Well no. Obviously. If that's what it is.' He turns and raises the lid on his laptop, which chimes as it wakes. 'Did you bring me that CD?' he says, and I take it from my inside pocket, pass it across. He opens the case, inserts the disk in the drive, and as the programme starts to load he sighs and concedes, 'There is more to it than that – there's bound to be – but yes, the mess is important. It hems you in. It weighs you down.' He purses his mouth, watches the screen. 'Living with Anna weighs you down,' he says quietly, as if stating an unavoidable fact, a regrettable truth, and of course it isn't for me to say otherwise. I keep my counsel, attempt to sit upright in his low chair, and breezily he says, 'So. What does this thing do?'

'It's the electoral roll,' I tell him, and realise the screen is too far away for me to see. Awkwardly I get to my feet, place my cup on the edge of his desk. 'It's the current electoral roll, plus the phone directory and the *Yellow Pages*, and you can search it various ways – on a name or a phone number, address, postcode, whatever. Or else you can type in an area – Westminster, let's say – if that's all you've got, and see who lives there. Or if you've got two people you know are living together, but you don't know where, then you can type in both names and it'll give you an address for them.'

Will is nodding, reaching for his spectacles. I place my hand on the back of his chair.

'So, we'll do a trial run first. Then an actual job. There's a couple of new ones I've just taken on – bread and butter stuff – and you can maybe choose between them?'

'Okay,' he says.

'It'll mean some phoning around . . .'

'Oh.'

'You're not keen?'

'Phoning? No.' He clasps his hands together, a doubled fist on his desk, and stares up at me. 'Not sure,' he says. 'Depends what's involved.'

'Lying, Will. You tell lies. You make up stories.'

He looks away, and drily he says, 'Do I now?'

'I'm afraid you'll have to,' I say, and he shrugs; he gives a slight nod. 'Okay,' I say, 'first one, this chap's acquired a TV on credit, six months ago – widescreen plasma thing, eighteen hundred pounds – but he's missed the first payments and can't be located. He's disappeared. So what we can do – what *you* can do – is enter his last known address to bring up the neighbours, then phone around and say you're from the warehouse and explain the TV's a dud, it's dangerous, and you really need to recall it, only you can't get hold of him. Just to see what they say . . . Perhaps someone will know where he's moved to.'

Will grimaces. He rubs the back of his neck. 'And the other one?'

'The other one,' I say, and reach for my coffee. I sip slowly, place it back on the edge of his desk. I take a breath. 'The client's married, okay. He's happily married, but he's wondering about this woman he knew years ago. He basically wants to know about her present circumstances, then maybe he can decide whether he wants to get back in touch with her. So we're to see if we can come up with a current address. Which'll be tricky if she's changed her maiden name. And even if she hasn't, there'll probably be others with the same name, so you'll need to phone around and say you're from the alumni office of her old university – something like that – and would she like to subscribe to their quarterly journal . . .'

Will is smiling. He flexes his fingers, sits straighter.

'You prefer that one?' I ask.

'Yes,' he says. 'Though it doesn't exactly ring true, Mike. He can't be *that* happily married, can he? Are you sure he's not just a stalker, this guy?'

I don't immediately answer, but point across him and say, 'So if you'd like to enter your own name, just there. Do that . . . With your middle initial if you've got one . . .'

I watch him. Then, 'Yes,' I say, 'I'm more or less sure. You can never be a hundred per cent, obviously. I've had husbands in the past employ me to trace runaway wives, either to know the identity of the guy they've gone off with, or just to confirm they're safe and well – so they say – and you just have to trust your instincts about them. There's always the chance she's run away because she's had to, because he was beating her up or whatever. I have turned a few down. But with this one, yes, I'm reasonably sure. I mean, we can never be certain, even about our own motivations, can we, not totally . . .'

I indicate the screen.

'Okay, so there you'll see it's come up with everyone by your name in the UK, with their addresses. And some with phone numbers too. Long list, but we know which one of them's yours, so scroll down . . . Click on your address . . . And then it comes up with a list of your immediate neighbours, and a handy map of the area so you can find it. And also, just there, it informs you who you ought to be living with. Anna C. Brown.'

'Except . . .' he says, half-smiling.

'It's not up to speed with marital separations.'

'Impressive, though.'

'It's good. The economics of this are pretty poor, you know, looking for people. Long hours, low fees. But it used to be worse – you'd have to traipse up to your local records library, or the council offices in some places, and search page after page listed by street and house number. Which was a real pain if you were looking for a specific name. And no good if you wanted some other constituency. So this is good, it speeds things along.' I reach for my coffee. '*Are* you separated, Will?'

He takes off his spectacles. He massages the bridge of his nose between his forefinger and thumb. 'Appears so,' he says.

'Just like that.'

'What other way is there?'

'It seems very sudden, that's all.'

'I suppose so. Maybe. But it's been coming for years, Mike.' He replaces his spectacles and looks at his details on screen, then begins to type in a new search. 'Have you ever read *The End of the Affair*?' he asks me, and rapidly taps out my name, followed by Jan's. He types in 'Janette'.

'No.'

'You should do . . . Actually, there's a private detective in there called Parkis. *The party in question was observed in a state of partial undress. Intimacy was imminent.*'

'I've seen the film,' I say.

'Right. Well, there's a line in the book – not one of Parkis's . . . *Love dies, affection and habit win the day.*' He glances up. 'Was that in the film?'

'I've no idea, Will.'

'*Love dies, affection and habit win the day*. Except with Anna and me there isn't much affection either, and I don't see the point in pretending there is, not any more.' I watch over his shoulder as my own address and a map of our neighbourhood come up on his laptop. Will holds open his hands, gestures towards it. 'You and yours,' he says.

'I can see.'

'Do you mind if I print off some of these, so I remember?'

I let out a laugh. 'Remember what? Who we're both married to? Where we live?'

Will inserts a cable in the back of his laptop. 'What the programme looks like,' he says, and then asks me, 'Have I ever told you about Philip Larkin and why he wouldn't make public appearances? Probably I have . . .'

Blank-faced I say, 'Why would you?' though I have heard him on this several times.

'Favourite quote. He used to say he didn't like giving public readings or doing interviews because he didn't like *going about pretending to be himself*. He felt he was impersonating himself, pretending to be this poet he'd heard of called Philip Larkin. Which is pretty much how I feel when I have to do any kind of publicity, like I'm acting in the third person. But it's a job, so I get on with it. It comes with the territory. Only that's also how I feel in my marriage. I feel like I'm putting it on, like it's not me. Even at home I feel like I'm someone pretending to be me.'

'I see,' I say, and watch as a page with my details feeds out from his printer. 'But that's a fairly common condition, isn't it, Will? I'm pretty sure most people feel like that at some stage in their lives, not just the poets and novelists. I feel it. Everyone does.' I pause. I take my coffee across to a window. 'I don't really see that as a reason to walk out on your kids.'

Will eases his chair back from his desk. Smiling, surprised, he folds his arms on his chest. 'I wouldn't worry about them, Mike,' he says. 'Nick and Nathan are smart boys. They'll survive.'

'I'm sure they will,' I agree, and gaze down on a railed garden, the landscaped area between this building and Rosa's. 'If that's the best hope you have for them. Survival. I'm not criticising, I'm just thinking of things you've said in the past . . .'

'It's okay,' Will interrupts me. 'Really. Look, Mike. With me out of the way their world will suddenly become that much clearer. It'll all add up and make sense. They'll have Anna to love and feel sorry for, and me to hate. Good parent, bad parent. Everything will be in black and white. You could say I'm doing them a favour.'

It seems he expects me to smile. I wait for him to continue.

'I'm serious,' he says. 'It might sound flippant, but I really do think they'll be better off without me. If I stay, okay? They'll grow up in this miserable poisonous soup of never being happy, never seeing their parents happy, always being afraid they're the reason for the unhappiness, and hating themselves because we're such a big part of who they are. So who gains? No one. It's alright feeling sorry for them, Mike, but I don't want to go through the rest of my life feeling sorry for *me*.'

'No, I can see that,' I say.

'It's a dead end,' he says.

I nod.

Will looks at me sceptically. 'You can't really see it at all, can you?'

'No, I can,' I say. 'I can see it.'

'But?'

'But . . . Isn't it just as likely they'll blame themselves for you leaving, and hate themselves for that? It's none of my business, Will, but that's equally possible, isn't it?'

He hooks his hands behind his head. He watches me steadily. 'It's possible,' he says.

'So then what? You'll never repair the damage. You'll only ever be able to chuck money at it. You'll become another one of these weekend dads, showering his kids with stuff they don't need. And they'll never refuse you, they'll let you spend as much as you like on them, but the money will never buy you what you want it to buy . . .'

'Yeah, yeah, and I'm sure I'd be a much better person if I stayed and endured the mess and the boredom and all the bickering and shouldered my responsibilities like a good citizen. I'm sure it would be personally improving, but no, you're right, it's none of your business, Mike, and anyway, I'm still here, I'm still available. They can see me whenever they like. And I'll make sure they do see me, don't worry. I haven't exactly gone anywhere, have I?'

'No,' I say. I look out of the window. 'You haven't exactly gone anywhere.' Enclosed on one side by the old city wall, the garden below is bright with rhododendrons in bloom and I notice a solitary young woman sitting on a bench in the shade, her head bowed over a book. Her hair is blonde and very long and parted in the middle. 'You're still here,' I say. 'But you can't really squat in your office forever, can you?'

'Obviously not.'

'So where are you going to go.'

'I haven't left in order to *go* anywhere, Mike. I've just left. Full stop. I've no commitment to staying, so I've left.'

'Just like that,' I say.

'Yes.'

'And there's no one else?'

'Ah.' Will smiles. He considers for a moment. He sucks in his top lip, raises his eyebrows. 'Just supposing there was someone,' he asks then. 'But not for me. For Anna. I'm curious, how would that register on your scale of moral disapproval, Mike? Better for her than if it *was* me? Worse? The same?'

'Why would I disapprove, in either case?'

'I'm guessing. I don't know that you would necessarily, I'm just wondering.'

'Anna hasn't got anyone,' I tell him.

'You sound very sure.'

'Aren't you?'

Will is smirking. He nods. 'Well okay,' he says. 'But I'm still curious. What *is* your line on all this. I'm wondering what you actually think of these "adulterers" you follow around everywhere?'

The girl's legs are stretched out before her and crossed at the ankle. She slips off a shoe, rubs the back of her calf with her toe, and I realise then that I recognise her. 'I don't think much,' I shrug. 'I'm not sure I understand them, exactly. I watch them. I learn quite a bit about them – factually speaking – but I'm not sure I know what drives them. And after a while it all gets to be a bit of a bore, to be honest. The shenanigans are pretty routine in a way. It gets messy, but it's always the same kind of mess. I don't really know why they put themselves through it.'

'Because they're in love?' Will suggests.

'Which is an illness,' I say. 'It passes. What's your quote? Love dies, habit sets in?' Outside the girl closes her book, begins to stand. I step away from the window and say, 'I think that's one of your neighbours, Will. The Sommers' daughter?'

He cranes his neck, partially lifts himself from his chair. 'Katie, yes,' he says. 'She works on the ground floor. Pretty girl.' He watches intently until she passes from view. 'Nice bottom,' he adds, and reluctantly draws himself back into his desk. He realigns his laptop, pushes his spectacles to the bridge of his nose. 'So,' he says then. 'This programme, who shall we look for?'

'You haven't answered my question.'

'Which was?'

'Is there anybody else?'

Will sighs. He turns and fixes his gaze on mine and I lean into his desk, fold my arms on my chest. I look down at him, the flakes of dry skin on his forehead, the specks on his lenses, and I wonder that anyone could find him attractive. 'Yes,' he says wearily. 'As it happens, there is someone else.'

'And?' I say. My heart scuds. 'Is this anyone I'd know?'

Will draws in a long breath. He slowly exhales. 'Let's just say it's someone I can't have, Mike. She's the right person for me, absolutely the right person for me. I feel *that* every time I'm with her. Which is something I've never felt with Anna, not even at the very beginning.' He is reddening, embarrassed. 'But with her – this other person – it feels exactly right, like *it was always meant to be*. Have you ever felt that? Is that how you feel with Janette?'

I stare but don't answer him.

'No? Yes? Well let me tell you how it is, it's like every crappy cliché there ever was. She's the last person I think of at night and the first person I think of in the morning, and every time I see her my heart skips a beat and my pulse starts to race. The world becomes a much sunnier place. It's all the romantic clichés you can think of, but *none* of the romantic circumstances. And it can't happen. Why? Because she's just like you, Mike. She's exactly like you.'

He is angry, it seems, and I nod. I don't look away. Will holds up his hand, counts out on his fingers.

'For a start, number one, she wouldn't walk out on her kids. Two, she probably wouldn't want to be with someone who'd walked out on *his* kids. And three, she's afraid of change, what she doesn't already know. She'd rather betray herself than betray her "responsibilities" to her husband and children. Habit and affection before love. Who knows, maybe she also thinks love is a fucking illness.'

'Have you asked her?'

'Yes,' he says flatly.

'And?'

'No answer.'

'I see,' I say.

'No you do not fucking see,' he says, and turns to his laptop. 'You don't see at all. You haven't the slightest fucking clue.' He glowers at the map of my street on his screen, his jaw muscles twitching, his lips tightly pursed. There are tears in his eyes and I decide I dare not pursue this. 'So,' he exhales finally, 'give me a missing person? Who are we looking for?'

I back away from him. I lower myself to his armchair. And when I speak I feel my own pulse accelerating; I hear the tremor in my voice. 'Okay, enter Sarah,' I say. 'Middle initial P. Last name, Quillan.' Which is the first time I have spoken her name aloud in all the years I have been married to Jan. And I repeat it; I spell it out letter by letter, and sit forward. I press my hands together and touch my lips to my fingers and watch as Will types it.

16

Like the Sommers before us, we don't know our neighbours, though I at least watch them. I know who lives where and with whom and if they have children. In some cases, a few, I know the hour they go out in the mornings and what time they come back and when they retire to their beds. I've seen the young couple at number 86 making love against the frosted glass of their front door, and the teenaged daughter of the woman at 82 squatting in the road with her skirt up, competing with a friend to see whose pee would trickle furthest down the hill. Her mother, red-faced and rotund, is frequently drunk. The single woman next door to them leaves the house every morning in her gym kit, and the two men beside her have recently opened a sixties-themed restaurant in town. The same cleaner tidies both of their houses. She comes and goes in a tiny red Fiat, rust-fringed and filthy.

Jan is aware of very little of this. She does not notice, or chooses not to be interested, and soon becomes muddled if I attempt to describe something I've seen: she won't quite know who I mean, or which house I'm referring to, or how this story connects with any others I've mentioned. I suspect she finds my own interest unhealthy, the amount of information I've gathered, though of course I could if I wished gain access to more, to names and phone numbers, credit ratings, even criminal records, all of which could be cross-referenced. Dossiers could be compiled. But in truth I wouldn't want to make that kind of an effort. For the most part I'm content to know as much, or as little, as can be seen from our windows, as much as might be noticed by anyone.

And on warm, still evenings like these there is a lot more to observe. Our neighbours will delay closing their curtains till bedtime – if they close them at all – and many will throw open their windows and doors and perhaps come to sit with a beer or a bottle of wine on their front steps. Families will stroll round the streets in their sandals and shorts. Children will be indulged, the antics of teenagers ignored. There will be parties in gardens, the smell of barbecued meat, the dark dusty fragrance of flowers. Late meals will be knocked up in kitchens. Voices will carry, the clatter of pans. Many varieties of music will mingle in the night air, and from Roger Mitchell's house – two doors up on the right, just over the road – there will come the melancholy circularity of the improvised jazz riffs he picks out on his electric guitar.

I am listening to him now, my boys beside me here on the sofa and our TV switched off, our sash windows raised. Or at least, Roger is playing and we can hear him, but the boys are just starting to drowse and my thoughts are drifting elsewhere, repeatedly snagging on my meeting this afternoon with Will, and on the print-out that I brought home with me – Sarah's listing in the electoral roll, and the street map showing her present location, and the name of her partner, her cohabitee.

Will dialled the number and got an answering machine. Expressionless, he held the receiver towards me and I listened to her voice and shrugged and said I'd try again some other time. He nodded. Soon afterwards I left. Agitated, the print-out folded in my pocket, I went and sat then for two hours in a pub and came home drunk and fell asleep on our bed. Jan made no comment, and though she doesn't appear to be annoyed with me, we have hardly spoken since I woke up.

She has been busy, sweeping floors and washing windows, polishing and tidying. For the third evening in succession this is what she's been doing, seemingly unable to settle, another yoga class missed, her marking neglected. Forty-five minutes ago she sent the boys downstairs from their baths, deciding that then was the time to change the sheets on their beds; it could not wait another day. Now her footsteps are crossing the ceiling directly above us. Evidently she's begun stripping our bed as well, and this is making me anxious. I left my jacket lying on the end of the mattress, the map still in my pocket, and I would like to go up and retrieve it.

But my boys have me trapped. Warm and sleepy in their pyjamas, Ben is leaning across me, his head about to drop to my lap, while Jack has one leg hooked over my knee, his head on my chest. My arms are loose around their shoulders. We are comfortable. I could not slip away from them.

*   *   *

There are some things I know about Roger, though not as much as I would like. His house is rented, or at least I assume so. Three students lived there before him, and very little has changed since Roger moved in. The posters have come down from the walls, but the same oval mirror hangs over the fireplace. The curtains and wallpaper and furniture all remain as they were. The paint continues to blister on the window ledges, the frames are in need of repair, and there are still several loose tiles on his roof. Work is required, but unlike most other properties around here, Roger's house is not being 'sympathetically upgraded'. I have never seen a hire skip parked by his kerb, and I could not picture him with a paintbrush.

His name I learned early, even before I first saw him, from a parcel I signed for one morning. White Arrow Express. *Roger Mitchell esq*. This was two years ago. I was just leaving for work, and left the package at the foot of our stairs. It was still there when I came home. Half the size of a shoebox, it was as light as any letter and made no noise – not the slightest vibration – when I shook it next to my ear. The plain paper wrapping – unmarked but for his name and address – gave no clue as to what it contained, and I was, I'll admit, tempted to steam it open and carefully unpack and rewrap it, just to know what was inside, as I have done with any other misdirected mail that's arrived here, including several dozen items addressed to the Sommers, none of them interesting. It does no one any harm, and satisfies my curiosity, and I haven't yet interfered with anything I've uncovered, but civic-mindedly sent it on its way, resealed and intact.

Jan however was watching, and shook her head at me. 'I'll take it across,' I said.

'Do that,' she replied.

It was four or five in the afternoon and Roger Mitchell was in no hurry. I rang, and knocked, and then waited as slowly he made his way down from upstairs. There was a chain on the door, a stiff bolt, a missing key to locate; I heard him sighing. Bleary-eyed and dishevelled, and wearing a vest and some track pants, he half opened the door but didn't look up from his name on the box. He scratched at his neck and mumbled his thanks, then quietly closed the door in my face.

And he hasn't met my gaze since, though we do often pass in the street, and sometimes emerge from our houses at just the same moment and climb into vehicles parked bumper to tail. He is someone I feel I should wave to, and bid a cheery *Good morning*, except that ours is not that kind of neighbourhood, and he and I are not that kind of person. On the one occasion I tried it, he simply ignored me.

There could be shyness in this; it may well be hostility. I have no idea. In the hunch of his shoulders, and the self-conscious clench of his jaw as he walks briskly by me, there is something 'furtive' about him, something evasive, like the man described in Will's jottings, his private detective. Yet Roger is also a person who very rarely closes his curtains – at least not when he's alone – and even my wife has noticed him naked, searching for an item of clothing in his upstairs front bedroom. Most of his meals are taken in front of the television, a can of beer by his side, and I have often seen him coming through from his kitchen, another drink in his hand. One week in three he appears to work nights – he goes out some time around nine – but wherever it is that he goes it's a place where the booze on his breath won't be noticed, or perhaps won't be queried, for always he drinks a can or two before leaving.

He is a drink-driver; more than once I have seen that. And of course he is drinking tonight. A moment ago he paused in his playing; I heard the snap of his ring-pull. He is sitting with his front door wide open.

Our telephone is ringing. Ben has stirred and sat upright; Jan is hurrying downstairs. Our answering machine will cut in after five rings, though it's possible her haste is simply to get there before me. These past few days, I'm sure, she has been unusually alert to the telephone, just as I've been alert to the tenor of her voice when she speaks on it. And something in her tone now, as she takes the handset from its cradle in the hall and carries it through to the kitchen, does strike me as odd – uneasy yet intimate, confiding but jittery. She closes the door. Her voice becomes indistinct, barely even a murmur, and I cup a hand to Jack's head, the other to Ben's, and hold them against me. I turn my face to the window. My boys will be happy to stay up this little while longer, and I am content for now to listen to Roger's guitar. He is playing a tune I think I recognise, and whatever my wife may be saying, I will eventually hear every word. Her conversation is being recorded.

A few days ago I did belatedly examine her mobile, then checked the memory on our home phone, and came across numerous calls to and from Will's office and mobile, more than I could account for. He and my wife have been talking, and the 'intercept' I have placed now on our landline is transmitting to a tape-deck upstairs in my office. I installed it this morning, before visiting Will, and if I have delayed for this long – if I have been complacent – I am sure that is not so unusual. The British, it is often reported, are more inclined than any other European nationality to have faith in their partner's fidelity. Amongst cohabiting couples, the figure is seventy per cent; amongst marrieds it is closer to ninety. No doubt you'll have seen the statistics; the surveys and articles are commonplace. Another appeared in the current issue of the trade paper I subscribe to, and was picked up in last Sunday's *Observer*. We are more trusting than our counterparts in Italy or France, Greece, Denmark or Holland, and yet we are also more often unfaithful. A quarter of Britons admit to having cheated on their spouses, though only a fraction of those have been found out, most of them men.

Women, of course, are better equipped to uncover adultery. This is the wisdom of almost every such article. They have the 'intuition' to recognise the signs, and they're more willing to seek the assistance of a professional. This much I know personally: most of my clients in this line have been female. And yet women are also far better at being unfaithful; they are more adept at the complex planning involved, and at concealment.

Unlike 'goal-oriented' men, they have a greater facility for 'multi-tasking', for juggling commitments, for lying, and soon enough, I suppose, I will know how far this applies to my wife.

She is standing now in the doorway, her cheeks flushed, her hair tied up in an old scarf. 'Boys . . .' she says softly. 'Time for bed.'

'Come on then,' I say, and pat the top of their heads. Reluctantly they unfurl themselves from my arms. I lean my hands on my knees and carefully push myself upright. My back has stiffened. 'Who was that?' I say, pressing my fists to my lumbar and flexing.

'Mum,' Jan replies. She reaches a hand towards Jack, caresses the nape of his neck.

'What'd she want?'

She looks at me, frowning. 'To talk?' she says, adopting an inflection she must have picked up from her pupils, insolent, American.

'And?'

'Just that. She talked.'

Pale and sulky, Jack squeezes past her. Ben flops against her belly, and for a moment it seems she might be about to say something more, then sighs and guides him out to the stairs. The door swings slowly behind her, and I wait a few moments, then turn off the light, half close the curtains, and quickly go through to our fridge for a beer.

I am not myself 'musical'. I could not be certain, but Roger doesn't sound to me to like a learner, or even a hobbyist, but someone who might once have performed professionally, though clearly he does not perform now, except of course for himself and the strangers around him, his neighbours.

In the two years that he has lived here I haven't once seen him leave the house with his guitar, and I do often look. Whenever I hear the particular thump of Roger's front door I will get up and note which direction he's going in, and whether he's walking or taking his car, and how he is dressed. Consciously or not, I will register the set of his face and what he is carrying and whether he's smoking – which is something he appears to have come to quite late, or perhaps only recently returned to: he inhales in short breaths, his grip on the cigarettes seeming stiff and uncertain. A few minutes ago I watched him light another. He took a single drag and laid it in an ashtray. Soon it will have burned back to the filter.

I don't know what he does for a living. Nor do I know where he has come from, or how long he'll remain here, though my best guess is that he won't be moving on for some time. What I do know is that Roger is a refugee from a failed marriage, and has two children, both of them boys, the oldest perhaps in his teens, the youngest now seven or eight. From time to time they will come to stay, the intervals irregular, maybe one weekend in five. The upstairs front bedroom is the youngest's, and remains from one visit to the next exactly as he leaves it – the quilt heavily mussed, the door open to the light on the landing – but there are no personal effects, nothing I can see from over here; he takes away whatever he brings.

And he doesn't bring much – an overnight bag, a stuffed toy, a scooter.

His older brother brings a skateboard. He brings his unhappiness. Always their mother will park her four-by-four some distance down the hill, and always their goodbyes will be prolonged. Minutes will pass before the boys emerge from the car, and once out they will linger a little while longer, still talking, before finally hoisting their bags onto their shoulders and setting off, waving to her as they go. Their most recent visit was just last weekend, and this was how it also proceeded, except that the journey from car to front door took over half an hour.

Three times the older boy turned back. He could not go in, and he could not go home, and so finally he dumped himself on the pavement, mid-way between his mother and father, sitting with his back to somebody else's garden wall, his head buried in his arms. He was sobbing. His younger brother stood over him. His mother came and crouched by his side. She patiently persuaded him onto his feet, and hugged him goodbye, and if Roger knew what was happening he showed no sign of it, but sat in his living room, watching the television. He didn't get up until they knocked. And he didn't glance in the direction of her car, but ushered the boys inside as their mother started her engine and pulled away, her gaze fixed firmly ahead as she accelerated past them.

She is a good-looking woman. Roger, I would guess, is several years her senior, closer now to fifty than forty, and doesn't seem much concerned with appearances, with matters of dress or 'personal grooming'. Thinner on top than I am, his hair at the sides and back is thick and unruly, as though he's still waiting on his wife's word to go to the barber's. He shaves infrequently, and is neglectful of his clothes, which are often shabby, creased and ill-fitting. But possibly this was always the case. Perhaps, like me, Roger has always been flattered by the match he once made; perhaps he too was the envy of his male cronies, if ever there were any. Certainly there are very few of them now. In all the months that he's been there I've yet to see him answer his door to a male friend, though there have been several women, perhaps half a dozen, and all of a type – mid-life and sturdily built, dressed for the occasion and bearing bottles of wine. I don't imagine they are paid for, acquired from an agency, though I do wonder where he finds them, and why they so rarely return.

That is one question I would like to ask him. And I would like to know too what went wrong in his marriage, and if he was to blame, and where he supposes his life might go to from here. Often I will stand and watch him through my slice in these curtains – my arms folded over my chest, a can becoming heavy and warm in my right hand – and I will wonder what were the circumstances that brought him to this moment, and if there are lessons for me in his story.

But of course I will never ask him. I have already observed far more of his life than Roger would ever be happy to know was on view, and very little of that, I suspect, comes anywhere near to the truth of his existence. It's what can't be glimpsed through these curtains that keeps me standing futilely here, and doubtless the real puzzle is not his life but mine; the real question is whether this is the only, inevitable life that I could be leading.

17

But for the three-hour drive that divides us, we might almost live in the same neighbourhood. Her street is not unlike ours; her bay-fronted house is built in much the same style. Regional differences are few. Some details are even identical: I recognise the keystone crowning the fanlight, the pattern of brickwork under the guttering. As in our own terrace, no two of these houses are exactly alike, though at first glance they might seem so. Hers is marginally wider than those to each side, and in her roof there's a dormer, an attic conversion. The windows of the house to her left are recent replacements, mock-leaded. The front garden wall to her right is being relaid.

In this street too, as in our own, there are vehicles parked up on both pavements, and the road – which is already narrow – has been squeezed to one lane. I am facing the wrong way in the only space I could find. That was at 7.08 this morning and though some gaps have since appeared we are very close here to the centre of town and for every local who leaves it seems an incomer is waiting to take up their place. The restriction is two hours, which I have now exceeded, though I wouldn't expect to be queried, not for a little while yet. The plates on the sides of my van say *Dave Lowery, Painter & Decorator*. The scrawled not in my window says *WORKING AT NUMBER 14*. Which is usually enough to excuse me, at least for a morning.

Sarah lives at number 25, six doors up on this side, from where a man of approximately my age emerged just over an hour ago, escorting two children, both of them girls. Watching through my rear windows, I estimated the girls' ages as eight and eleven and noted their time of departure as 8.23. Fair-haired like their mother, they were dressed in a school uniform of white and pale green: a white-belted green pinafore, white ankle-length socks, a green-ribboned straw bonnet. Many other children have since passed by my van, all dressed in blue or red T-shirts, baggy trousers and shorts – nothing remotely as formal – and so I would guess that Sarah's girls are enrolled somewhere private, or even religious, which perhaps ought to come as more of a surprise than it does.

The younger of the two was holding the man's hand, the elder dawdling behind him, and they proceeded away from my position towards a bottle-green family saloon, whose registration I noted as Y114RRY. The man was 'smartly attired' in a light grey suit and polished black shoes, a white shirt and blue patterned tie. His height I estimated at five ten, his build medium-to-portly, his weight perhaps fourteen stone. His complexion was ruddy and his hair was distinctive – a strikingly blonde 'mop', unruly and in need of a trim. He repeatedly jerked his head to shift the fringe from his eyes. And what I felt as I photographed him, and then as I jotted these notes, was the same degree of passing or 'professional' curiosity as I might feel on any other assignment, the same degree of detachment. I knew in advance not to expect Anthony. I naturally assumed there would be children.

Of course this man may not be Sarah's first husband, or even her second; they may not be married at all. Conceivably he isn't Cameron Wilson – the only other adult listed for this address – but a recent 'usurper', or merely a visitor, a family friend. Possibly he isn't the father of these girls, just as Sarah may not be their mother. At present all is conjecture, assumption, though my strongest hunch is that he and Sarah are indeed married, a long-standing couple, and the girls their legitimate offspring. Short of asking directly, which I may yet be able to do, such guesswork could only be confirmed by extended surveillance and further enquiries, which is one eventuality I have allowed for. So far as Jan is concerned I am here to establish a case of cohabitation and may not be home for some days. She knows where I am, and which motel I've booked in to, though not that I'm spying on Sarah. She no doubt believes I am acting on instructions from Rosa.

Certainly there is much about my situation today that is familiar, including my discomfort in the rear of this van, the ceiling a fraction too low for me and my back already beginning to ache in this foldaway chair. Close at hand on the wheel-arch there's a pair of binoculars. Two of my cameras are here on the floor at my side, my camcorder and zoom. I have ample food and water, coffee in a flask, a bottle for my urine. My clipboard is resting on my lap, my log of departures and arrivals. All of which is routine, a standard 'scenario'. I am regularly employed to keep surveillance in this fashion, usually on a 'missing' or former spouse to determine whether he or she is now living with a new partner. Maintenance payments are generally at issue rather than any more intimate concerns, and often I would be in possession of a recent photo or pen portrait of the main 'party in question'. I might also be aware of where they work and what type of vehicle they own and perhaps have some idea as to their likely movements. But while such advantages do not apply in this case, what makes it most different is that I would not normally be deceiving my wife in order to be here. Nor would I be quite so impatient for my 'target' to make an appearance.

I reach again for my binoculars and focus on the bay window, but the angle is unhelpful and the sun's glaze deceiving. The dark form I can see is a jacket laid across the arm of a chair. At 7.42 I mistook this for a person; at 8.28 I thought it might be a reflection.

I pan up to the bedrooms, where the blinds remain closed, and then to the dormer, but still there's no movement; there is nothing for me to record. Sarah may be ill, or taking a lie in. She may have risen early and left the house before I arrived. She could be sitting in her kitchen, sipping tea as she contemplates a day spent tending her garden. It is possible she has gone away for a while, visiting relatives, or receiving treatment in hospital, or presenting a paper at some conference. Until I find otherwise, each of these things is equally feasible, and really I ought to establish at least whether or not she's at home. I ought to have done this before now.

I lay down the binoculars and take my phone from its pouch. It is already switched on and Sarah's number punched in. The 'script' I will use is ingrained, the one I recite every time: I am selling insurance. But still I delay, as I have done all morning. I run the pad of my thumb over the buttons. I look down at the display – *CONNECT?* – and close my eyes and feel my pulse quicken. Slowly I inhale, counting to five, and then slowly exhale, counting backwards from seven. I complete another long breath, and gently I press with my thumb. I incline my head to the phone. The dialling tone rings out and mentally I continue to count as I breathe – one up to five . . . seven down to one – and then she is there. Her voice is warm in my ear.

'Hello. Sarah Quillan,' she says, and waits for me to speak. 'Who is it please?'

But this is a question I find I can't answer. I am unable to speak. My nerves, I fear, will betray me; she will know at once who I am. With Sarah, it seems, 'professionalism' is no protection; I cannot pretend detachment, or pass myself off as someone I'm not.

'Hello?' she says, more quizzical now, a little annoyed. 'Hello?'

And holding my breath I carefully hang up. My hands are shaking. I pocket the phone and edge my chair away from these windows, as if suddenly I have made myself obvious, pinpointed my position. The time is 9.43. *Subject answered phone*, I jot down; *confirmed identity*.

My pen is retractable; I click it on, click it off. I drink some water. Three minutes elapse and I lean forwards. Nothing moves. Sarah's door does not open and she does not appear at her windows. My own windows are mirrored and the curtains behind me are black: there is no way that she could see me. I shift my chair closer, back to where it was previously. I pick up my SLR and focus the zoom on her front room. The jacket on her chair is an adult's anorak and appears to be turquoise; I make a note of this.

Few among us, I'm sure, will have a definite philosophy on life, a set of clear rules that we live by. Most, like me, will stumble along, try to be good, try not to be crooked. In the course of my work, as I have said, certain 'situations' will sometimes arise. There have been opportunities, and I have been tempted, but always I have cautioned myself to be wary. If I've paused to consider at all, I have counselled myself to take the long view – meaning, I suppose, 'Don't get excited, don't react, because this moment will pass, and a month from now, a year from now, it will have faded from memory.' Which is a tidy way of avoiding any unnecessary upset, any emotional upheaval, but also, I do realise, a way of avoiding any real engagement with life; it's a way of not living, of looking ahead to a time of forgetting.

And perhaps it is this – the avoidance of risk or complication – that has governed my choices in all the years I've been married to Jan. I wouldn't say I've ever been wholly content with my lot, but neither have I felt much desire to change it. In both spheres of my life – at home and at work – I have always been *happy enough*. I am not a 'driven' person. Even before I met Sarah, I was never especially ambitious or enterprising, and I haven't since felt particularly motivated to make more of myself than I am. At one time this seemed somehow virtuous. Now it seems less so. My passivity has become a burden to me, and also, I suspect, an aggravation and a disappointment to Jan. It's become a flaw, a character trait I needn't be proud of, and clearly, it isn't a readiness to go with the flow or a willing acceptance of fate that guides and defines me, but inertia and a good deal of fear.

And no doubt it is fear that has kept me from tracing Sarah till now. I have always known I could track her down if I chose to, and always this has been something I've shied from. Being in love in that way was disturbing, unsettling, and I've only ever wanted to be settled, secure; I've only ever wanted to be somebody's husband, trustworthy and stable in a marriage that lasted. This is what I am best suited to. Many of us are, and I congratulated myself on realising that early and making my choice. No chance was being missed. Jan was much less confusing than Sarah, and more comfortable to be with. She was more capable, dependable, organised. And if I wasn't quite certain I loved her, I was hopeful that in time I might come to.

Of course there is love and there's love. One is all head-spin and nerve-ends, a mental derangement, a sickness. The other's a palliative, a balm, the antidote to all that. Ideally, it runs deeper, a low thrum of contentment, though it's possible that Jan and I have become so used to the thrum that we no longer hear it; it's possible the monotony has induced its own symptoms, its own kind of illness, and perhaps in our familiarity we have become somewhat complacent. Certainly there must have been a time – unnoticed then and unidentifiable now – when I grew out of the habit of attending to Jan or expecting to learn new things about her, when I came to think of myself as sufficiently 'fluent' in her moods and responses that I needn't make any allowances for how she might change. I settled for what I already knew, and what little that amounted to has come to stand for all of her.

Which is, I suppose, typical of any lengthy 'relationship' and I do wonder, as I sit here, whether Sarah's years with Cameron have been as companionable as mine have with Jan, or whether her marriage has been marred by suspicion and friction. I wonder, in fact, if she really has ceased to be the Sarah I once thought she was, if she has now become as faithful a 'partner' as I always took Jan for.

My seat is a striped nylon beach chair, chrome-framed and creaky, and my back is complaining; I cannot sit still. Outside, the last high wispy clouds have dispersed and there are cats drowsing on ledges, butterflies flitting across these front gardens. This is the longest day of the year, and surely one of the warmest so far. Here in my van the heat is becoming unbearable. I would like to rest for a while now in the front passenger seat with my windows wound down. I would like to climb out for a stroll.

The time is 10.18 and some minutes ago a young man ambled past my position, beating a tattoo on the side of the van. He appeared from my blindside – sun-tanned and sandalled, a salmon-coloured shirt tied round his waist – and proceeded towards the far end of the street, where a couple of young mothers were wheeling pushchairs in this direction. His gait was loose-limbed and swaying, and as he passed by them he made a partial pirouette and appeared to say something admiring. They concentrated their attention on their sun-hatted children, toddling along at their sides, and ignored him. Progress was slow, and as I watched their approach through my binoculars – their skimpy tops and transparent wraps, their easy unhurried movements – I tried to imagine either one of them as Sarah.

But however youthful such women now seem to me, the Sarah who remains in my memory is six or seven years younger still, just twenty in the few photos I have of her, twenty-one the last time I saw her.

She did not like to be photographed – few women do – but neither would she thrust the flat of her hand at the lens, or turn away, or attempt to hide her face with her arms. Instead she would fix her gaze on the camera. She might draw in her cheeks and pout, or press her mouth to a smile, or simply stare without flinching, and the effect was subtly unlike her – unflattering, and deliberately so. She wouldn't offer a likeness, anything to remember her by, but a kind of mask of herself. And though

I have kept a couple of envelopes of snapshots from that time – not only of her but of our housemates, and some of the demos we went on – whenever I take them out from their hiding place I find I'm frustrated. The Sarah I hope to retrieve from the pictures has gone, or was never there; she always eludes me.

Despite which, I can't help but expect someone of similar age and appearance to emerge from Sarah's front door this morning, and when at last she does come there's a drag of surprise, a long second's adjustment, and I don't for a moment quite trust that it's her. Which isn't unusual. For all my expectancy, the target's appearance very often wrong-foots me. There is always this pause, this blankness. Then comes the adrenaline, and though I can't yet be certain it's Sarah, I grab for my zoom and fire off a series of shots as she lifts the latch on her gate and steps through and turns in my direction. She is walking briskly, and hastily I swap the zoom for my camcorder. I train the cross-hairs on her face and just as she goes by my van, just before she disappears, I finally have her in focus, the ghost of her former self quite clear in her features. It is unmistakably her, though middle-aged now, not the Sarah I've preserved in my mind, but someone just old enough to be that young woman's mother.

I look at the watch my wife bought on my birthday. The time is 10.25, and as I enter this to my log I almost fumble my pen. My hands are trembling. I lift my knapsack from its hook and drop the camcorder inside and climb from the rear of the van. My legs too are unsteady. I fasten the doors as quietly as possible. Sarah is already turning right at the end of her street, heading, I believe, in the direction of town, but she may yet double-back, remembering something she's left, and so I cross over the road and follow along the opposite pavement, feeling in my knapsack for my disguise, my blue floppy sunhat.

In certain situations there's no harm in the subject of my enquiries being aware of my presence, so long as they don't suspect my true purpose. It's even possible to remain in close proximity for lengthy periods of time, particularly in busy locations, such as a town centre, and not actually be noticed, or 'burnt'. The key in most cases is to avoid making eye contact. Even fleetingly, this is the most memorable of acts, leaving an imprint, however unconscious. I might stand beside you in the same queue, travel on the same half-empty bus, visit several of the same shops, later drink in the same pub, and still I would not expect you to show any signs of discomfort. Providing your gaze did not meet mine, I would not expect to be recognised.

My blandness of appearance is an asset of course, and while I do own a couple of wigs and false beards, it's some years since I last wore them. The simple rearrangement of a few basic items – a change of headgear, a cagoule pulled over a jacket and tie, the removal of a pair of sunglasses – will usually suffice to protect me. In addition to my sunhat this morning I have packed some dark glasses and a flimsy grey rainmac that folds into its own pocket, but Sarah has yet to glance over her shoulder, or linger near any windows that might contain my reflection, and won't yet be aware that a man in a blue hat is consistently ten or twelve yards behind her, a gap I closed as soon as we came near to these shops, and will need to close further if the crowds become any denser. The street she is leading me down is long and wide and pedestrianised, a major parade of multi-tiered 'emporia', and there are countless side alleys and openings, any number of turnings she might take or stores she might enter. I would not want to lose her; I haven't been here before, haven't reconnoitred the area, and wouldn't be able to guess where she might re-emerge.

She has no definite purpose, it seems, no clear itinerary. At first I assumed she was hurrying to make an appointment, but then – some way short of the shops – she started to dawdle, as if realising she had nothing to rush for, no pressing engagements. A narrow bridge brought us over a dual carriageway that skirts the centre of town, and there she began to hurry again, the metal steps rattling as she descended. For a short distance I thought she might break into a trot. A few minutes later, in the dappled shade of some trees, she almost came to a stop. And this has been the pattern in the half-hour since, the sudden quickening or slowing of her pace apparently in tune with her thoughts – now excited, now dreamy; now agitated, now reflective – and though I would very much like to know what she is thinking, the only means to that end would be to engage her in conversation, after which I wouldn't be able to keep her under surveillance; I couldn't continue to scrutinise her without myself being scrutinised.

And I am enjoying this unhurried pursuit, fascinated by the

mundanities of her movements and the details of her appearance, the simple fact of this being Sarah, at home in a life that does not include me. I am invisible to her, and happy enough to be so, but she is, I suspect, another of those women who will complain that she too is becoming 'invisible' as she grows older. She has for instance just passed through this late-morning crowd without attracting the attention of anyone but a professional canvasser, a woman of similar age and 'attire' who stepped forward with her ID and clipboard as soon as Sarah came near her, and seemed deflated when she shook her head and slipped by. I have been watching, and there has been nothing else, no second glances or compliments, not even from the men on the market stalls arrayed along here to our left.

And perhaps in other circumstances I would not notice Sarah either. She is weightier than she once was and her features less clear, in some way smudged over. Her hair, which once hung to her shoulders, has been cut very short, and is several shades darker, presumably dyed because it's gone grey. Her eyes and jaw-line have become as pouchy as mine, and she has thickened around the hips and buttocks and thighs. The clothes she is wearing fit loosely, the style and colours quite plain: muted orange and brown, cut simply. She is 'homely', even 'mumsy', and though she would surely hate to be told so, her homeliness is attractive I find, another reason to feel tender towards her.

A little way beyond the market there is a confluence of streets and a cluster of circular benches, each enclosing a spindly tree in a tub, where Sarah pauses to buy a copy of the *Big Issue* from a young woman who's struggling to be heard above the amplified noise of some buskers nearby, a rockabilly band whose slicked heads I can just see, none of them much younger than I am.

With a brief smile, Sarah waves away the change the girl is holding towards her, and quickly I narrow the distance between us as she starts to ease through the crowd round the band. She doesn't look across at them, barely looks up at all, and I observe only her, becoming so close at one point that I can see the softness of the down on her neck, the pinkness at the back of her ears. I inhale deeply, but can't locate her scent among so many others, and the urge to touch her then is so strong that I can feel my palms tingling. The thin leather strap of her shoulder bag is dragging on her cotton top, exposing the pearly white of her bra strap, the paleness of her skin, and just as the buskers come to the end of their set I thrust my hands deep into my pockets to stop myself from reaching out to her.

The audience, most of them smiling, have begun to applaud and disperse, and I notice Sarah, released from the crush, depositing her *Big Issue* in a litter bin. She heads towards the open double doors of a bookshop and I take off my hat, wipe the sweat from my brow, and follow her in.

The store is large, and there are very few customers. Sarah weaves past carousels of postcards and fridge magnets and novelty bookmarks, then several tables piled with 'recent releases' and 'three for two' offers, casually touching the covers but not pausing, and as she begins to climb the stairs to the next floor she looks over her shoulder, across to the doors we have just entered, and seems almost to be expecting someone to be there. Her step falters; it seems she might be coming back down, and reflexively I turn my face to the shelves. I stuff my hat into my knapsack and incline my head, scanning the names on the spines in search of one of Will's books. I take down the only copy there is and pretend to read the review quotes on the reverse, all the while conscious of the staircase and the doors, but no one comes in, and Sarah does not descend. She continues up to *Non-Fiction*, and casually I crease the spine on the book, re-shelve it some distance from where it should be, then cautiously go after her.

Holding on to the bannister, I fix my gaze on the steps as I climb, afraid in my nervousness I might trip and attract her attention. I am not quite ready to feign surprise should she approach me; nor am I yet sure that I want to approach her. On the upper level there's an aroma of coffee, and momentarily I mistake Sarah for someone much older – a woman carrying two white cups towards a low leather sofa – but then find her again at the edge of my vision, standing in the *Health & Healing* section, her head bowed over a book and her posture protective, as though unwilling to reveal what she is reading. I turn in the other direction.

There are many more people up here than on the ground floor and I position myself in *New Age & Religion*, a dozen other browsers between us, and surreptitiously watch her. For some minutes she reads, several times licking her thumb to turn over a page, then examines the cover, and jounces the book in both hands as though testing its weight, and finally decides not to buy it. As she slots the book back on its shelf I notice a patch of sweat under her arm. She glances at a young assistant nearby, edges apologetically past him, and I track her slow, pensive walk across to the cafe. She doesn't order a drink but selects a table overlooking the concourse below, and while her attention is taken by the scene through the window, I move quickly to where she was standing, the location of the book she was reading firmly fixed in my mind.

There are sex manuals on the shelves above, and a section on addictions below, but Sarah's interest was in dieting. I don't trouble to look at the title.

I turn instead to where she is sitting, immersed in herself and the space that surrounds her, and even at this stage, having travelled this far, I could very easily persuade myself not to go any further, as I tend to persuade myself against most things. I could imagine the type of conversation we might have: the suspicion and puzzlement on her part, perhaps disguised by politeness; the hesitancy and embarrassment on mine. I could imagine far worse, in fact: she might be openly hostile, or pretend not to know me. And in the end it isn't courage or determination that gives me the spur to approach her, but something more like fatigue: I am tired of myself, of my habitual caution, and when I do finally cross the wide store to her table it's because this is less wearying than to remain where I am, looking on and prevaricating.

*   *   *

220

'Sarah,' I say, bending a little towards her. It isn't a question, and I don't attempt any other inflection. 'Hello,' I say.

She has been distractedly toying with a sachet of sugar, which she returns now to its bowl. I am standing, and she is seated. I have surprise on my side. I ought to have the advantage. But in the long seconds it takes before she recognises who I am, my scant confidence leaves me, and though I am not normally someone who blushes, I feel my face burning. My upper lip twitches.

'Mike,' she eventually says, and gets to her feet. She touches a hand close to her throat, allows her mouth to fall open. There's a wedding ring on her finger, a simple gold band. She is wearing nail polish, which I would not have expected. 'My God,' she says, and makes a small noise like a gasp, a stifled half-laugh. She widens her eyes and shakes her head very slowly. 'How bizarre,' she says, and gives me to believe, in the tone of her voice, that she is not exactly unhappy to see me, merely caught unawares.

'I was just browsing,' I say, and gesture lamely behind me. 'Over there. I thought I recognised you.'

'Well,' she laughs, and her eyes flit away to the shelf-stacks, as though to confirm where I sprang from. 'You did well to. I've changed a bit from how I was.'

'A little,' I say. 'Not much.'

Sarah smiles at me sceptically, tilting her head.

'I think we've all changed,' I add.

'Yes,' she agrees. 'Haven't we.'

She regards me with something close to amusement, and I fold my arms on my chest. I look briefly away, look back, and I notice the fine lines above her top lip; I notice a polyp to one side of her nose. I shrug – I can't think what to say – and our silence is broken by the sound of a ring-tone, a brief muffled chirping. Sarah reaches for her bag and rummages inside. 'Sorry,' she smiles, and takes out her phone, consults the display. People drift by on the concourse below. I am aware of two women talking at another table, their voices urgent, near-whispers. I am conscious too of Sarah's physical presence, just a short step away from me, and fleetingly I am struck by a memory of her kneeling on my bed in her dressing gown, taking hold of my wrist between her forefinger and thumb, lifting my hand to her breast.

She drops the mobile back in her bag and refastens the clasp. 'You're looking very well though, Mike,' she says then.

'Thank you,' I say. I transfer my weight from my left foot to my right. I unfold my arms, push my hands in my pockets. 'So are you,' I say.

And Sarah laughs, politely, at that. She hangs the strap of her bag over the back of her chair. She is, I suppose, considering her options. In a second or two she may well invite me to sit with her, or suddenly remember somewhere else she should be. She might refer to her text message. 'So how have you been?' she asks then. 'What've you been up to?'

I hesitate. 'For eighteen years?'

'No, really?' she says. 'It's that long?'

'I think so.' My mouth is dry and I swallow. 'About that . . .'

'What a horrible thought,' she says, quickly scanning the other people around us. 'Eighteen years . . .' She glances over her shoulder, down at the shoppers outside, and belatedly it occurs to me that she is waiting for someone: another man, I suppose; maybe even her husband.

'Look,' I say, 'if this is an awkward time . . . You can't have been expecting me to leap out on you like this . . .'

'No, it's fine, Mike,' she says. 'It's good to see you. A bit of a shock, obviously . . .' And again she widens her eyes, jerks her head backwards, a mime of delighted surprise. But this, I'm sure, is a kindness. Her colour has not risen; her attention is calmly appraising, and I find I still can't disguise my discomfort or control my expression. If I could I would smile. I would match her easy gaze with my own, and ply her with questions and hope to regain some semblance of composure, after which, perhaps, we might begin to find our way back to some deeper connection. But my heart is pounding and my legs are unsteady. I feel the sweat prickling my forehead, and it occurs to me that I ought to leave now, before I am tempted to confide the real reason I came here. The Sarah I once knew would have wanted to hear that; we never used to have secrets.

'So,' she says. 'What *have* you been up to, Mike?'

'Sorry?'

'Married? Kids?'

'Yes, one wife, two boys. Jack and Ben. Ten and six.' The mention of my children momentarily lifts me. 'How about you?'

'Two girls,' she confirms, 'a little bit older – twelve and just-turned-eight. Jemima and Esme . . .' But her voice is trailing away. Her gaze briefly flares at someone behind me. She has made eye-contact with whoever is coming to join her, and I suspect my presence here can only be an inconvenience, a nuisance she would rather not have to deal with. And yet still I continue. With an edge to my voice that surprises me, I tell her, 'I got married to Janette actually. Do you remember Janette? Jan?'

Sarah looks at me dimly, and then, as if the meaning of my words has been a fraction delayed, she says, 'Oh that's nice! I thought you would, somehow. And you're still together?'

'Yes,' I say, frowning. 'She's Jack and Ben's mum.'

'Oh that's nice,' she repeats, and fondly smiles at someone behind me. 'I'm glad about that . . .' she says.

'You weren't at the time,' I say quietly.

'Hmm?'

'You weren't glad at the time,' I repeat, more quietly still.

And Sarah nods, as though to encourage me. She is waiting; it appears she is quite prepared to allow me to continue, if that is what I would like. She will listen, if there are things I feel I must say, even here, in front of whoever has joined her. And I let my shoulders drop; I exhale. I concede and say nothing.

'Jan was lovely though, wasn't she?' she says then, and reaches towards me, almost touching my arm. 'I always thought you two suited each other. You went well together.'

'Thank you,' I murmur.

'I'm glad it worked out for you,' she says, and clearly, for Sarah, any words will suffice now. As far as she is concerned, nothing much is happening this Monday morning that she will not very quickly push from her mind, just as soon as I have departed. Whatever significance I was hoping to find in our encounter – and however much importance I might have wished to accord her – the reverse clearly does not apply. She will not allow it. She is not the person I was hoping to find. That Sarah has long gone – outgrown or discarded by her – and plainly there's little more for us to share beyond these pleasantries, and our 'news', which will always be insufficient for me, and rather more than she will have time for.

And when finally she asks me, with the barest note of genuine interest, 'But what about the writing, Mike, are you still doing that?' I shake my head and glance round. The momentum is lost, and no part of me now wishes to persist with this.

'No, I'm in insurance,' I say, and make room for Cameron Wilson, who is standing just a few feet away and regarding our conversation with untroubled interest, his hands in his pockets and his jacket pulled open, his blue tie riding over his paunch. Still flustered, I nod, and wait to be introduced to him, after which I will gladly make my excuses and leave; I will apologise to Sarah and her husband and go back to my life and hope that what follows is not further regret, but relief at having brought something here at last to a close. This is my firmest wish for myself now, that this strand of my 'story' will soon be concluded and this episode as quickly forgotten by me as it will be by Sarah.

'Cam,' she says then, 'this is Mike,' and I accept the firm hand that he offers me. I try not to flinch from his gaze. 'We used to know each other,' she says.

18

'When you smile?'

'Yes.'

'There's this crease appears along the underside of your top lip – it's quite hard to describe: there's a sort of fold, or a kink . . . It's quite sexual. I'm not sure if you'll know what I mean . . .?'

She doesn't reply. I take my left hand from the wheel, adjust the fit of my earphones. When I listened before I could hear the hiss on the tape at this point, but the noise now from my van is too great. I am speeding, I notice. I glance to my wing mirrors, ease back down to seventy.

'Hello?' he says.

'No, I don't,' she says then. 'I don't know what you mean.'

'Well . . . it doesn't matter. It's just that it's very pretty. If I you asked me to choose one thing about you, I'd say that was my favourite.'

'Will, please,' says my wife.

'So, what I've been doing lately, whenever I've been in your company? I've been staring at the stains on your teeth, the ones at the sides – they're quite badly stained. But probably you know that? I think you must do, I've noticed how you try correct yourself when you smile . . .'

'Thanks,' she laughs.

'They *are* your worst feature though. If you *have* to have a worst feature – that's probably it, your incisors . . . So that's what I've been doing – whenever I've been with you and you've been smiling, I've been trying to focus on your teeth, as a kind of turn-off, so I wouldn't feel so attracted . . . It's a kind of aversion therapy.'

'And has it worked, do you think?'

Her voice is deadpan, his buoyant, and I realise he may well have been drinking.

'No, it hasn't worked!' he says. 'That's just the thing, it's had the opposite effect, it's made me feel quite sorry for you, in a way. Or not sorry exactly. But . . . you know.'

'Will,' she sighs.

'Yup.'

'Can you promise me something?'

'Yes.'

'*Don't* put me in a book.'

There's a pause, a choke of laughter in his voice. 'Do you know, you've asked me that once before, the first time you two came over to ours for supper . . .'

'Yes, I do know. And I meant it. Don't.'

Will's pause this time is longer, and I remember listening upstairs in my office, gazing down at the tape as it turned. By chance I happened to be standing at my bench when he phoned.

This wasn't last Friday, the evening I sat with my boys on the sofa – that call really did come from Jan's mother – but yesterday, Sunday, as I prepared for my journey to Sarah's. Possibly Jan thought I'd already packed and departed. My appearance on the stairs a little while later seemed to surprise her.

'You know, you can't legislate for this,' Will says at last, a sombre note in his voice that sounds to me practised, a tone I assume he must adopt for his readings, interviews, public pronouncements. 'Whether a writer intends to or not, these things will creep in. It happens. If you feel strongly about something, or someone . . . Either now or later it *is* going to affect what you write. It will leave *some* kind of emotional residue. And that eventually seeps in to the work . . .'

'Just try not to describe me, Will.'

'Oh I'll disguise it, don't worry. I'm a master of disguise in that sense.'

He laughs, my wife doesn't, and I pull out alongside a lorry, a juggernaut. There are two more trucks up ahead. The road curves lengthily around to our right and I grip my wheel tightly, concentrate on keeping my line.

'But can I tell you something?' Will's voice continues. 'This is the hardest thing. I was thinking about this earlier. When I went out with this girl at uni – *before* I went out with her, when I first began to fall in love with her – I used to sit on my own in my room in the evenings, staring down at this two-bar electric heater thing, and I'd hold these imaginary conversations with her. I'd whisper out loud all the things I wanted to say to her. Quite intense, heartfelt stuff. And that's what it's like now. I'm having these pathetic late-night whispered conversations. Constantly. And not just at night. With you, I mean. And normally, if I really needed to talk to someone about something, the person I'd confide in, usually, would be Anna. But this is the last thing we could ever discuss. Especially now, obviously. And I can't discuss it with you either!'

'You *are* discussing it.'

'On the end of a telephone.'

'What else do you expect, Will? Honestly?'

'I want you to come over and see me.'

I am gaining on the last lorry, but my exit from this dual carriageway is fast approaching and I'm in the wrong lane. I force the accelerator, edge ahead of the cab, and as soon as I think I am clear I cut across to my left. The lorry, suddenly huge in my mirrors, blares its horn. My van, I can feel, is vibrating. And then I am racing into the slip-road. I brake and release, brake again. Road markings, saplings, flash by.

'I'm not coming over,' says my wife. 'I'm just not.'

'I want you to.'

The slip-road descends to a roundabout. I press my brake fully down, drag back through my gears, and just manage to halt at the white line.

Jan sighs in my ear. She speaks quietly, distantly. 'That isn't going to happen, Will. I'm sorry.'

And somewhere in the silence that follows one of them

appears to be crying. I listen harder. Previously I missed this. So far as I can recall, neither of them speaks again; the tape will run on now until one or the other cuts the connection. Who is crying, and who ends the call, these are things I might determine at home. I could analyse the channels.

Instead I punch the eject on the tape and hurl it away from me. It hits the windscreen, the passenger door, and drops to the seat at my side. I tug out my earphones and indicate left. There is nothing behind me, nothing approaching. My heart is racing, and I take a deep breath and move off.

I have mentioned *Rear Window*, and the ease with which Jimmy Stewart keeps the lives of an entire tenement block under observation with the aid of little more than a long lens and his plucky, well-heeled accomplice, Grace Kelly. Thelma Ritter, his nurse, also assists him, though she initially is more sceptical of his motives, having chided him already for his interest in 'Miss Torso' and the other 'bikini bombshells' on view from his windows. The New York State sentence for a Peeping Tom, she warns him, is six months in the workhouse. She refers to his camera as his 'portable keyhole'.

This is, as I say, one of my favourite films, though a truer, less comforting depiction of the nature of surveillance is to be found in *The Conversation*, which I think I might like even more. There Gene Hackman plays a private detective called Harry Caul, shabby and serious and lacking any of Stewart's charisma or charm, but nonetheless, as a competitor says, 'the best bugger on the West Coast'. In the opening scenes he is shown to possess the most sophisticated battery of watching and listening devices – many operated by associates in unmarked vans, or positioned on the roofs of tall buildings – but none of them sufficient to provide anything more than a few distorted snatches of ambiguous conversation which will then require many hours of lonely, concentrated attention in his workshop – a bleak, wiremeshed corner of an unused warehouse, furnished with state-of-the-art electronic signal-enhancing devices, and reminiscent for me of the breezeblock 'unit' in which Sanjeev and Kuldip have their business.

The film was made in the seventies, in the era of Nixon, and Hackman is never entirely certain who he is working for, or quite who he is spying upon, or why. There are no panoramic perspectives, no easy explanations. Nothing is obvious, and none of the people he meets or observes could ever be summed up in a simple nickname or phrase. His own assistant, introduced early, is next found to be working for his nearest professional rival, the goading Bernie Moran, who has been hired by the very people who hired Hackman, with instructions to keep tabs on what Hackman gets up to. The watcher is being watched. And the subjects of Hackman's surveillance – a young couple he believes to be the targets of a murder plot – turn out to be the instigators of the plot; they turn out, in a roundabout way, to be his employers.

There is much in all of this that's intriguing; I do find the intricacies absorbing. But it's the accuracy of the portrayal of

Harry Caul that appeals to me most, or perhaps most appals me. Unexpressive, enclosed, Caul is a man who keeps his private life scrupulously private, his home devoid of all 'personal things'. Unlike James Stewart, his nights are disturbed not by the comings and goings of his neighbours, but by mist-shrouded, guilt-ridden dreams. And unlike Stewart, he is never simply an observer, but always in some way implicated in what he is watching. Paranoia defines him – paranoia and guilt – and even his girlfriend doesn't know where he lives, or what he does for a living, or how to contact him by phone.

What she does know is that he keeps secrets – of which she is just one – and that he spies on her from the staircase to her apartment, and listens in on her phonecalls. Spying, it seems, is as close as Harry Caul can come to real intimacy, and though he yearns to make some kind of connection, he is unable to confide in her; he cannot allow his private self to be so exposed.

Instead, on his birthday, as he sits drinking scotch on her bed – still wearing his crumpled brown mac and his shoes – he denies that he's hiding anything from her, and insists, not for the first time, that he's a 'freelance musician'. Which is at least partially true. Harry Caul will often pass the evenings at home on his own with a saxophone. And in this, as in his dowdy appearance, he bears a strong resemblance to Roger Mitchell of course, though there is also, I now realise, some correspondence with another made-up detective, the 'Harry' described in the notes for Will's latest novel.

The Conversation concludes with an isolated Hackman

mournfully playing his sax in a derelict room after he has – at first methodically, then frantically – dismantled and dismembered his entire apartment. The floorboards have been ripped up, the wallpaper stripped down. Every cable has been torn out, every appliance taken to pieces. Nothing remains intact, and yet still he has been unable to locate the listening device that has allowed his former employers to pry into his private world. Bernie Moran, it seems, has in the end been able to penetrate his defences.

I have reviewed my videotape of this film any number of times, searching like Hackman for the bug that betrayed him, and it is, I believe, built into his spectacles. This became evident to me some months ago, the last time I replayed the film, and though it isn't important – it's the answer to a riddle, nothing more – it is those final images of Hackman destroying his apartment, then sitting defeated in the midst of the debris, that are fixed now in my mind as I drive home from my encounter this morning with Sarah.

Of course, unlike Hackman, I have been exposed to no one today but myself. Sarah, I'm sure, will have dismissed the coincidence of our meeting almost as soon as I shook her husband's hand and departed. There was no third party observing us, and my own life is not under surveillance. But my closest rival, it's clear, does have the ear of my closest companion, and her thoughts are currently as much occupied by him as by me. I have the evidence for that on this cassette, and though it might easily be wiped, what I know of what it contains could not. I could no more erase it, I suspect, than I could escape the person I have become, or the life I'm about to return to.

I have been speeding for most of this journey, taking risks I would not normally take, and now as I approach the outskirts of town I find I'm being trailed – whether deliberately or not – by a car I am certain I passed some forty or fifty miles earlier. It was cruising then at just under the limit and made no move to pursue me, and the reason I can recall it so clearly is that it's identical in colour and make to the vehicle that Cameron Wilson got into this morning. He isn't the driver of course, and neither is the registration the same: the heavy curtains just behind me are open, the view from my mirror uninterrupted, and I have checked.

The coincidence however is unnerving; so too the straight ahead gaze of the driver as I lead him onto the ring road and over two roundabouts and into the left lane at this first set of red lights. He is a man of my age, tidily moustached, and seemingly determined to appear unaware of my scrutiny. With the curtains open, my rear windows are not so reflective, and I would expect him to try to look in. Most people do. I adjust each of my mirrors, conspicuously realign them and stare hard at his face, but still he does not react. Gently he taps his right hand on the steering wheel.

The lights have turned green. I indicate to go left, and when he indicates to follow I proceed straight ahead, only mildly surprised to find that he stays with me. The road here has two lanes and if he wished, he could easily overtake me. I slow down to twenty, and notice then that he's begun talking to someone. Presumably he is wearing an earpiece; there must be a microphone clipped to his tie. Which may mean nothing at all, or that he has an accomplice – someone further ahead or behind us – and when I see the shopping parade coming up on our left I begin to accelerate, drawing him with me, then suddenly brake and pull in sharply to park. I stop outside the hairdressers – *Curl Up 'N' Dye* – and watch as he continues straight on. He doesn't appear to glance in his mirrors, and no other vehicle slips in beside me.

He disappears from view and I wait a minute or two longer, then turn and head back in the direction I came from, though this time at the lights I do take the turning I indicated earlier, which will lead me not towards home but into the centre of town. Whatever the 'trigger' in what's just occurred – if indeed anything has happened at all – I feel I would now like to test the transmitter I left in Will's office.

Being so 'compact', and with such limited power, the bug's range is not great and though anyone could intercept the signal on their car radio they would first need to be in the locality, and tuned to the right frequency, and preferably clear of any obstructing buildings. The spot I had in mind was the upper deck of the carpark that can be seen from Will's tiny kitchen, but as I rise now through the tiers I decide that this would be too conspicuous and so settle instead for the low-ceilinged gloom of the level below. The time is just after four and many of the bays are unoccupied. I park against the perimeter wall, but it seems I will need to get out and stand if I also want to look down on his windows. There's a concrete stanchion between us, and the wall is higher than I anticipated.

I search the FM band and locate what I assume to be his office at 107.8. The interference drops; there is something like silence. I turn up the volume and unfasten my belt and push back my seat. I stretch out as best I am able. Folding my arms on my belly, I let my chin drop to my chest and lower my eyelids, but my back is as sore as it has been in weeks, and I have cramp in my left leg. I sit up and consider returning home after all – there is no reason not to – but then I hear a faint knocking, irregularly spaced, and a snuffling sound such as a small creature might make. For a brief moment I picture a rodent on top of Will's cupboard; I imagine it gnawing through my transmitter's antenna. Then a man grunts and I reach for the volume control. I raise it a notch or two higher. The knocking continues. A woman gasps. And with a start I find my heart racing. I lurch across to my glove compartment and scrabble about for my headset. A torch falls out, a pen, a packet of batteries. But the cable is here by my side, where I dropped it when I was driving. Fumbling, I manage to plug the jack into the radio socket. The *thwop* of the blood in my ears is almost as loud as the hiss from the earphones, but there can be no doubt what I am hearing, and it isn't remotely what I expected.

Conceivably, this could be my wife. She might have walked

here from work; it doesn't take twenty minutes. Jack and Ben could have gone home with Anna, which is our usual arrangement. We do take care of each other's kids after school; on occasions we have them sleep over. It is conceivable, but I don't believe it is plausible. This isn't a scenario I would expect William Brown to include in one of his novels, for instance, given the nature of the protagonists and the lives that we lead, for even if my wife were to consent to such an 'assignation', she wouldn't first arrange for Anna to look after our children. She isn't that calculating, or callous. She isn't that kind of person.

And yet, as I listen to the increasingly rhythmic gasps from Will's office, I allow myself to imagine how it might be if this were in fact Jan – if this is how she might sound as she comes towards orgasm – and immediately I find that I'm aroused; I begin to get an erection.

Of course, if Jan were to have an affair, I would then be released from my obligations to her, licensed to do as I pleased. Whatever scruples I have previously lived by, these would no longer apply. And neither would Anna be constrained by any loyalty she might feel towards Will. If I have read her correctly, she has already hinted that she would be receptive to me. That possibility has been in the air for some time, pressing, unsettling, and perhaps our spouses – the ones I imagine coupling on the floor of Will's office – would wish us nothing but joy. Except that scruples alone cannot account for my faithfulness to Jan: as Anna might say, I've also lacked sufficient sense of 'adventure'.

And besides, this isn't my spouse I can hear; these gasps are clearly not hers.

I search again in my glove compartment and take out a blank tape. I press it into the slot and set the machine to record. This will be my audio evidence, should Anna require any, and in a few minutes' time, I am sure, I will also have a photo of whoever her husband has in there. I kneel around in my seat and reach into the back of my van. I drag my camera case closer and as I lift it gingerly over the seatbacks the cable becomes wrapped around my arm. The radio jack tugs free, the connection is broken, and my van is suddenly filled with the sounds of their coupling.

Quickly I lower the volume. I sit and listen, staring out at the concrete wall of the carpark, and the only word I can think of is 'desperate'. For each of Will's pounding grunts, his partner responds with a noise like a sob. I imagine both of them sweating, their faces flushed and contorted, eyes tightly closed. And then there's a cry, almost a squeal, girlish and final. Will gives out a last groan, and they fall silent, desolate, and quietly, as though they might hear me, I unclip my metal case and lift out my zoom lens – my portable keyhole – and re-attach it to the camera I used on Sarah this morning.

I open my door a few inches, place one foot on the tarmac. I continue to listen but neither of them sighs, or laughs, or murmurs, and finally I reach over and switch off the signal. Cautiously I stand by the side of my van. So far as I can see, there is nobody observing me from any other vehicle, and no one looking up from the offices below. The ornamental garden – where last week we saw Katie Sommers – appears to be empty. I locate each of the benches in turn, glance over my shoulder once more, then lean in close to the stanchion and support my arm on the wall.

From this position, I can see the whole of one side of Will's building. The blinds are fully raised on his kitchen. And though the connecting door to his office is presently closed, his toilet is at the end of that narrow space and I expect they will each need to visit it shortly.

I bring my left eye to the viewfinder, poise my finger over the button, and the instant she comes through the door I snap and wind on. Even before I have quite registered that this is Anna, and just before she slips from view to my right, I snap and wind on, snap and wind on. I capture her three times. She is in a state of partial undress, of course – wearing only a dark tee shirt – and what's imprinted now on my mind, as on my film, is her exposed lower half. I see the broad width of her pelvic bone, the thickness of her pubic hair, the slenderness of her thighs. I see her hand cupping her crotch as she quickens from sight. And I am disgusted, betrayed.

19

There isn't much crime in our neighbourhood. Robberies are rumoured – there is always that fear – and periodically we will find police notices attached to our lampposts, warning of burglaries, suggesting precautions. But I don't personally know of anyone who has been affected. What we suffer from mostly is nuisance – in other words, students – though of course it's the students themselves who suffer most of the burglaries, the robberies and late-night assaults. Their houses are less secure, and they're more inclined to be out in the evenings.

Recently our local newspaper – once homely, its readership ageing – reinvented itself as a 'campaigning', sensationalist tabloid, and several alarming stories have since appeared on its front pages, giving details of rapes, drug seizures, and shootings. But these, it seems, nearly always happen elsewhere – in the city centre at night, on the peripheral estates, in towns and dormitory villages that we only pass through – as do the petty offences that are listed inside, the weekly tally of mis-demeanours run up by the shoplifters and drug dealers, kerb-crawlers and prostitutes who routinely appear in our county's three magistrates' courts. The only incident I can remember lately that occurred anywhere near to us concerned a white male, aged twenty-two, a recent graduate, who was caught climbing onto the flat-roofed extension of a house a few streets along, hoping to spy on the female students who lived there. The police had been looking for him. Several other girls had reported similar incidents, and stolen underwear was later found in his bedsit.

This also made the front page – a 'stalker' story – but otherwise we live in an area where the crime rate is low and house prices are continually rising, where unemployment is rare and most incomes above average, where every indicator of social advantage tilts in our favour. We are by no means rich, but we are comfortable. And just as we are rarely the victims of crime, neither are we often its perpetrators. Should a fridge-freezer break down, or a camera be 'lost', our insurance claims will of course be exaggerated. Our tax returns will be 'finessed'. There will be fiddles on expenses, stationery items pilfered from work, freelance commissions completed on company time. Most of us will have claimed state benefits that we weren't entitled to. Some of us will still be using 'soft' drugs. But these, we would argue, are victimless crimes. They are technical, or trivial, and we remain far more likely to serve on a jury – or to appear before it as witnesses or advocates in the course of our work – than to depend on its verdict.

As I have explained, we are law-abiding, responsible citizens who assume the best of each other, and so I would not expect to arouse anyone's suspicions in taking the side alley to the rear of

Anna and Will's house this afternoon. It is five minutes to five, and sunny, and my very visibility, I feel sure, will serve as my disguise. I have already made myself conspicuous. I have knocked on their front door, peered in through their living room window. I have stood back on the pavement with my hands in my pockets and looked up to their bedrooms, and if my face is not already familiar to whoever might be watching me, I am confident that my complacent demeanour – as well as my collar and tie – will help to reassure them. Should I be challenged I can plausibly claim to have come straight from work to pick up my children; I can say I was expecting them to be here, playing with Nathan and Nick. Fathers do often get into such muddles with their domestic arrangements.

The spare key to the Browns' kitchen is hidden, I remember, beneath a blue-glazed plant pot in which Anna is growing some parsley. I lift it from the saucer and open the door, then replace it just as I found it. Anna can puzzle later over how the door came to be unlocked, assuming I go out by the front. It isn't my intention to cause any damage or to leave any obvious signs of intrusion. For the moment I merely wish to look around. And now that I am in here, I pause and take a deep breath; I savour the distinctive smell of their home – its vaguely meaty odour – and notice as well something cleaner and crisper: a bowl of fruit warming in the sunlight by the windows, a dozen apples and oranges, a bunch of grapes, an avocado.

I pluck a grape and suck away the flesh; I spit the seeds at the floor. The litter bin – stainless steel and tall – is almost over-flowing. I press on the pedal and look down, and immediately I recognise a gas bill, smeared with ketchup, and what appears to be an autoteller receipt. I finger the bill, but in truth I feel little inclination to examine it more closely. Already I can see that it's a final demand, and the receipt, I don't doubt, will show a negative balance. Anna and Will have always lived in debt, and always claimed to be at ease with that. It is something 'known' about them – something they allow to be known – and I'm now as wearied by this as by every other aspect of their lives, from the clutter in this kitchen to the messiness of their marriage.

Despite which, I can't help but glance in each of their cup-boards and drawers, and what frustrates me is not the absence of anything of interest but the persistence of my curiosity. I slam the final cupboard shut and drum my fingers on the worktop and then realise that I'm staring at a bottle of red wine, already uncorked. Anna always has booze and would not begrudge me. I rinse a glass at the sink, pour myself out a large measure, and as I sip the wine I run my gaze along her shelf of cookbooks until I come to a packet of photographs, a bulky yellow envelope slotted beneath a pile of paperbacks. I note its position and which way round it goes, and carefully I remove it. I check for any negatives, and tip the pictures into my hand.

They make a fat pile – enough perhaps for three or four films – and briskly I sift through them, disappointed to find that most are unpeopled. Their purpose is to record the appearance of this kitchen before, during and after last year's conversion, and though one builder or another does now and then appear, captured working and seemingly unconscious of the camera, he is always incidental. Many of the images are indistinguishable, and none are very interesting, but tucked in towards the end there's a clutch of snapshots of Will posing – I suppose ironically – beside their new 'soft-sheen' units and their 'retro-styled' mint-green fridge, and then, at the very back, a single picture of Anna on her knees, pausing to smile as she paints – I think – a wicker rocking chair.

She is wearing a white vest, her arms and shoulders bare, her cleavage just on show. The focus is sharp on her eyes. Looking sweetly up to the lens, her cheeks are flushed, her hair in disarray, and it occurs to me that this could be Will's view of her during oral sex, and that probably they were aware of this; that this was why he took the photo. I angle it away from the light and scrutinise her face – the lines wrinkling her eyes, the grooves around her mouth – and perhaps because I can imagine the circumstances so clearly, or because I know them both so well, I have no sense of being included in her gaze. Unlike my photograph of buck-toothed Helen Slater, this face does not invite me closer; Anna is smiling for Will alone.

The fridge shudders behind me, begins to hum, and regretfully I replace her in the pile. I return the envelope to its shelf and pour out some more wine and briefly I do have second thoughts; I consider keeping the photo, but of course the message it conveys will always be the same, and always be excluding, and with a sigh I turn and wander into the hall – as I have done

here at parties, searching for a comfortable spot, an inconspic-
uous place to stand – and turn towards their back room, whose
door – I make a mental note – is presently closed.

Bright today with sunshine, and facing out to the garden, this
used to be where they took their meals, and though the same
circular table remains, it's been given over now to scissors and
gluesticks, felt-tips and crayons, paintbrushes standing in jars of
black water. Drawings and paintings are everywhere, and on
either side of the fireplace the shelving is stacked from floor to
ceiling with board-games and toys, jigsaws and books and
transparent plastic storage boxes that are filled to the brim. I
can see a ram's skull with horns, a stack of computer games, a
pair of rollerblades. There's a stuffed bird in a bell jar. A hefty
PC, covered in stickers – a toy arrow rubber-suctioned onto its
screen – occupies an old lidded desk. An upright piano stands
against one wall, and a giant cardboard construction – an
assemblage of shoe boxes, egg cartons and cereal packets –
lurks in one corner, a sentry of sorts.

This then is the boys' activities room, and much as I envy the
Browns the size of their home, I do also recognise in here an idea
of childhood that is shared by most in our 'community',
including Jan and myself. Ours are the privileged children of
parents who 'oppose' privilege, and while some of us claim to
feel guilty about this, we will still pay for them to attend private
violin and piano lessons, tap and ballet classes, trampoline
courses, drama clubs. We will take them on hiking and horse-

riding holidays, camping trips abroad, city breaks. From an early age they will be familiar with arts festivals, puppet theatres, Shakespeare in the park. They will be tolerated at dinner parties. And though, like everyone, we will allow the TV to nanny our kids when we are too tired or too busy, we will also feel uneasy about this and forbid them from having TVs in their bedrooms or staying up beyond the watershed. Similarly we are 'against' convenience foods, and dinners on trays, and we take care to limit their consumption of sweets, crisps, burgers and 'fries'. We approve of reading, craft activities, enquiring minds, and in order to enrich their experience of childhood we will buy them microscopes, telescopes, even airguns and catapults. Above all we value politeness and will make a point of praising our children for their kindness and consideration, the ways in which they ape our own best behaviour.

Possibly you could add to this list. And perhaps Will is right to suppose that Nathan and Nick can survive his departure unscathed – if indeed his going is genuine – given the advantages they already enjoy and the extent to which they are provided for. Materially I doubt their circumstances will alter. Emotionally, I'm sure, they have always relied far more on their mother – Will being so self-absorbed, so often 'at work' – and this is bound to continue. It is possible they won't miss their father unduly. And should some deeper damage occur, some more lasting disturbance, this may even be to their advantage, shaping their characters in 'interesting' ways. Too cosy or stable an upbringing may not actually be the best preparation for life. Or at least, I can imagine Will taking this line, arguing – as he did in his office – that he's doing his children a favour by walking out on them.

Softly I close the door on their playroom and stand for some moments quite still – my hand on the doorknob and my head slightly bowed – gazing down at these pitted, scuffed floor-boards, and though it's none of my concern and these are not my children, I do feel something of the sadness that comes over me when I put my own two boys to bed – sad that another day has gone for them, and oddly sad too for myself, that my duties for that day are done.

And it's this, I now realise, that most disturbs me in Will – not his seeming indifference to the hurt he will visit on Nathan and Nick, but his readiness to contemplate a life in their absence, his lack of reliance on them. Their bikes are still here in the hall, propped against the wall. A pair of soiled sports socks lies by the door to the kitchen. The downstairs toilet, directly behind me, is furnished with clipframes of photos from when they were babies. And he will not be back; I am suddenly certain of that. His idea of himself does not depend on these things.

I sip from my wine, wipe a thumb over my eyes. This has been a long day for me and I'm beginning to wish I had napped in my van, or gone straight home to my wife. Yawning, I return to the kitchen and top up my glass, and as I come back through to the hall I hunker down and pick up the socks, then stiffly stand and nudge open the door to their 'utility room', a large windowless space next to the kitchen in which there's a washing machine, a tumble drier, various brooms and mops and a vacuum cleaner. I tuck the socks into a linen basket whose lid is askew.

Before the Browns moved here, eight or nine years ago, this room was a pantry and it still smells dimly of raisins and flour despite the powders and detergents on the shelves and the mound of floral-scented ironing on the worktop beside me. I place my glass on a shelf and switch on the light and half-heartedly I search through the ironing, finding only sheets and school clothes, T-shirt and jeans, and then without pausing to consider what I am doing I remove the lid from the linen basket and rummage about in the damp towels and scrunched clothing until I come to a pair of black panties. They are flimsier and lacier than anything Jan would wear and I hold them like a handkerchief to my nose, and what repels me is not the slightly pissy smell but the mustiness they've picked up from so many other moist or stale fabrics. I stuff them back in the basket and replace the lid as I found it.

Cursorily then I look in on the next room along, a dark L-shaped sprawl of sofas and cushions whose only window faces into the space between the garden wall and the back of the kitchen – a dark mossy corridor of bricks and drainpipes and bins.

They call this room the 'snug' and it's where they have their TV and where Will displays his own published works, including his foreign translations and the various anthologies he has appeared in, but these are of no absolutely interest to me, and neither do I feel much inclined to re-examine the family photographs on the walls, having surreptitiously scrutinised those on other occasions, coming in here to entice my children away from a video or on the pretext of seeing what they were up to.

I leave the door as it was, and though I do glance round the living room it is merely to confirm that nothing has altered, and that no one is in there. However thoroughly I might 'investigate', I am fairly certain there is nothing new or particularly surprising to be found in these 'reception' rooms – and for that I am grateful. My true purpose isn't quite clear to me, but I suspect I ought not to be lingering. Anna will be home soon enough, perhaps with Nathan and Nick.

I smell the scent of her briefs on my fingers, wipe my hand on the back of my thigh. The old wardrobe in the hall is still laid out on its side. I sip some wine and edge around it, and as I begin climbing the stairs I notice in passing how skilfully the carpet has been laid, and how much better this fabric has worn than our own. Coarse-woven, straw-coloured, it is similar to the sisal matting we had in our previous home and though clearly hard-wearing it is – as I remember Anna discussing with Jan – extremely awkward to vacuum: the dirt becomes trapped in the weave.

No doubt there are many purchasing trends that include or even identify us, however much we might like to think of ourselves as individual, thoughtful and discerning consumers. We are wary of 'fashion' and use the word 'trendy' disparagingly, but we are also less sure of ourselves than we might once have been – though admittedly with more social graces – and so take a deeper interest in our visible assets: the solidity of our bricks and mortar, the style and durability of our furniture, our fixtures and fittings. The relative merits of floor-coverings are one staple of our conversations, and while Jan and I have opted for terracotta tiles and wood laminates – our stairs and landing excepted – the general preference would be for stripped and varnished floorboards, though lately it appears these might not be such a reliable sign of 'refusal' or back-to-basics authenticity but are in fact ubiquitous, not only a cliché and all too predictable in 'people like us' but equally popular with people unlike us, who presumably take their inspiration from the 'makeover' shows on TV that most of us watch and affect to cringe at.

Acid-stripped doors are another common feature of our homes – the original panels and woodgrain revealed – and here at the top of the stairs I find there are five of them, plus two more that are yet to be treated. None of them are open. The landing is bannistered and dark, the only daylight filtering through a small stained-glass window above the door to the bathroom. A red-tinted rhomboid falls across the white-glossed door that conceals the staircase to the loft – Will's former office – and though I'm intrigued to know what might be up there now, the attraction of the bedroom he once shared with his wife is much greater. I turn the doorknob without making a sound.

The curtains are drawn, the light coarse-textured and blue, and it is airless in here, cloyingly milky and feminine. I want to open a window; I think I might like to lie down. The room is dominated by a giant brass bed and is in a state of such disarray it looks as though recently ransacked by some other intruder. I doubt I could make it much worse, but still, as I step across to the window I take care not to tread on the books, clothes and newspapers that are strewn about the floor. I part the curtains just enough to illuminate the bed and what I glimpse then is my own face in a mirror. It seems I have caught the sun on my excursion to Sarah's and now have the livid appearance of someone drunk or deeply ashamed, though my posture too is a factor: hunch-shouldered, I am slouching again.

I place my glass on a chest of drawers, next to a couple of bowls such as we have in our bathroom, containing pebbles and seashells, dried starfish and cuttlefish, bits of bleached bone. Like the other furniture around me, the chest is reconditioned, the wood a pale blonde, sanded and waxed. The mirror itself is framed in pewter or tin, and is too small to give a proper impression, but there's a taller mirror behind me, free-standing and tilted. I turn and confront myself as I did in Stella's surgery, my arms at my sides, my feet squarely planted, and though on this occasion I am fully clothed, the rightward slope of my torso is quite obvious – so too the mound of my belly under this shirt.

Sighing, I loosen my tie and attempt to stand properly. I remember undressing for Stella, and consider taking off my clothes now: my shirt and trousers at least, my shoes. I imagine Anna watching me, waiting, and I turn my head to the bed, as if I might find her. She would be sitting with her knees tented under the sheet, her arms loosely cradling her legs. Her breasts would be bare. She would not be embarrassed.

I tug my tie from my collar and push it into my pocket, then release the button on my trousers and pull my shirt from my waistband. Holding on to the bedstead to steady myself, I untie my laces and take off my shoes. My feet are swollen, my socks patchy with sweat, and perhaps that is enough; I am comfortable. On either side of the bed there is a cabinet of shelves. One is starkly empty, the other extremely disordered. I pad along to what I assume is Anna's side of the bed and draw back the sheet and sit on the edge of the mattress. I smooth a hand over the place where she sleeps, as if over her body, and notice several tight curls of dark public hair. I pick one away, drop it onto the floor, then reach for the next.

Minutes quietly pass, and as I busy myself in this way – picking at hairs, crumbs, bits of grit and fluff – it occurs to me that I'm now as close to Will's wife as I may ever come. Even if I were freed to behave as I pleased – even if Jan were to give me that permission – it is possible I would choose to remain as I am. There isn't a new version of me to be found in this bed, where Anna presently sleeps alone. What she would discover of me is precisely what I would discover of her: the person we each have become. After which, the usual me and the usual Anna would have to conduct our usual business, suddenly more complicated now than before. Sex in itself would never be enough; anything more than that might just be too much.

I straighten a ruck in the sheet and stretch out on my back. The bedsprings creak and I draw up my knees, lay my hands flat to my stomach, and as I watch the shifting patterns of light on the ceiling I remember Stella in her close-fitting tunic, enfolding my bare leg in her arms, then Anna kneeling by my side at the fun run, her moist hand holding mine. That afternoon she was wearing a fuchsia-pink dress, taut across the span of her belly and hips, slightly frayed at the hem. One thin strap repeatedly slipped from her shoulder. Will and my wife were elsewhere with our two youngest children, and Anna, drunk, recited a rhyme about the burdens – I think – of reaching middle age.

I turn my gaze to the wardrobe, whose doors are both open, but can't identify that dress among so many other bright fabrics. Then I notice an undergarment tucked beneath the pillow beside me: a negligée the colour of old-fashioned stockings, American tan. It is cool and silky, and I hold it out by the shoulders and allow it to fall softly over my face. I inhale her bedtime smell of sweat and stale perfume, and closing my eyes, I try to picture her as she appeared just one hour ago, naked from the waist down. I remember the noises she was making. And I unzip my trousers; I slip my hands inside my underpants.

Of course the logic of my coming into this bedroom is that I should masturbate. The logic of my behaviour today – and perhaps for much longer – points to that outcome. And I think I probably would, here on Anna's bed, but for the voices outside.

They arrive before they quite register. A man speaks first. A woman laughs and calls a few words in reply. He is closer. She appears to be approaching from the direction of the town centre, and with a jolt of alarm I swing my legs from the bed. Still clutching Anna's negligée, I grip my trousers to stop them from falling and immediately I tread on something jagged and small – a piece of jewellery, an earring perhaps – and give out an involuntary cry. Eyes smarting, I crouch and find it – a brooch in shape of a beetle – and drop it into my pocket. Hurriedly I limp to the window.

On the other side of the street, Mr Sommer is waiting by his front gate, a leather zip-file under his arm, a corduroy jacket slung over one shoulder. I lean my forehead into the curtain and peer in the direction he's facing – towards Katie, his daughter, who is strolling towards him, smiling and 'shapely' and evidently returning from work. Dressed in a white short-sleeved blouse and a white pleated skirt, her arms and legs are tanned, her blonde hair glinting in the sunshine, and when they meet she presents her cheek to him, stooping a little so that he can kiss her. Her shoes have cork soles, built up in a wedge. They make her seem slimmer, and a year or two older.

Neither goes inside. Instead they stand and talk by their gate, their voices lowered – conscious perhaps of the neighbours – and quickly I survey the windows directly behind them, then along to each side. I make a rapid inventory of those rooms whose curtains are parted and whose interiors are lit at this hour by the angle of the sun as it slants over these rooftops.

No one except me appears to be watching, and I step aside for a moment. I reach across to the chest of drawers for my glass and finish what remains of my wine, and when I look out again I see that Katie is leaning back against their garden wall, her hands half-hidden behind her and one knee slightly raised – an arched posture which thrusts her chest and pelvis forward. She lowers her eyelids, tilts her face to the sun, and as I gaze down on her from this, Anna's bedroom, my mouth slowly moistens, my heart beats a little faster, and I begin again to get an erection.

I let go of my trousers, allow them to fall around my ankles. Lazily I stroke myself – Anna's negligée clutched near to my crotch – and what returns to me then is Will's remark about her backside. I remember the way he watched her, looking down from his desk, and dimly I wonder if Katie is someone he has already begun to pursue, and whether he is now capable of fucking this young woman as well as the wife he's supposedly left – and indeed my own wife, should she ever allow him.

Fleetingly I picture Katie naked on the mat on his floor, her legs entangled in his, and then Anna as I imagined her earlier, desperately grinding against him, and finally I think of Jan, getting dressed to go out, absorbed in herself in her mirror. And in fact it is this familiar image of my wife – the only woman I have made love to in all the years of my marriage – that I focus upon as I close my eyes and determinedly, frantically attempt to make myself ejaculate.

But it is hopeless. It may be the wine I have drunk, or my tiredness, or the inescapable tawdriness of what I am doing, but my erection softly wilts in my hand and I have no choice but to stop. Resignedly, I toss Anna's negligée across to the bed and tuck myself into my pants. I pull up my trousers and fasten my zip, and as I tuck my shirt into my waistband I notice that Katie has opened her eyes. Yawning, she says something short to her father and he raises his head, squints upwards. He appears to frown in my direction. And though I'm quite certain they won't be able to see me in the dark of this bedroom, I step swiftly out of the way and stand for several seconds with my back to the curtain, staring down at the mess round my feet and hardly daring to breathe.

Their front door slams and I glance out. They have gone, and I feel for Anna's brooch in my pocket. I search about her room for a jewellery box and eventually locate a tangled collection of chains and bangles and earrings in a drawer inside her wardrobe. I suppose the brooch must belong there, and that these doors really ought to be shut. I turn the key in the lock, and then pick up her negligée and tidily fold it. I tuck it back under its pillow, and take hold of her bedsheet – my arms spread wide apart – and flap out the creases and guide it gently down onto the mattress. I straighten the edges. And then – as only a husband would trouble to do – I pad about in my socks, gathering her clothes from the floor and briefly sniffing each item to determine which is soiled and which clean. I make one pile of clothes to sort and return to their drawers. I make a second pile to take downstairs for the wash.

20

Will might well have invented me. Even the most favourable of reviews for his books – the ones I have kept in my file, and which I have here now on my lap – take issue with his male characters for their 'passivity', their 'undemonstrativeness', their 'slowness to act'. Imprisoned by their ordinariness, it seems his heroes are far from 'heroic'. The ways in which they are good are the ways in which they are weak. They are good because they are cowards.

This is the theme of at least two of his novels, including the first, which my wife has read and I haven't: whether the effort to stay 'true' to those who most love us – or simply depend on us – means we must then betray some deeper truth in ourselves, and whether such faithfulness is admirable, or in some degree pitiable. Often drunk and incapable, sometimes in therapy of one kind or another, a typical male in the fiction of William Brown is a man struggling against his own mediocrity. On the evidence of these clippings, he is 'risk-averse' and short on ambition, but also frustrated by his personal failings, his lack of imagination, his indecision. He is, according to a review in *The Times*, someone who feels himself to be 'constantly measured, constantly tested' but is 'lacking the instruments to calibrate or correct the extent of his dissatisfactions, the scope of the absence within him'.

All of which doubtless reflects something of the nature of Will's own inner life; it represents what he himself 'knows'. And possibly, having acted at last – having taken a chance on his future good fortune as a man without ties – his next novel will affirm the moral value in being 'true' to oneself, regardless of the consequences for anyone else. His book about a gumshoe called 'Harry' – about a man much like myself – will be an argument against the commonplace 'virtues' that I would subscribe to, against a life as dutiful as mine has become. This would not surprise me, and I trust my 'contribution' will be properly recognised, as in previous books he has honoured so many others, the dedication brief – to his soon to be ex-wife – the acknowledgements a fulsome page or two at the end.

Presumably too he will favour me with a copy of the book – 'personally inscribed by the author' – and on this occasion I may even read it, though I wouldn't then trouble him with my thoughts as to its accuracy, or indeed quality. Once, some years ago – soon after he had published his collection of stories – I stood near to him at a party and watched as he attempted to deflect the admiration of a tipsy young woman who had just made the connection between Will, her neighbour, and William Brown, an author she was sure she had heard of. Affecting embarrassment, he referred to his work, I remember, as 'nothing special, really; English provincial realism', and then described himself as a 'mid-list mediocrity', and I suppose we are all of us that, whatever our 'field', though I personally would still rather be a middling author than a middling auditor or solicitor or private investigator.

As would William Brown of course. Self-deprecation is a style he can afford to adopt, and while he pretends not to enjoy his small measure of fame, and insists it is anyway a very small measure, I have no doubt he has always been secretly pleased with himself, warmed by the thought of his 'public', eager for such praise, and quietly confident of more, much wider acclaim to come.

It is Sunday morning, early, and the light is still watery, the sky vaporous and grey. A pigeon is cooing on the roof of a neighbouring house, a blackbird relentlessly chirping. Insects are stirring, the first traffic sweeping by on the ring road, and I am sitting on the bench in our garden, a mug of black coffee beside me.

I have not slept well. In the week since I journeyed to Sarah's my nights have not been easy. If I dream, I dream only that I am still awake. I might perhaps drowse, then find that my eyes are wide open. If I change position – reverse and beat my pillow, cautiously roll on to my side – the relief is always shortlived. Aches will develop, my thoughts become fretful, and I will have to get up and go to the bathroom, swallow some aspirin, swill my mouth at the sink. In the early hours I will wander the house, checking that the windows are closed, the doors locked, all our appliances switched off. I will try not to remember my encounter with Sarah; I will try not to dwell on my visit to Anna's, or the sound of weeping on my tape of Jan and Will talking. Instead I might drink a herbal tea and gaze at the television. I might do some exercises. And then I will climb again to our bed, and if my wife should be disturbed by any of this she will lay a warm heavy hand on my arm, squeeze gently, and abruptly fall back to sleep.

She is sleeping now. For several long minutes this morning – the light through our curtains deceiving – I sat up and watched as she breathed: the soft pulse at her throat, the tiny pinch and flare of her nostrils. Half-turned towards me, her left arm was crossed over her chest, her hand resting near to her shoulder, and as I gazed at her I became transfixed by her fingernails, almond shaped and tapering, as pretty as they ever were, and by the back of her hand, which is becoming old now, the skin roughened, faintly netted with wrinkles. I looked at the whorls of her knuckles and thought of all the chores her hands had performed, all the scouring and scrubbing, the house-painting, mending and cooking, the tending to our children. I thought of all the work she had dedicated to the idea of 'us', to our family, and a kind of sadness came over me. I was touched, momentarily, and grateful.

Then sighing, I left our bed and stepped into my track pants and pulled on a sweatshirt. Quietly I went upstairs to my attic.

I am not, I think, a sentimental person, though lately I might seem so. In all the years of my marriage I have, I'm sure, expended far too much energy policing myself for signs of foolish 'emotionalism', and I have, at least until recently, avoided becoming overly nostalgic for the intensity of feelings I once experienced with Sarah. Such intensity was anyway too confusing and painful to live with, and Jan was my escape from all that. She offered herself as a refuge, and I suppose I have always felt in her debt.

Our marriage, it occurs to me now, was founded partly on gratitude, partly also on guilt, and my faithfulness has always been in some respects dutiful, an atonement, and has always carried some undertow of resentment – though that too is an emotion I've been careful to marshal. From the beginning I've been content to settle for trust, consideration, fondness; I've been happy enough with affection and habit.

And yet I have also preserved in my office, in files I rarely take out, more of my old correspondence than I've been prepared to admit to – least of all to myself – including the letter I once drafted in longhand to Sarah, and which she never read. I have kept in addition maybe two dozen pages of 'creative' writing that survived my earlier 'winnowings', plus a small burgundy address book at least eighteen years old, most of its entries now obsolete but others potentially useful: the parental homes of various friends I've lost touch with, the first points of enquiry should I ever wish to locate them.

Not that I now ever will. Like the gumshoe sketched in William Brown's jottings, much of my spare time this past week has been spent examining and questioning every last snapshot, postcard and keepsake that connects me in any way with the person I used to be. I have rooted out, too, all the academic and professional certificates I've acquired through the years, and the school exercise books I've held on to, and the great many redundant or superfluous reports that I've written and pointlessly archived in the course of my work, and though I have tried to find a single good reason to keep each one of these items, none of them – not even my letter to Sarah – has held the slightest interest for me. Whatever their previous purpose or importance, they too are now obsolete, and so I've destroyed them. I have fed everything through the shredding machine in my office and bagged it all up for the binmen.

What I haven't yet disposed of are the reviews I've kept of Will's books, which I placed on my desk some evenings ago and didn't get round to re-reading until I went up there this morning. In a moment or two I will burn them. I have a small box of chef's matches. And then I'll decide what to do with these tapes – my recordings of Will on the phone to my wife, and of Will having sex with his own. After which, possibly – who knows? – I will be freed from the shadow he appears to cast over me; I will be released to get on with my life.

Sunshine is forecast for later, temperatures in the mid-twenties, and perhaps this afternoon Jan will suggest we drive out to the seaside, treat the boys to an excursion. We might find some 'attraction' we haven't previously been to, and take some new photographs, collect some more trinkets, and hope that this 'family day' at least can pass without quarrels, the usual tantrums and tiffs, our customary bickering.

Alternatively, and preferably – if Jan is agreeable – I might make a start on what remains of our conifers, the stumps and roots I left in the ground on my birthday, six weeks ago. The tool-hire shop is open on Sundays till twelve, and Jan herself has already booked a skip for the debris that remains on our lawn, her patience exhausted, though this won't be delivered until Tuesday. I expect the job to take us three evenings, maybe three skips in total. The boys, I'm sure, will be happy to help me, and my back should just hold out, if I am sensible.

My mound of branches is beginning to rot, and I expect the grass underneath it has died. We should not delay for much longer. Soon the schools will be closing, and then we will be packing again for our holidays, our two weeks of grey skies and brown seas in North Yorkshire. Time is passing, and already the streets around here are much quieter, most of the students departed. The house that backs on to ours is deserted.

One afternoon in mid-week, returning from work, I came out to the garden and stood and breathed deeply, and as I turned slowly about, my arms stretched wide to each side, enjoying the sunshine, I realised I wasn't alone. Where previously the student had stood with her hairdryer, a woman in a blue housecoat – a contract cleaner perhaps – was smiling down at me. Taken by surprise, I waved to her, and daintily she waved back. Then she ducked and climbed on to a chair. Still smiling, she began to unclip the curtains.

Somewhat stocky, and plain-featured, she was several years older than I am – what I think of now as 'middle-aged' – and my interest in her was not sexual. Yet immediately I went indoors, and for half an hour then, from the vantage of my attic, I watched as she vacuumed and dusted and polished. I used my binoculars, as on other occasions I had used them to observe the student as she typed, or chatted on her mobile, or applied her make-up in front of the mirror. I noted the clench of the cleaner's brassiere under her housecoat, and the swaying earrings she wore, and the fixed curl to her hair. I noted which cleaning agents she used.

Of course the student was much younger, and prettier, and though her dressing and disrobing always happened in another part of the room – tucked away from prying eyes such as mine – I can't pretend I never lingered in the hope of catching her in an unguarded moment. I did find her attractive. But still, that alone could not account for my attentiveness, and I do wonder now if I wasn't equally drawn by the mystery of her everyday existence, the puzzle of her private life, for even after the cleaner had removed the last vestige of her presence from that room – and then gone home herself – I continued to stare down through my binoculars, examining every surface – the freshly gleaming furniture, the bared white walls, the brand-new mattress on her bed – mentally inhabiting the space where she had been, as fascinated by her absence then as by anything I had seen in the two years or so that she was there.

*　　*　　*

I strike a match and apply it to this first twist of newsprint, but there's more of a breeze than I realised. The flame catches and dies, and I try it again, the paper inverted. Threads of smoke spiral away from me, black flakes of ash, and I turn the paper around. I hold it upright, pinched between my forefinger and thumb, and watch as the flame burns steadily down. Then I drop the stub to my feet and take up the next cutting, twist it into a column, and ignite the next match.

In this way I work through Will's reviews, surprised to find that my print-outs and photocopies are just as combustible, disintegrating equally readily, though they produce much more smoke and less flame. In each case, I let go of the final few centimetres, and when the last of the sheets has been burnt I kneel and gather these fragments into a pile. I poke several lit matches amongst them and lean forwards with my elbows on my thighs and my hands clasped at my knees and blankly I gaze into the fire, which is over in seconds.

'What are you doing?' asks Jan.

Startled, I look round. She has come from the kitchen in her nightgown, a knee-length cotton shift so old it is almost transparent. Her feet are bare, slightly splayed. She is yawning and her hair is thickly dishevelled.

'Having a clear-out,' I say, and find that even this short time on my knees has caused me to stiffen. I get to my feet, supporting myself on the bench. I lay a hand over my cassette tapes and slip them into my pocket and sit down. I move my coffee out of the way. Jan perches beside me, puffy-eyed and pale, and I glance at the roll of flesh around her middle, the soft clear shape of her breasts. Blearily she looks to the sky and stifles a yawn. Then she grips the bench on either side of her thighs and stretches her legs straight out before her. She flexes her toes. There are freckles on her white shins.

'Of what?' she asks quietly.

'Hm?'

'What are you clearing out?'

'Stuff,' I say. 'Superfluous stuff.'

Jan sighs. She lowers her feet to the grass and looks round at me, her chin nudging her shoulder. 'Burning seems a bit drastic, Mike. A bit final . . .'

I nod. 'I wanted it to be final.'

Her mouth forms a small o. She lets her gaze drift away, towards the flecks of charred paper littering our lawn, the spent matches I threw there. 'So what were you burning?' she asks me.

Some of the scraps are identifiably newsprint, which Jan can surely see, though it's hardly possible that she could guess what they are. Even so, I am momentarily lost for a plausible lie; I can't think what to say. Certainly I would not wish my wife to know the full extent of my interest in Will's writing; that truth would be too shaming, and so I offer another disclosure instead: 'You remember the lad who got caught peeping into girls' bedrooms, the student? The one in the paper?'

Her frown is puzzled, amused. 'Yes . . .'

'I kept the clipping,' I tell her, which I did, for a few days, and

267

with just this intention: 'I thought I might try and write a short story about it.'

Jan gives a sudden laugh, a small yelp, and sits around on the bench, tucking one leg under the other, folding her arms. She is grinning at me, displaying the kink in her top lip, the discoloration of her incisors.

'Only I changed my mind,' I say, returning her smile. 'So I burned it, and some other odds and ends – notes for stories, that sort of thing.'

'Mike, I thought you'd given up on that sort of thing years ago.'

'*I* thought I had,' I say. 'It's just . . .' I shrug, and look away from her, up to the student's bedroom, then across to the next house along, where some curtains have recently been parted, perhaps in the last minute or so. The gap is narrow and dark and possibly someone is watching us. A pigeon takes off from the roof and I follow the dipping arc of its flight across the neighbouring gardens and up into the crown of a sycamore. 'Some things are hard to shake off,' I say. 'Especially from that time, from years ago . . . They linger. You know?'

Jan does not speak, and in her silence I sense – or imagine – some quality of understanding, and a willingness perhaps to hear more. She appears to be waiting. I take a long breath, and find myself yawning. My coffee is cold and it crosses my mind to slip indoors and make a fresh jug. I could allow this moment to pass. I could, if I wished, continue to behave as though nothing out of the ordinary has occurred in the weeks since I turned forty. I could pretend, even to myself, that the days since my birthday have been as unexceptional as the days and weeks and years that led up to it, and erase from my mind the visit I made to see Sarah, and the extent of my prying into the lives of my family and friends, and rely instead on what I suppose must be Jan's habitual assumptions, based on our familiar routines, our usual story.

But I have come to take comfort from the idea that I am transparent to Jan, that she alone can see through me, and it's disturbing to realise I am not as thoroughly known as I once thought I was, that my sense of myself is no longer shared or confirmed by my wife. She trusts me, I'm sure, but I am not the person she believes me to be, not quite. And I would like her to know this; I would like her to realise that something about me has changed, that I have behaved in a way she might not have expected, and so at last I confess, 'I've been to visit Sarah, Janette.'

'Sorry?'

'Last weekend, when I wasn't here. I traced her whereabouts. I went to find her.'

'Oh, did you?'

Her tone is neutral, polite, and she watches me steadily, her eyes unblinking. If she is surprised – or apprehensive, or angry – her expression gives no sign of it. There is nothing in her face or posture that I can read clearly, and this, more than any hint of annoyance or distress, is unnerving. Her hostility, I'm sure, would be easier to cope with.

'I thought it was . . . it seemed about the right time.'

'Did it? Okay.'

I nod. I look at her directly. In the course of my work I have become accustomed to aggressive questioning from Counsel in court, and have become adept at keeping my temper under cross-examination, adopting the appropriately courteous tone. But Jan's mild stare gives me no guidance; I am not sure what to withhold and what to reveal, and so I begin on my birthday; I offer a tentative account of my dream, and when Jan continues to watch me, blandly absorbs what I tell her, I admit to Sarah's persistence for years in my thoughts, and to the impulse that led me at last to locate her. I describe tutoring Will in the use of the electoral roll, and watching as he typed in her name. I mention the phonecall he made, and the print-out he gave me, and as I speak about him – about his role in my search – I'm sure I do notice some small shift in Jan's attention, the merest compression of the lines round her eyes, the slightest tightening in the line of her mouth. Her composure appears for a moment to waver. Then she links her fingers and hooks her hands over one knee, and casually she enquires of me, 'And did you explain to Will who Sarah was?'

'Does it matter?'

'I'd be interested.'

'No,' I say, 'I just used her name as an example.'

'And he got through to her answering machine.'

'Yes.'

She nods, and folds her arms again beneath her breasts. 'And then you . . . what? Arranged to meet her?'

'No,' I say carefully, and can't prevent myself smiling. 'No. I went and observed her. I made a professional job of it, Jan – clipboard, cameras, binoculars . . .'

My wife too gives a wry smile at that, slowly shaking her head, and then, before I can reveal any more of the nature of my surveillance, or describe my pursuit of Sarah in town, or the awkwardness of our eventual encounter, she leans towards me and places both hands on my thigh. She grips lightly and gazes into my eyes and calmly she says, 'You don't have to tell me, Mike. Whatever happened – good, bad, indifferent – I don't want to hear it.'

'But I would *like* you to hear it,' I say, surprised by myself, the plaintive note in my voice. 'I want you to know what happened . . .'

'No, really,' Jan insists, and heaves a long sigh. She pushes herself upright and sits round on the bench and for some moments then she gazes at the clematis tumbling into our square of garden from next door. A tiny white butterfly jinks over it. A breeze quickens the leaves and Jan shivers; she rubs her bare arms and glances towards me. She smiles. 'The trouble is, Mike,' she says. 'I don't really care. It's just *you*, isn't it? Carrying a torch all these years, tracking her down, spying on her . . . Nothing you could tell me about it would be a surprise. And it wouldn't *bother* me, either. That's the terrible thing. It just would not bother me.'

'No matter how bad it was?' I say.

She regards me evenly. 'No matter how bad it was, Mike.'

'I see,' I say.

'No. I don't think you do,' she sighs, and slumps back on the bench, allows her knees to splay outwards. She cups her hands in her lap and dismally stares at the stumps of the trees. 'I'm not sure you ever do,' she says quietly, as though to herself, and I glance round at our house, certain I heard some thump or shuffle indoors. Our boys do not usually wake until a quarter to eight. It is still barely seven.

Jan looks at me. Her eyes rove over my face, and sadly she says, 'Do you know what I think, Mike? I think you've never stopping taking me for granted. Have you? I think you've always just assumed I'm contented with things – that I'm contented with you, contented with our marriage, everything. Because I was the one who always wanted it, wasn't I? I chose you, I suggested we get married. . . . So it's always been me, and you've always thought . . . what? That you just need to stick around, and do all the things you *think* I want you to do – like decorate the bathroom, or fetch the boys from school, or chop down these fucking trees – and that way you'll keep me happy . . .'

'Janette,' I interrupt her, 'I *did* take down the trees to keep you sweet – if you remember, I admitted it – but then you turned round and said you weren't fussed either way. "I'm not un-happy," you said. *Not* unhappy, Jan. That's what you said.'

She shrugs, concedes. 'Well I'm not. I'm not unhappy, Mike. It's true. And I don't make a fuss. And I'm always here, always dependable, and I never surprise you . . . Which is how you like it. It's what suits you, isn't it? You don't want surprises, and if you think about me at all – if you actually notice me – you always assume I'm *not unhappy* because of you. Only it's not like that. If I'm contented, it's not because of anything you *do*, Mike. Or anything you *don't* do.' She looks at me and grimaces: a gesture of apology. 'And I do want surprises,' she says.

'Me too,' I protest. 'And I don't assume as much as you think, Jan. I don't take you for granted. I think you're wrong about that . . .'

She purses her lips, faces away from me. Frowning, she stares at the mess of our garden, and when indoors something tumbles she does not react; she appears not to notice. The boys have definitely woken, and I suppose they will shortly be coming to join us, Ben thrilled to find his mother outside in her nightgown, Jack more cautious, distrustful. And oddly what returns to me then, as I strain to listen for their footsteps, is the memory of a phonecall I once took from Anna, perhaps the first time she dialled my mobile, soon after we'd first exchanged numbers. It was a school day, this early, and I was already awake. Anna wondered if I might be able to recommend a good electrician. In fact I knew of several, and her thanks were effusive. 'Not at all,' I said, 'it's nothing.' Which was true. I did no more for her than rummage about in a drawer and read out some names. But afterwards, once our brief call had ended, I was glad, absurdly glad, to have been of assistance. I was cheerful, even elated, and came to sit for some moments just here, on this bench in our garden, my hands in an attitude of prayer – my thumbs supporting my chin, my lips pressed to my index fingers – and happily gazed into the encircling green of our trees, rehearsing in my mind the entire script of our conversation and speculating on her motives for phoning.

Of course it wasn't impossible that she was impatient to have a bad situation put right, and had found the range of electricians in the *Yellow Pages* bewildering, and had called on me as someone who might, in view of my profession, be acquainted with a reliable workman. But equally, she may simply have encountered some minor problem which had provided her with just the excuse she needed to call me. It could have been that she, too, was becoming impatient for some fresh turn in her life, that her 'story' had also come to seem stultifying. She might have decided that her 'conversation' with Will was unable to advance any further, and that no matter how many words they continued to share they would never again be able to articulate anything new or 'surprising'.

All of which, no doubt, is common to most long-lasting marriages, and doubtless too there will be moments in every lengthy relationship – however outwardly harmonious – when one or other partner will yearn for some new intimacy, when this will seem exactly the thing that's required if either of them is to connect with who they once were, or once hoped they'd become, as opposed to the tired, outdated roles they'd taken on and worn through. And if I didn't act then, if I lacked the inclination to pursue the opportunity she held out to me, it was not – I now realise – because I didn't care to spend the time and energy required to learn about her, or because I was fearful of where that might lead, but because I must already have known that no future acquaintance was going to help me arrive at a more suitable, authentic, or more richly rewarding version of myself, that there only ever could be my wife.

And this, above all, is something I would like to share with Jan now; this, more than any other, is a truth I would like her to hear. But when I murmur her name and reach a hand to her shoulder she doesn't for a moment respond. She does not move. 'Jan,' I repeat, and wearily she straightens. She looks askance at my hand, and I remove it.

'You know,' she says softly. 'I *do* want surprises, Mike – I do want new things to happen for us – but I just don't think you can bring them about. That's the saddest thing. You could get on the phone to Sarah now. You could jump in your van and go and spend the week with her – you could spend the rest of your life with her – and I really don't think I would mind in the least.' Bleakly she stares at me. 'I just would not care,' she repeats. 'Not any more, Mike.'

'But I *want* you to care,' I tell her. 'Jan, I want you to care.' And what grips me then is something like panic, something perhaps closer to terror; it comes and goes in an instant, and immediately I take the tapes from my pocket and sit forwards, my forearms on my knees, a cassette in each hand, and prepare to make plain to her as much as there is to be known of me, the full extent of my intrusion into the privacies of others, including the recordings I made of her phonecalls to Will, and the tape I possess of Will fucking his wife, and the hour I then spent in the Browns' bedroom. I prepare to tell her these things – to take that risk on whatever remains of us – but something in the intensity of my wife's gaze stalls me, and I realise she does not need to hear this. The fact is, she can guess; what she does not already know, she can easily imagine, and with a brief, cold glance at the tapes, her voice tight with emotion, she warns me, 'Get rid of them, Mike.'

I nod, but don't move. Jan's stare is unwavering, and I cannot look away; I continue to face her until at last our boys come out from the house. I clear my throat; I manufacture a smile for them. 'Hiya!' I call.

Unselfconscious, Jack is holding Ben's hand, and his younger brother, it's clear, is not at all thrilled by this scene, but apprehensive. 'What're you doing?' he asks. 'Why are you here?'

They stand before us, their faces pale, eyes puffy with sleep, and I smell the warmth from them, the hours they've just spent in their beds. Reflexively I look at their feet. 'Where are your slippers?' I chide them.

'Why aren't you in the house?' Ben persists.

'Because we're in the garden,' I smile. His pyjamas, I notice, are becoming too small for him. His belly button shows between his top and his trousers.

Jack takes half a step closer, looks down at the tapes. 'What're they for?' he asks me.

'They're just old ones, Jacko,' I say. My hands are trembling, but with the nail of my smallest finger I manage to hook out a short loop of tape from each of the cassettes. 'Here,' I say, and present one to Jack, offer the other to Ben. I touch his tummy with it, and cautiously he grins. 'It's a competition,' I tell him. 'You have to pull out the rest of the tape, see who can get it all out the quickest. It's a race.' Which of course is all the incentive he needs. Copying Jack, he goes about his task with sudden determination, furiously gripping and yanking, until very soon both my boys have accumulated a large crackling ball of tangled brown plastic.

'Look Mummy,' Ben laughs, and holds his bundle towards her. 'Mummy, look,' he insists.

'Oh yes,' she says lightly. She cups her hands to receive it. 'It's like a bird's nest, isn't it?'

'Yes,' he agrees.

Jack looks at me. I make a bowl with my hands, and with a shrug he gives me his tape. 'I'll throw it away,' I say. 'It's no use now. And then if you like we can go and get the axe and the saw again – and some shovels – and make a go of digging out these tree stumps, and the roots in the ground. What do you think? Would you like to help me with that?'

Quietly Jan gets up from the bench. She steps across to the mound of sawn branches and discards her tape. She smoothes the creases from her nightgown. 'You'll hurt your back again,' she says, and kisses the top of Jack's head, gently touches his cheek.

'I'll be careful,' I say.

She kisses Ben too, but does not look towards me.

'Can I do the axe?' asks Jack.

'You can have a go,' I say. Then, 'Jan?'

'Can I as well?' says Ben.

'You can,' I nod, and then add, 'We'll be careful, Jan.'

But she does not reply. She walks slowly past us, her hands clasped before her as though bound, her head slightly bowed. Without another word she goes back down to our house and I turn to watch her, dumping my tangle of tape on the grass, and it occurs to me for the first time that her age is now beginning to show in the weight of her step, in the heaviness of the life she is carrying, and as she disappears inside, shutting the door softly behind her, the emerging sun glints from the glass and I sense our story has changed, that something between us has shifted. She will not leave our marriage, I'm sure, but I know that I have lost her. For now, at least, she is lost to me, and I get to my feet and open my arms to my boys and draw them towards me. I hold on to them tightly. I hold them for a long time, though whether to prevent them from fleeing, or their father from falling, I could not say; I do not know.

Acknowledgements

The words quoted on page 38 are Rolf Hochhuth's.

I am grateful (again) to the Authors' Foundation, and to the Arts Council England, East, for financial assistance during the writing of this novel. *What I Know* also won an Arts Council England Writers' Award and I am very grateful for that.

For their help and encouragement (and patience) I would especially like to thank Georgia Garrett and Carole Welch.

What little I know about being a private investigator I owe to Steve McIlroy of Tracker Investigation Services, Kettering. Thanks, Steve!

This book could not have been written without Lynne Bryan.